Talk Nerdy to Me

AMULET BOOKS
NEW YORK

TIFFANY SCHMIDT

BOOKISH BOYFRIENDS

Talk Nerdy to Me

Cataloging-in-Publication Data has been applied for and may be obtained from the Library of Congress.

ISBN 978-1-4197-4010-7

Text copyright © 2020 Tiffany Schmidt
Lettering copyright © 2020 Danielle Kroll
Book design by Jade Rector

Published in 2020 by Amulet Books, an imprint of ABRAMS.

Printed and bound in U.S.A.
10 9 8 7 6 5 4 3 2 1

Amulet Books are available at special discounts when purchased in quantity for premiums and promotions as well as fundraising or educational use. Special editions can also be created to specification. For details, contact specialsales@abramsbooks.com or the address below.

Amulet Books® is a registered trademark of Harry N. Abrams, Inc.

ABRAMS The Art of Books
195 Broadway, New York, NY 10007
abramsbooks.com

FOR ANN-WITH-AN-*E* HELTZEL,
A TRUE KINDRED SPIRIT.

AND TO ALL THE STEM GIRLS OUT
THERE: YOU WILL CHANGE THE
WORLD. I CAN'T WAIT TO SEE IT.

Gilbert took from his desk a little pink candy heart with a gold motto on it, "You are sweet," and slipped it under the curve of Anne's arm. Whereupon Anne arose, took the pink heart gingerly between the tips of her fingers, dropped it on the floor, ground it to powder beneath her heel, and resumed her position without deigning to bestow a glance on Gilbert.

—Lucy Maud Montgomery, *Anne of Green Gables*

1

I spun the dial on the fine focus lens of the microscope, wishing it were as easy to bring clarity to my life as it was to the bacteria wet-mounted on the slide. The bio classroom hummed with conversations happening at a half dozen lab benches. The clink of slides, the snap of stage clips, the clatter of laptop keys as observations were recorded—these made up the soundtrack of both my favorite part of the day and the best memories of my childhood.

"How would you describe this color, Eliza?" My best friend, Merrilee Campbell, pointed to the cluster of Gram-positive bacteria we'd stained with crystal violet and mordant. "Ink-spilled twilight? Wine-crushed shadows?"

"Purple." There was no one in the world I'd rather have as a lab partner, but Merri and I disagreed about the amount of descriptive language I'd tolerate in our reports.

I squeezed the bulb on our eyedropper and added a bead of safranin beside the cover slip of a second slide. I watched the capillary action of it draw under the glass to mix with the liquid containing our specimen.

My life was supposed to be as simple as this Gram-staining assignment—one I'd first completed at age eight under my parents' scrutiny in the laboratory that dominated the first floor of our house. Back in second grade, I'd followed the steps and gotten the correct answer.

Eight years later, I still had clear directions, but outcomes felt less certain. Not for this experiment, but for my life. My parents had rules for everything I did: nutrition, sleep, exercise, socializing, studying. They weren't technically around to see if I followed them, but they remotely monitored the data collected by my iLive LifeTracker wristband and recorded in my daily log from wherever they were working—currently Amundsen-Scott South Pole Research Station.

But nowhere in their restrictions and guidelines did they account for the feeling of restlessness that was spreading beneath my skin like an allergic reaction to my regulated life.

Merri grinned and nudged me, pointing to her laptop. "'Purple' is boring. I already had 'aubergine'—I was checking to see if you were paying attention. You've been fiddling with that slide for five minutes. Everything okay?"

I forced a nod. The last thing I needed was Dr. Badawi sending an email. The desire to be acknowledged by celebrity scientists frequently led my teachers to be overzealous when communicating with my parents.

Last year my math teacher had reported I'd seemed "withdrawn." My parents had asked for the lessons being taught that day, then responded: *What you're describing as "withdrawn" is more precisely known as "boredom." Eliza has been capable of solving for the volume of a tetrahedron since she was nine. If you'd like to see her engaged, provide material that challenges her.* This was one of the many reasons I'd left the all-girls charter school I'd attended from sixth to ninth grade and was now a sophomore at Reginald R. Hero Preparatory School—aka Hero High.

I handed Merri the slide I'd prepared. "I'm fine. This is done. You should be able to see the Gram negative bacteria in pink."

"Want the first look? Or have you already done this experiment a million times?"

"Only once." My parents had no patience for repetition. I learned lessons the first time, or I figured them out on my own in secret. I'd had to memorize picture books on their first read, because there were no endless nights of *Curious George* or *Harry the Dirty Dog*. Instead I'd gotten lectures on the bad science in the first ("No real anthropologist would behave like that!") and the lack of observational skills in the second ("The premise is they don't recognize their dog because he's dirty? They aren't fit pet owners. They shouldn't be allowed to raise children.").

My parents were experts at being judgmental—even in areas where they lacked expertise. Raising children? Not unless you counted child-rearing-by-proxy. We hadn't shared a roof for more than a week in eight years. Not since the disaster in Brazil.

"Ohhh! Pretty." Merri didn't move away from the eyepiece, but she kicked my stool. Her sister Rory had painted dogs in top hats on the toes of Merri's canvas shoes. I had a pair with double helixes in my closet. They were next to the shoes I wanted to be wearing right now—my sneakers. Preferably with my treadmill beneath their soles. "Brand-new-eraser pink? Or kitten's tongue?"

I laughed, pulling my thoughts away from the workout I had planned for tonight. Not the one I'd record in my log for my parents, but the additional miles I'd run after I'd taken off my iLive wristband. They'd think I was showering or studying for the hour it charged; instead that time was *mine*. A whole sixty minutes where I was breaking rules and setting my own pace— literally and figuratively.

"Kitten? Who are you and what have you done with Merrilee?" Tobias May, her other best friend, turned around at the lab table in front of ours. He was annoying, but he wasn't wrong—Merri was a canine person to her core, courtesy of her parents' specialty pet boutique, Haute Dog.

"Kittens' tongues are pinker." Merri stated it like a fact—she was good at selling self-invented "facts" as truths. "Plus I couldn't think of other pinks. I'll have to ask Rory."

Toby grinned. He'd started dating Merri's younger sister eight days ago on New Year's Eve. This had made him more tolerable, both because he'd finally gotten over his unrequited crush on Merri and because he was around a lot less. Also, he and Rory were endurably adorable—I'd been scrutinizing how the traits that irritated me about each of them seemed smoothed when they were together.

I was very observant—I would've made a great pet owner: able to identify my dog dirty, clean, shaved, dyed, etc.... if I'd been allowed to have one. But lately my observational skills had been focused on all the couples around me: Toby and Rory; Merri and Headmaster Williams's son, Fielding; his sister, Sera, and her girlfriend, Hannah. The more people that paired up, the more the walls felt like they were closing in on me.

"So, how are things going at the BBB?" Merri asked Toby and his lab partner.

"Don't encourage him," I muttered, but it was too late. Curtis Cavendish grinned over his shoulder. He nicknamed everything. Five-foot Merri was "Short Stack." Toby was his last name, "May." Thin ballerina Sera was "Tiny Dancer." Our cafeteria table was "the Lunch Bunch." They weren't clever nicknames—that would be expecting too much.

He'd tried giving me a nickname once—I'd made it clear that repeating it would be at his own peril.

Their lab table was "BBB"—"Brown Bros' Bench"—because Toby was Latinx and Curtis was biracial: white dad and Egyptian mom. They could call themselves whatever they wanted; my problem was with the person who'd turned around to fully face us, almost knocking a box of slides to the floor as he leaned his elbows on the lab bench behind him. Curtis crossed his long legs at the ankles, highlighting his red-and-yellow-striped socks and bright red sneakers. At least he'd finally stopped wearing flip-flops. It was January in Pennsylvania. No one wanted to watch his brown toes turn blue.

"'Sup, SPP?" he said with a nod that made the top of his hair bob. It'd grown longer since September—swooped upward in a style that defied gravity and suggested his grooming routine consisted of globbing on product and twisting the hair out of his eyes while running out the door.

"I told you we're not responding to that." Beside me, Merri shrugged, then nodded to show her loyalty.

"I get that I can't call you"—I raised an eyebrow, and Curtis winked before continuing—"that other thing, but SPP—'Smarty-Pants Partnership'—what's not to like?"

I pointed a finger directly at him and ignored Merri's kick to my ankle. Back in September, after a memorable first meeting where Curtis had practically stared at me and drooled, he hadn't looked at me directly for weeks. It had been a bombardment of furtive glances, and he'd stammered whenever he spoke. Now he did the opposite, pinning me with direct eye contact that made me feel like he had the fine-tuning capacity of a microscope. Like he could see all my details and flaws. He paired this with one of those smiles people called "infectious." But it wasn't actually contagious. It was facial mimicry. An evolutionary mechanism caused by our brains' desire to create emotional connections.

I ignored the impulses of my striosomes, looking away to pick up the tiny squares of tissue paper that had separated our coverslips.

"It was better than my first idea: P-G-I-G. Pronounced *pee-gig*." He popped his collar, a move that would've been obnoxiously egotistical on anyone else. On him it was purposely over-the-top. "Pretty girls in goggles."

If Merri weren't standing next to *me*, she would've laughed. She might've let him call her "P-gig" or joked that it was an upgrade from "Short Stack," since she wasn't a fan of references to her height. But the way she felt about "short" was the way I felt about "pretty." So, instead of smiling, she watched me with concern.

I knew what I looked like—but I'd done nothing to earn the blue eyes and blond hair and curves and eyelashes that made people pause. It was genetics, not some divine blessing. And, yes, there was privilege that came with beauty, but there was also a cost. Blonde jokes weren't compatible with being taken seriously as a scholar, and I'd had enough post-puberty conversations where people's eyes slid below my chin to know my body had become a distraction.

If experiential evidence weren't enough, my parents frequently reminded me beauty was a liability for any female in their field, telling me I'd have to work twice as hard to "transcend" my appearance. I always bit back the reply I wanted to give: "Maybe other people should work twice as hard at not being biased or lacking in self-control."

Instead I settled for uniforms slightly too big, hair scraped back in tight ponytails, no makeup. Which was fine. I mean, it made my mornings more efficient, so I shouldn't complain.

"P-gig?" Toby groaned. "That might be one of your better ones, Curtis."

"It will stand for 'perfectly genius intellectual garroting' if you say it again." There—that was an almost civil response. Toby and I were reactive in the best of circumstances, with both of us in competition for Merri's time and attention. But lately—post-him-plus-Rory—we'd found a tenuous peace. I was trying to maintain it.

He snorted, but it was Curtis who responded. "Is your issue specifically with nicknames, or are you opposed to fun in general?" When I ignored him and unplugged our microscope, he turned to Merri. "I'll entertain all thoughts and theories."

Merri claimed we had "friendship ESP"—which was nonsense, of course. But still, hers was broken, because she blurted out, "Nicknames. She hates them."

Curtis bit down on his lower lip, but it did nothing to hide the curve of his smile. "Oh, I'm guessing you had a good one then."

If by "good one" he meant "one that had haunted me for years at Woodcreek Charter School for Girls," then, yes, it had been "good."

Brandi Erlich had coined "Brainiac Barbie" with the targeted cruelty of a sixth grader whose popularity is untouchable. I'd spent years with it chasing me in whispers, giggles, and hair flips. When I protested, the usage escalated to questions about if my "plastic face melted in the sun" and charades of mincing high-heeled footsteps.

I straightened the strap on my safety goggles. "This conversation is over."

"Now you've got me intrigued." Curtis tapped his chin. "May, who do we know that goes to their old school?"

My throat tightened. I was supposed to be done with days of scraping Barbie stickers off my locker and finding little plastic shoes in my bag. Retorts raced through my mind, but when I opened my mouth all that sputtered out was a shrill, "*No!*"

Dr. Badawi turned from where she was demonstrating something to Sera and Nicole. Merri pretended to look in our unplugged scope, I nudged my laptop out of sleep mode, and Toby capped his bottles of stains. Curtis didn't bother pretending to be occupied, but he did shoot me a look that might've been contrite.

I turned away.

"It's awfully noisy in this corner." Dr. Badawi peered at us through glasses that were cartoonishly thick and permanently smudged.

"We were discussing our results." Merri's wide-eyed panic screamed *liar*.

"Oh?" Dr. Badawi pointed to the guys. "Tell me what you've chosen as a real-life application of this experiment."

Curtis straightened. He towered over our teacher, but not in an intimidating way. He was too indolent, too smiley to intimidate. "Pharma. When there's a contaminant found in a production process, they use Gram staining to narrow down the type of bacteria to help determine the source and if it's pathogenic. Gram-negative organisms are more likely to be harmful. Gram-positive organisms are only potentially pathogenic if cocci, not rods."

I narrowed my eyes at Toby. He was capable—clearly the one who carried the weight at their lab bench—but I'd never heard him express interest in pharmacology. Yet the answer Curtis had rattled off was mirrored on the laptop screen between them on the bench. His gaze slid to me. He raised his eyebrows and grinned at my skeptical expression.

"Very good, Mr. Cavendish," said Dr. Badawi. "But I'm concerned about the level of chatter between the partnerships in this corner of the room. I think I'll shuffle you to see if it helps with focus."

"That's not necessary." My words came out firm—and without foresight. Had that sounded like an order? This woman lionized my parents and fawned over my work. I didn't want to abuse that, but... switching partners? No.

"I'll give you one more chance." She held up a finger, then used it to point at each of us. "In the meantime, get packed up."

I glared at the bench in front of ours as we put away our materials, grateful Toby wasn't in my next two periods and that Curtis wisely decided to give Merri and me space as we all walked to our shared history class.

"Too bad Fielding's not in bio. So many YA novels start with two people sharing a lab station, creating their own sort of chemistry..." Merri trailed off to smile at whatever scenario she was imagining. "Maybe it wouldn't be so bad if she mixed us up."

"Don't start." I wasn't in the mood for teasing, not while fearing I'd manipulated the power dynamic with my teacher in unintentional ways. If Dr. Badawi didn't change us, I'd worry I'd influenced that. If she did... "Her assigning partners undermines the meritocracy. I work with you not because we're friends but because you're good at science and do your share."

"And because of my write-ups, right? Wait until you see the Gram positive–versus–Gram negative star-crossed love story I'm putting in our report for you to edit out."

I laughed, and the muscles in my shoulders loosened. Merri's romantic vignettes had their own folder on my hard drive, and her writing skills were approaching those found in the books that filled her room. When her name was on a cover, I'd be first in line to get my copy signed.

A lanky figure darted past us and onto the lawn to catch a red ball being thrown from across the quad. We weren't allowed on the grass. The guy tossed the ball in the air, then put it in his mouth. Gross. My smile dropped. "I cannot be paired with Curtis. On any given day it's as likely he'll ingest the experiment as complete it."

Merri snorted and opened the door to the humanities building. "I think Curtis would be fun to work with."

"'Fun' is not a quality I want in someone who impacts my grades. I can't afford for them to suffer because his life goal is being named 'Class Clown.'"

Someone called Merri's name, and she waved. She knew almost every person at Hero High. I knew only our direct classmates. But thanks to a big article in the summer newsletter about my parents and my transfer, everyone on campus knew of me.

"Hey." She paused, and I realized she wasn't greeting someone else; she was getting my attention. Merri waited for me to meet her eyes and unclench my jaw. "You'd be fine."

There was a slap-bang-laugh behind us, and we turned toward the commotion: Curtis. Greeting someone on his lacrosse team with a leaping chest bump that resulted in dropped books and guffaws like it was comedic genius. How could anyone make that much noise just entering a building? At least I'd been wrong about one thing—it hadn't been a ball he'd caught and gnawed on the quad. An apple hung loose in his large hand. When he caught me staring, he held it up with a smile. "Bite?"

I turned away in disgust. It wasn't possible—it was the sort of detail Merri would include in one of her stories that I'd make her edit out for realism—but even from half a hallway away, I could smell that apple and feel his eyes on the back of my neck.

I rubbed at the spot and filed into the classroom, where he'd sit two seats behind me. It was only second period; there was so much school left. But all I wanted was to get home and trade my uniform for workout clothes and run until this restlessness stopped chasing me.

2

've never gotten nervous before oral presentations. Never sweated through a shirt or held note cards in shaky hands. I didn't do stomach butterflies or sleepless nights before exams.

I prepared. I learned the material. I did well. It was simple cause and effect. A pattern positively reinforced by years of As.

Around me I could hear the complaints of my math classmates. "My parents are going to kill me," intermixed with "What'd you get?" and "There goes my weekend."

I stared at the paper Mr. Neumoyer had placed facedown on my desk. I hadn't finished the test—no one had—so I hadn't thought it would be a problem. But even through the back of the page I could see the red pen circle and the number inside. Eighty-nine.

I was an A student.

That number was incontrovertibly a B. Only one standard deviation above average. There was a pulse of pain between my eyebrows as I tried to focus on Mr. Neumoyer's speech about failing tests needing signatures. I should feel pity for those classmates, but I couldn't spare any from myself.

Merri's eighty-five was faceup. She frowned but shrugged it off. I couldn't shrug. Not then. Definitely not after school when the email I'd been expecting hit my inbox.

Eliza—

Your latest math test was posted. We're concerned and will be calling tonight. Make yourself
available. Be prepared to communicate a reason for
this grade as well as steps you'll take to prevent
similar scores in the future.

It was from Dad's email. Not that he'd signed it. No time for
closings or sentiment when their offspring had performed in a
substandard manner. Actually, no time for sentiment ever.

They hadn't given a time for their call, which meant it hovered over my plans for the night. I could do today's prescribed
workout: thirty minutes of yoga and twenty minutes of weight
training, paired with an audio file of a research article they'd
chosen. But there was no way I could sneak in *my* run. The
one I'd been looking forward to since I got off the treadmill
last night, dripping and wobbly legged but mentally lighter,
capable of completing the rest of the tasks on my to-do list
and sleeping.

My parents weren't delaying the call to make me anxious.
Telephone communication at South Pole Station was dependent
on the positioning of satellites. Other Antarctic bases had more
consistent access, but Amundsen-Scott was remote—*at* the
pole—and if there wasn't a satellite in range, they'd have to wait.
Sometimes the access window narrowed to a few hours a day,
unless they used the station's iridium phones.

I never wanted to get one of those calls, because they were
only for emergencies. I couldn't think about that—about the
times when a medical emergency *did* occur at their base and
how transportation from the South Pole wasn't always possible. When those fears hit, when I had flashbacks to Brazil that
left me quaking, I reminded myself I was safe in Pennsylvania

and that, of the places they'd traveled, Antarctica seemed to be among the safest.

No snakes, I reminded myself. No poisonous spiders. I rubbed my hands up and down my arms. No street gangs.

I was making dinner when my phone rang. I alternated cooking nights with Nancy, the latest in my string of doctoral-student guardians, but she wouldn't care if dinner was late. She was so deep in dissertation mode, I doubted she'd notice. I pulled the pot of bulgur off the stove and rested my knife against the piles of onions and tomatoes I'd been dicing. The salmon could stay in the oven, but I turned it off, then snatched up my phone, treading the fine line between delaying and missing their call. "Hello."

"We're both here." Mom's crisp voice emanated from the receiver. Dr. Violet Gordon was the parent who was sterner, more pragmatic. My dad, Dr. Warner Fergus, had two modes: chummy, or distracted. I preferred them two on one; individually they were too intense.

"How are you?" I asked.

"We're well," Dad answered. "I wish I could say the same about your math grade."

"Present the facts, Eliza." It was what Mom always said, a throwback to when I'd tried emotional arguments for why I should have a later bedtime or be allowed to attend a slumber party, or eat ice cream, or join the soccer team. But I was no longer a second grader clutching a soccer permission slip and whimpering, "Everyone else is doing it," only to be faced with "I guess 'everyone else's' parents don't care about the brain health of their children." Because facts like "girls' soccer has the highest concussion rate of youth sports" always trumped "but I like it."

I sat up straight on my kitchen stool. "It wasn't a qualitative problem; it was a quantitative one. I understand the material perfectly. There were more problems on the test than could be solved within the class period. I didn't get any wrong; I simply left some incomplete."

"You mismanaged your time, that's what I'm hearing," said Mom.

"There wasn't enough time. No one finished. But Mr. Neumoyer grades on a curve; my class average is a ninety-seven."

Dad *hmm'd*, and I imagined him nodding, his shaved head reflecting any overhead lights. I closed my eyes. I didn't know what their current lab looked like, but I could picture other ones, where mini-me had had her own stool.

They'd let me help as much as I could. Had asked for my observations and written them down like my findings had as much merit as their own. And when I hadn't been able to be a hands-on participant, I'd had my own assignments—sometimes just coloring on copies of the periodic table. There'd been a place for me with them...until there wasn't.

Dad asked, "Was yours the top score?"

"I was in the top."

"Your voice has gone up, which means you're being evasive," Mom said. "It's times like these I wish we had video capabilities so I could analyze your body language."

If I didn't satisfy them, they'd email my teacher. Merri called them "'Space-station parents'—because they're too far away to be helicopter, but they're still right on top of you."

Ironically, I had fewer rules and more freedoms during their rare visits home. "Mr. Neumoyer mentioned one person scored above ninety."

"Which student? Merrilee? She's quite competent at math." I was waiting for the day they revolted against my best friend. Her rampant imagination and spontaneity were the antithesis of their priorities, but whenever they spoke about her, Mom would slip in something closer to a compliment than I ever got. "Quite competent at math" was high praise. On their last call Dad had dubbed her "formidable."

Blast! I was gritting my teeth, a habit I needed to break. "Merri got an eighty-five."

"I can email Dr. Walton at Princeton and ask if she has a doctoral student who's available to tutor you," Dad said, but Mom disagreed. "She's more than capable."

I gripped the counter with white knuckles. In our family, needing help was akin to failure—academic achievement should be independent and appear effortless. I'd grown up overhearing stories of their colleagues' disappointing offspring: *Dr. Feinstein's son didn't get into MIT. Have you met Dr. Ramos's daughter? She's an "artist"—I wonder what they even talk about? Dr. McNamara's twins are taking an SAT prep course—a prep course!*

"I don't need a tutor."

"Good." I was relieved for a half second before Dad continued. "Then is it how you're allocating your time? Perhaps we should do a, let's call it an 'energy audit,' where you record your day in fifteen-minute intervals and we evaluate how you're—"

"That won't be necessary." I had only the illusion of privacy as it was—if they added this new demand, I'd lose even that. My jawline tightened in the distorted reflection on the window across from me. I forced the muscles to relax. Everyone who said I had a great poker face didn't factor in how much time I'd had to perfect it while staring at my miniature on a computer screen. Antarctica might not have video-call capabilities, but most of their previous locations had. "This was one assessment. It's an anomaly, not a pattern."

"Patterns start with one anomaly," Mom said.

"But in this case...," Dad began, and in the pause that followed, I imagined them exchanging looks, maybe even passing each other notes, "we're going to accept your assertions—"

"—with the caveat that your next score is back where it belongs."

Dad continued over Mom's interruption. "Mr. Neumoyer also confirmed that this was a more difficult assessment and there was only one Λ."

I ground my teeth again. So it had been a trap to see if I'd tell the truth. Though they'd call it "verification by additional sources."

"Eliza." There was a change in Mom's voice—it went from inquisitive to informative. "We've never expected a school to be in charge of your education. That's our responsibility."

"I realize that." It was the explanation they gave for the work that filled my weekends and school breaks. They'd been home for only three days over Christmas, but in the rare moments they weren't meeting with colleagues, they'd piled on assignments.

Merri kept waiting for some clichéd teenage rebellion where I trashed our home lab, but I liked science. I found the processes and exactitude of experiments calming. Sure, my parents and I might not always overlap in the scientific topics we preferred, but it gave us something to talk about.

Dad cleared his throat. "We had, however, expected your preparatory school to do a better job of rounding you."

"We're not unaware that our educational efforts tend to be one-sided." Mom's laugh was a dry titter. Dad's was closer to a cough. When I truly laughed, it was a wild honking sound that made them both freeze and blink. Luckily we weren't a family that joked. In most instances, I could get away with a flat "Ha."

"If we were ignorant of cognitive neuroscience, we might make a humorous comment about your 'creative left brain' needing work."

Mom groaned. "How can people still believe that myth?"

"Can you give me the bottom line?" I asked, because satellite phones weren't always reliable, and if I was going to be reprimanded, I'd rather it happen before the signal dropped.

"You need to do more," Dad said.

"You've accomplished nothing extraordinary since beginning at Hero High. Now that cross-country is over, do you have a single obligation outside of class?"

That was the crux of it. Merri's parents told her "Do your best." I'd seen them praise Rory for a seventy because they'd known she'd tried. Mine expected "extraordinary."

And I'd done "nothing." Besides homework, their assignments, their workouts, their logs. Cooking, shopping, cleaning. Driver's ed and getting my license. Following their rules and directives and fitting in my secret workouts.

Bracing for their reply, I asked, "Do you have a club you'd like me to join?"

"Oh, that's your decision," Mom insisted. I waited a beat, swallowing a sigh they might hear through the speaker. "But we've narrowed it down to three you may choose between."

They'd used the word "choose," but they'd have an obvious preference.

"There's robotics club, chess club, or academic bowl team," Dad said.

"The other option we discussed was if you should form your own group."

"It would be a good way for you to hone your leadership and interpersonal skills."

I closed my eyes and counted by fives, then by sevens. I'd trained myself not to react during these calls. Not to show emotion when their criticisms dug deep, or flinch when some data I'd reported didn't measure up to their standards. When *I* didn't measure up to their standards. But "leadership"? "Interpersonal skills"? They must be talking about their other, fictitious daughter, because those weren't traits I possessed.

84, 91, 98, 105... "Academic bowl sounds promising."

"Good," Mom said. "Well chosen."

The signal was holding, and I wanted to keep them on the line. I wanted them to ask me questions—real questions, not the data-entry ones from my log. Who cared about my blood pH or REM cycles or the protein-to-carbohydrate ratio in my diet? How about my day? How about the project my English teacher, Ms. Gregoire, had said she'd announce in class tomorrow? When she'd teased it today she'd added, "Some of you in here are skating...but not for long," while looking in my direction. If I told them this, would they hear me, or would they jump to asking, "*Are* you skating?"

I wanted to snicker over burnt suppers when Dad attempted to cook local cuisines. I wanted to fall asleep listening to them debate the merits of Darwin versus Wallace, Edison versus Tesla. But I wasn't eight anymore. And they were nine thousand miles away.

"Nancy can sign any permission forms," Dad said. "Put her on the line, would you?"

16, 32, 48, 64, 80, 96, 112. "Sure." I knocked on the door of her office and held up my phone. "My parents." Into the receiver I said, "Here's Nancy."

She straightened from where she'd been bent over a laptop, her short black hair in disarray from absentminded finger furrows while she edited her dissertation. Taking my phone, she said, "Hello?" then nodded that I should leave. So I shut the door on a conversation that was likely about me, because what choice did I have?

That's what passed for goodbye with my parents. There was no "Miss you," "Love you," or "Talk soon."

They cared. They did. They wouldn't spend their precious time analyzing every facet of my life if they weren't invested in my well-being. They just communicated their affection in a different language than the Campbells' good-night hugs and the notes they snuck in Rory's and Merri's lunches. Small talk wasn't in my parents' skill set, and I didn't need them to hand me the perfect-temperature cup of chamomile tea, look me in the eye like they had all the time in the world, and say, "Catch me up on you."

I never knew how to answer when Mrs. Campbell did that. Or how to process my disloyal yearning when Mr. Campbell called me his "fourth daughter."

After Nancy returned my phone, I'd call Merri and tell her we'd be joining the academic bowl team. But first I unplugged my headphones from their charger and filled a water bottle. Dinner could wait. Four miles. That was my estimate for how long it would take to chase away these feelings. So that when I spoke to Merri, I could present this like it was something I wanted to do. If I didn't sell it, she'd be in their inboxes with a passionate defense. But Merri never realized that for every battle she won with them—permission to have a doughnut on the first day of school, assent for the occasional sleepover, the privilege of no longer turning in my cell phone to my guardian before my designated bedtime—they added additional restrictions to some other aspect of my life. If she protested this, I'd be forced to start my own club.

I practiced the words in my empty kitchen. "Academic bowl sounds fun. Doesn't it?"

Better make it five miles.

3

My English teacher's black wrap dress was covered in pairs of antique keys that crossed in *X*s all over the fabric. Her red lipstick outlined a half-moon smile as she waited in the classroom's doorway. "Come in and get settled. I need every second of class time to go over this assignment."

Merri was captivated by Ms. Gregoire's personal style. A staple of our drives home was my best friend deconstructing her outfits: the printed dresses ("They're so glamorous, not cute like you'd think. I mean, bicycles on clothing sounds like it'd be cute, but it's glam!"), her shoes ("Did you see her heels? How does she glide around the room on such high heels?"), and her hair ("I've always wanted to be a redhead; Ms. Gregoire's hair makes me explode with follicular envy").

Personally, I thought the heels were a poor choice that would lead to joint and back pain as well as shortened Achilles tendons. But I'd admit to being intrigued by her dresses and elaborate hairstyles.

That day was no exception. Her hair was in a loose side braid that looked purposefully messy. I didn't know how to do that. I could do a braid or a bun, or any other style that required precision. But anything that was beachy, or casual, or involved random pieces hanging or wafting was beyond me.

"Get seated," Ms. Gregoire announced, and Merri practically squealed as she settled into her desk between Toby and me. This was the only class our whole lunch table had together. Hannah Kim and her girlfriend, Sera Williams, sat on my other side. Curtis—the only person who could make shy Sera laugh out loud—was next. To his left was Lance Volgate. They'd been Toby's friends, and since Merri was friends with him and I was friends with her, it was where we'd melded when she and I transferred. If Merri and I had started at Hero High as freshmen, it's probable we'd eat lunch at a different table and my group texts would come from different numbers.

The non-lunch table members of the class—Ava, Michael, Randolph, and Nicole—were already in their seats. It was Curtis who was holding things up, sharpening his pencil with the most lackadaisical twists of the handle. I gritted my teeth as he pulled the pencil out and blew shavings off the tip, then, apparently dissatisfied with the point, reinserted it.

Finally, he flopped in his chair and Ms. Gregoire began. "Many of you have had big opinions about the books we've studied this year. That's the difficult thing about constructing a curriculum: Should I choose books that say a little something to everyone? Or books that are monumental for a single student?"

She clasped her hands behind her back and began to pace around the center of the circle formed by our desks. For as vibrant as her clothing and personality were, the room was drab. It didn't matter, since it was a rare moment when our eyes strayed from her during class. She was a good teacher, a captivating one. English would never be my favorite class, but she made it tolerable—despite the fact that Merri had a ridiculous theory she was some sort of "story sorceress" who made book plots manifest in reality.

"Some of you in here have already had the experience of a book changing your life." She paused to wink at Merri. "But you should all have the chance to grow as people through the lessons you glean from literature."

I appreciated her enthusiasm for the material she taught, but demanding we find fictional books personally relevant was a step too far. Before I could arch my brows, she'd stopped in front of my desk. "Some of you need the opportunity to choose your own path. Your own story."

Her eyes were soft with sympathy when they met mine. I was the one who had to look away first. Choice was a luxury for people whose parents were not the doctors Gordon and Fergus.

"That brings us to our new project." She spun around, her dress flaring in a way that Merri would gush about later. "Drumroll, please, Mr. Cavendish." Curtis was only too happy to oblige, hammering his long fingers against the edge of the desk and adding bonus noises that were supposed to be cymbals, until she held up a hand. He finished with one last "*Boom-tish*."

"Your free-choice independent-reading assignment!" She flicked her wrists outward in a ta-dah motion. "There are a few simple rules. One: this class is Brit lit, so your book needs to be tied at least tangentially to that theme. Two: poetry and plays are fine. Three: your project, presented in whatever form that calls to you—as well as response journals—is due the week before spring break. Four: you must get your book approved before you begin. Five: everyone must read a unique book; no duplicates." She picked up a stack of handouts from her desk. "I have a list of titles to get you started, but before I distribute these, any questions?"

Lance was first. "Can it be something you've read before?"

"No, but I'm going on the honor system."

Randolph called out, "Does it have to be fiction?"

"A novel, play, or poetry."

Ava's black hair was arranged in perfect curls that she shook over her shoulders as she announced, "I have a question."

"Let's hear it." Ms. Gregoire was infinitely patient, but I rolled my eyes at Ava's constant need for fanfare.

Curtis caught me. He grinned and made a *blah-blah-blah* hand under his desk. I turned away as Ava whined, "So we pick a book, no duplicates or partners, etc., and then we do *any* sort of project? How will you grade them?"

"The same rubric we've been using, but I'll factor in the effort your project represents. A shoebox diorama is not going to earn the same grade as re-creating a key scene as a contemporary movie."

"But if we want to do a standard paper, will you accept that too?" Merri's question was for my benefit, because she would likely be writing a sequel to whichever novel she chose.

Ms. Gregoire smiled at me. "Of course."

It was a straightforward assignment: choose a book, write a paper, turn it in. I should have been relieved, but it felt like fingertips were walking up my spine; the sensation was so strong I leaned back against my seat and looked left at the only person who would play that sort of asinine prank. But Curtis was in his seat, doodling in his notebook.

"I want you to make this assignment personal." Ms. Gregoire paused for so long that I looked around the room. Lance was staring out the window—not at the old stone mansions that made up the campus buildings but at the athletic fields. Merri was making a list of book choices; Nicole was sketching an intricate design on the back of her hand; Toby had his laptop open, and I'd bet he was stealthily messaging Rory. Sera and Hannah had their pinkies linked between their desks. The others were in various states of attentiveness, but no one else appeared to feel our teacher's words humming like electricity across their skin. I rubbed my hands together, but the sensation didn't fade.

Ms. Gregoire stopped directly across the circle from me, tapping the toe of her shoe in a rhythm that seemed to match the pulsing in my temples. "I want your project to show how you've connected with your chosen work. How you've identified and found yourself in the story, and how you've changed because of it."

The hair on my arms rose in goose bumps below my white button-down and navy sweater. My muscles contracted, my heart pounded, and I started to sweat. My hands went cold. Adrenaline. My body was reacting to an emergency that didn't exist.

"But no pressure to pick the perfect book, am I right?" asked Curtis.

My inner crisis popped like a balloon. I sat back in my seat and took slow, even breaths. The joke wasn't funny, but Toby laughed. I leaned around Merri to raise my eyebrows at him. Curtis was not to be encouraged.

But he was accidentally correct. It *mattered* what book I chose. Especially if Ms. Gregoire thought I was "skating." I couldn't afford less than an A, but her "let's make this personal" expectations felt like a cryptic minefield.

"Some of you may find this...uncomfortable." Her smile was bright as she aimed it at each of my classmates. Everyone but me. The thing was, Ms. Gregoire was very deliberate about her eye contact. She made it a point to go sequentially and include everyone. It was something I'd noticed on our first day of class, and I hadn't seen her skimp since. It was how Merri had gotten caught using a messenger app on her laptop. It was why Toby was reckless for still daring to do so. But when her eyes jumped from Hannah on my left to Merri on my right without even a millisecond of connection with me, something tightened in my stomach.

"I'm sorry this assignment may cause some of you pain. It may change the way you see yourself or the world—certainly your place within it. But that growth mind-set—pushing through the experience and getting to the other side—will be worth it, I promise." It was only then that her eyes came back to mine. She maintained contact a beat longer than necessary, so I couldn't escape seeing the sympathy in her gaze.

On the first week of school when she'd used this sort of language—*Literature is powerful. Anything can happen when you open yourself up to it.*—I'd expected it to be met with a chorus of snorts and scoffs. It hadn't been. Instead Merri had been convinced that "book magic" was happening—that plotlines from stories were appearing in her life.

I'd told her she was overidentifying.

Then Rory Campbell, who was *not* prone to wild flings of imagination, had come to the same conclusion about the books Ms. Gregoire had assigned her in freshman English.

I'd heard the rumors from others on campus. Even Trenton Rhodes, Hero High alumnus and the oldest Campbell sister's new husband, had made cryptic comments about Ms. Gregoire steering his path to Lilly. And if asked to describe Trent, I'd have said "rational" or "logical."

I pulled my shoulders back and lifted my chin. I was not going to get caught up in the Ms. Gregoire-mythos frenzy. Books were static. They were words on paper, written and unchanged. They were of a time, from an author. They had no power beyond that which the reader granted. I didn't give them permission to bestow anything but good grades.

"Respectfully, Ms. G, you're making this assignment sound about as appealing as the Convocation where Nurse Peter shared pictures of athlete's foot and ringworm."

It was Curtis. Of course it was Curtis. I didn't need to look to know his legs would be stretched out past the edge of his desk. His feet would be crossed at the ankles, creating an obstacle Ms. Gregoire would step over as she paced the inner ring. Each time, she'd smile at him.

Once, during cross-country practice, I'd grumbled to Merri about his manspreading, and she'd laughed so hard she'd had to stop running. "Whose space is he spreading into? He's a foot taller than me, and I barely fit under desks." She'd wiped tears of laughter from her eyes. "It's okay not to like someone—you don't need to justify it."

Which was easy for her to say; Merri liked everyone.

Hannah nudged me. I took a book list before passing the rest to Merri.

"It's not an exhaustive list—feel free to propose your own," Ms. Gregoire said before retreating to sit atop her desk. "I'm here for consultation. You know I've got opinions!"

My eyes skimmed, skimmed, skimmed—stopped on the S surnames. From what I knew of this book, it had science, it had horror, it had zero romance, and it was written by the daughter of one of the first feminists. Written on a dare, because the men in her life teased her that she couldn't.

My hand shot in the air.

"Oh. Already?" Ms. Gregoire's forehead wrinkled as she approached my desk. "I had some suggestions I was going to make for you."

"No need." I tapped a finger on the list. "I'll do *Frankenstein* by Mary Wollstonecraft Shelley."

Her smile turned concave. "I strongly advise you to reconsider."

"Is it too easy?" My stomach sank. *Some of you are skating...*

"No. Nothing to do with academic rigor." She paused, then crouched before softly adding, "I understand the appeal, but I don't think it's an emotionally healthy choice for you."

My cheeks flamed red. I already had one set of adults dictating ninety-five percent of my decisions. *Eliza, you must get at least eight hours of sleep a night. Consume sixty ounces of water each day. No caffeine. No processed sugars. Do these workouts, chart your menses, graph your weight. Join a club. Eliza, make sure to charge your iLive LifeTracker; there was a gap in yesterday's data. Eliza, report every detail of your existence for us to scrutinize. Sacrifice your privacy and autonomy on the altar of science.*

Ms. Gregoire had told us we could choose our own book. I'd chosen mine. I'd even chosen one off her list. I ground my teeth. "I'm happy with this choice."

"I don't think you'll be happy at all." Ms. Gregoire trailed a finger down the list. "What about..."

I wanted no part of her selection or literary-matchmaking schemes. If I chose a book without romance, then I was eliminating that possibility—not that I believed it was actually possible. Magic wasn't real. But I wasn't going to feed into the hype or give Merri fodder to spin into a fantasy.

"Is Eliza done yet?" Ava whined. "Because I'm ready."

"She's all yours, Ava." I slid the paper from under Ms. Gregoire's hand and folded it in half. "I'll consider what you said, but for now I'm content with *Frankenstein*."

"Okay." Ms. Gregoire gave me a small, concerned nod. "But my door is always open if you change your mind."

4

'd lost Merri during the exodus from Convocation—Hero High's tradition of ending each day with an all-school assembly for announcements or lectures or performances. Today the student government presented a fund-raiser for the prom. It involved buying carnations, but when I saw the hearts and cupids projected on the screen, I tuned out the rest.

Merri reappeared beside my locker, wearing a wide grin and her bright red duffel coat. "I chose my book! Ms. Gregoire just gave me the thumbs-up." Merri enthusiastically demonstrated this gesture, then turned pink and dropped her hands.

"Well, I'm glad one of us met her approval." I shut my locker hard and turned to exit the building. "What did you pick?"

She bounced on her toes. "*Maria; or, The Wrongs of Woman.*"

I tilted my head. I didn't recognize the title, but I was intrigued by it.

"It's by Mary Wollstonecraft—the mother of *your* Mary. I did some preliminary research during media class. I know you're anti-dating—"

"I'm not allowed to date." It was in bold print on the list of things my parents forbade, cross-referenced with studies about the connections between adolescent romantic relationships and lowered achievements and self-esteem. "Also, I'm not interested. Especially not in your teacher-matchmaker theories."

"Like I said—you're not feeling the romance-novel angle. And you're probably miffed Ms. Gregoire pushed back against your pick—but now we're like a literary family. Mother-daughter book club."

I froze on the path outside the humanities building. Sometimes I felt like everything inside me was calcified—figuratively, of course—and that my emotions were fossilized from disuse, or of an entirely different chemical makeup than Merri's effusions or Rory's transparent hurts and barbs. But then Merri would do something so thoughtful it made me feel like the muscle fibers of my heart had melted and were going to leak out my eyes. If I let her, she'd hug me. If she hugged me, I'd cry.

"Merri, I want you to choose a novel you'd like to read."

"I did." She shrugged. "It's done."

But she hadn't. She'd chosen *me*—over kissing scenes and her favorite teacher. I sniffled, trying to cover the sound by crunching my boot on a piece of ice.

She swung her satchel so it bumped against my legs. "Team Eliza," she said softly. "Till the end."

"Team Merri," I whispered back. "Always."

She whistled. "Now let's hope we make this quiz bowl team. Well, that *I* make it. You're a lock. Fielding told me it's ridiculously competitive."

"You're ridiculously well-read and intelligent," I reminded her.

"I'm, like, come-up-with-an-answer-at-your-own-pace smart. Or, come-up-with-a-creative-answer-then-convince-everyone-it's-right smart." Merri grimaced. "Not buzzer smart. But how fun will buzzers be?"

"You'll be fine." I hadn't thought about buzzers. I hadn't done much thinking about this, period. Merri had texted me five minutes after she agreed to join: Fielding knows the team captain. We can try out tomorrow after school. And I'd let it go. Let it be a worry for another moment—but that moment was *now*, and Merri was pushing open the doors to the science building so we could enter the classroom where the team practiced. It was one we knew well: the bio lab where we started each morning.

"What are the rules?" I asked Merri.

"Um, be smart and press the buzzer?" She snorted. "We can still run away and pretend we were kidding."

"Actually, 'be smart and press the buzzer' is a pretty good summary."

We turned toward the voice, and I rolled my eyes. "What do you want?"

"To be smart and press the buzzer," Curtis repeated. He was eating an enormous cookie. There were crumbs on the collar of his gray peacoat, and I suppressed the urge to brush them off.

"Well, it's good to have a dream," I told him. "Maybe if you're nice, they'll let you press the buzzer anyway."

Merri coughed into her elbow, but Curtis laughed outright. "I'll cross my fingers you make it. You'd be amusing to have around."

"No way." I gaped. "You cannot be on this team."

He shrugged, his smile not losing any of its intensity or obnoxiousness. Was it normal to have so many teeth? I was tempted to count them but didn't want him to think I was staring. I wasn't. "We were mid-Atlantic champs last year."

I narrowed my eyes. "Are you the manager or something?"

Curtis threw back his head and laughed. It made me want to lock him out of the bio room or push him down a flight of stairs.

Ugh, violence was the lowest form of counterattack. He brought out the *worst* in me. "Nope. But let's see if you can *manage* to unseat me." He crinkled his nose. "That sounded punnier in my head."

I blinked at Curtis like we'd never met, and my voice wavered. "Sorry, but...Are you really on the team?" He was jokes and grins and calling out non sequiturs that our teachers met with frustrating good humor. He was making disgusting food combinations at the lunch table and daring Lance to eat them.

But worst of all, he was the second person Merri and I had met on our first day at Hero High, and within thirty seconds he'd blatantly ogled me and confirmed my parents' grim predictions about coeducation, ruining my morning and my hopes for the school.

"Really, truly. I've got the team T-shirt and everything," Curtis said. I realized I was grinding my teeth again. Next time my dentist asked why, I'd send him a picture of the boy who was currently hanging from the classroom doorframe, doing an impromptu pull-up before swinging inside. "Come on. Bartlett has a thing about punctuality."

Bartlett turned out to be a pale, freckled boy about my height—five seven. He was standing by the lab tables with a folder and a plastic bin of buzzers. He scrutinized us as we walked in, narrowing his eyes as Merri chirped "Hi" and waved her blue sparkly nails.

She was petite with a perky nose and voice. Her dark hair made her large gray eyes pop. Her mouth was small, her chin pointy. Merri hated words like "cute" and "adorable"—but they weren't inaccurate descriptors. I'd seen far too many people use her appearance and personality as an excuse to underestimate her. They'd do it *once*. Merri was no pushover.

When Bartlett turned to prejudge me, his dismissal was even more apparent. His eyebrows went up and he gave a silent snort, but he pulled on a smile he probably thought was charming. "Hey, gorgeous, I'm—"

"About to make an epic mistake," Curtis interrupted.

Well, he would know. I glared at him.

"Hi," Merri said again. "We're here to try out. Fielding said you could use more players."

"Fielding." Bartlett scoffed, "He quit the team because it interfered with fencing practice. Like fencing's going to get him anywhere."

"Well, he's nationally ranked and being recruited by Ivies, so..." Merri shrugged. "He's also my boyfriend, so maybe rethink whatever you're going to say next." She paired this with a smile while boosting herself to sit on a lab table. It was a low-key Campbell superpower—Merri and Lilly could simultaneously correct you and defuse a situation.

He dropped a buzzer back into the bin. "I'm Bartlett Ashcroft. I'll be your team captain if you make it. I'm good at history. And Fielding's a lucky guy."

"I think so." Merri's voice always went a little dreamy when she talked about Fielding, but she blinked a few times and added, "Merrilee Campbell. That's Eliza."

"Is there a test or something you need us to take?" The getting-to-know-you time-wasting portion of the afternoon was over. I needed to be on the team, not know his life story.

"Sure, but let's talk specialties. I told you mine. The questions in competition tend to fall into broad categories we need covered: literature, science, history, geography, mathematics, fine arts, religion...and they throw in a few on popular culture."

"Literature and mathematics," Merri said.

"If that's true, that's excellent. We need support in both. Especially lit."

"*If* it's true?" I sharpened my gaze on Bartlett. "Merri finishes books more often than you brush your teeth."

"I hope not; my mom's a dentist." He grinned, revealing a shiny, perfect smile. "But people usually aren't as smart as they think they are. What are your specialties? Pop culture?"

I swallowed back a lecture on the way society evaluated the worth of knowledge, and the problematic bias in terms like "smart" and "intelligence." A lecture that would make me a hypocrite since I'd just aimed those words at Merri, Curtis, and myself. "Science."

He glanced at Curtis with his eyebrows up. I swear he was one second away from making a blonde joke. In which case I'd be one second away from eviscerating him. Curtis shook his head in warning, and Bartlett turned back to me. "We don't need a science person. How's your fine arts knowledge? Musicians, painters, philosophers?"

I took a step back, my hip hitting the table where Merri was sitting. My family didn't do fine arts. While my parents never directly stated they thought these were wastes of time, Mom frequently said things like, "Rory's artistic talent would be useful for making field sketches; it's a shame she has no inclination for botany or biology."

"Just give them the test," said Curtis.

Bartlett picked up two stapled packets. "So you know how this works: quiz bowls are on weekends a couple times a month—we go against other schools in the area, then after we beat them, we'll progress to the state, regional, and national competitions."

Merri was digging in her satchel for a pencil, but I kept my eyes and chin up. This guy could underestimate us all he wanted; he'd lose the condescension when he saw our scores.

"The test is long. You have twenty minutes, and that won't be enough time to finish. I'll warn you when you have ten minutes left."

Merri was still elbow deep in her bag; she'd rejected at least four writing implements, so she must've been searching for some lucky one. I wished she could take her nervous energy and weaponize it. Or that there was a way to kick both guys out of the room so I could give her a lecture on owning her abilities and not allowing others to project their biases onto her emotional state.

Since I couldn't do either, I offered her my pencil. It was a plain yellow #2, but well sharpened, and maybe she could tell it was imbued with my faith in her, because she grasped it like a life vest and smiled.

"Then I'll correct them and we'll see if you made it." Bartlett dropped a packet next to Merri and handed one to me. "Any questions?"

"Is the team all male?" I asked. "How many of you are there?"

"No, and five. Ideally we'd have six. We need to cover the subjects I mentioned, and there's no room for redundancies."

"Lynnie went home with a migraine," Curtis said. "André's visiting Howard University."

"Lynnie? Boy Byron's twin?" asked Merri.

Curtis nodded. Apparently he knew the story of Merri's parents owning a dog named Byron, and thus her giving our classmate a nickname to designate him the human version. "There's also Norman—but I don't know where he is."

"I told him to go home." Bartlett was setting a timer on his phone. Curtis had picked up a buzzer and was clicking the top like a pen. That was going to get old fast. "He doesn't need to watch these two take a test."

"Can you not?" I pointed to Curtis's hand. He dropped the buzzer back in the bin and switched to tapping his foot. Ugh. I turned to Bartlett. "So we need to score better than one player to both make the team?" It was a necessarily obnoxious question, because Merri looked peaked, and I didn't want her to have what she called a "nervous puking episode."

"But if we beat them, do they lose their spot?" she squeaked.

Bartlett chuckled. "Worry about scoring high enough first. If you earn a spot, you earn it." He pointed to a table across from Merri's. Curtis held out a pencil that I accepted only for expediency. The sooner this was over, the sooner Merri could relax. If she didn't make it, I wasn't joining. If we both made it and she found it stressful, then we'd quit. There was no part of her well-being that I was willing to sacrifice to this new demand of my parents.

I nodded a thank-you to Curtis for the pencil—see, I could be civil. I should get bonus points for that. Not that they'd be necessary.

Bartlett tapped his phone screen and said, "Begin." Curtis called out, "Good luck."

Ugh. Like luck was real. Like we needed it.

I worked through the packet in order, glancing over at Merri every few minutes to check that she wasn't too green. Science was first. I didn't bother wasting time guessing on the ones I wasn't sure of. I'd rather leave them blank than be wrong. I peeked at Merri again—her head was bent over scratch paper, her fingers flying through calculations. Knowing her, I was pretty certain she would've started with her favorites. Good. She'd nail them, and that would calm her down.

With five minutes remaining I reached the math portion. If I'd had more time, I could've solved all the problems on the page, but I'd answered enough questions across all the sections that my cumulative score had to be more than sufficient.

I smiled smugly when Bartlett called out, "Time. Pencils down."

5

Bartlett handed Merri's packet to Curtis, and the two of them bent over an answer key. I tried to distract her by asking about her work schedule at Haute Dog.

"It's not bad lately," she said. "Lilly's picking up a lot of shifts because she misses being around and next year she won't be. I already hate law school and—"

Bartlett cleared his throat. "Well, I have good news for one of you."

Merri's bottom lip was between her teeth. Would it be inexcusably rude to grab her arm and leave right now? Did I care if it was? I wasn't joining without her.

"Congratulations." Bartlett held his hand out...to Merri. She looked as confused as I did, blinking at him until he dropped his arm.

She pointed at me. "She's Eliza. I'm Merrilee."

"I know. You got eighteen out of twenty on lit and a decent thirteen on math too. We need you on the team."

Merri shook her head. Her words tumbled over themselves. "But—how? Eliza—"

"Didn't make it." Bartlett turned to me. "You missed our team's high score in science by one. It's laudable, but I told you we can't have redundancies. You don't bring enough to the table."

"But Eliza's smarter than me," Merri protested. "She's smarter than anyone."

"I answered thirty-nine questions," I stated, not sure how to point out that this was higher than Merri's thirty-one without making it look like I wanted to beat her.

"Cumulative score doesn't matter—it's about the individual sections and team needs."

"You might have *told us that*." My voice was still level but growing tighter.

Curtis had been unusually quiet. I glanced over to see him paging through my test and wanted to swipe it from his hands. I hadn't made the team. I was going to have to tell my parents. My hand clenched around his pencil. How was this even happening?

"Barty—you gotta look at this test again. She nailed everything she answered."

I winced. Curtis was sticking up for me. I shoved the pencil in my backpack and grabbed my coat. One of my gloves fell out of the pocket, but I didn't stop.

I needed to run. Miles and miles and miles until I was able to make sense of this.

"I don't know what's so hard about 'Don't call me *Barty*.'" He fumed. "Fourteen in science is good, but she had to beat fifteen."

"Fourteen?" I froze with my coat gathered in a jumble. "I answered fifteen science questions."

"You got one wrong."

"Not possible." I'd answered only things I knew with complete certainty. I snatched the packet from Curtis. There was an X through question three: *An organ is composed of two tissues, is self-contained, and performs a specific function. What is the largest organ within the human body?*

I checked my answer. It was legible, and more importantly—"This is correct."

Bartlett rolled his eyes. "Don't be one of those people. You can try out again next year."

I pressed on. "What answer is on the key? Because the liver is the largest organ in the human body."

"You're wro—"

"Just check, Barty," Curtis said. "I'm curious too."

He sighed like I'd assigned him a Sisyphean task, but ran his finger down the answer key before smiling smugly. "It's not the liver. It's skin."

My answering smile was equally smug. "That's wrong. It can't be."

"Give it up." Bartlett's ears were red, but Curtis was looking at me with raised eyebrows.

"Why can't it?" he asked.

"What is the largest organ *within* the human body?" I read from my test. "The skin is the largest organ, but it's not internal. The liver is the largest organ *within*."

Curtis whistled. "She's right."

I shot him a piercing glare. "Of course I am." Merri was sitting on the tabletop. She'd taken grapes out of her lunch bag and was popping them in her mouth as she watched us, eyes wide.

"I remember answering 'skin,' so I got that wrong," Curtis added.

I rolled my eyes at the walls, trying to summon extra patience from a poster of the water cycle. "No offense, Curtis, but who cares?"

He drummed his fingers on the lab bench. "I had fifteen right, and now I have fourteen. You had fourteen and now have fifteen. Your score is higher than mine."

My jaw dropped. "You? You're the highest science scorer? I assumed you were pop culture or fine arts." I winced as those words came out of my mouth. They sounded like something my mom would say.

"It doesn't matter," Bartlett protested. "You gave the answer that would've been accepted during a match."

"If she gave her answer with her explanation—which is correct—it would've been accepted on appeal." I hated that Curtis was defending me, but I didn't know enough about the rules to make my own arguments.

"Still, you're our top math scorer too. She'd be redundant."

"Math?" My world was spinning. No. Curtis was a class clown. He was the one who avoided answering teacher's questions through any antic possible. Last week he'd juggled whiteboard markers instead of solving a problem. The only times he raised his hand in math were to ask to go to the bathroom or if we could work with partners. I'd assumed the first was escapist and the second was because he couldn't do the work by himself. I scrutinized him, trying to see beyond the ever-present goofy grin. If he was capable, why would he put so much energy into masking it?

I stared at him until he ducked his head, running a hand over his tousled black hair and grasping the back of his neck.

"Eliza." While I'd been studying Curtis, Merri had slipped off the table and come to stand beside me. She had her coat on and she'd picked up my glove. "I peeked at his paper. He got the A on the math test," she whispered. Except Merri couldn't whisper, and her words hit Curtis like a dart to the spine. He stiffened and ducked his head further. I tried to close my mouth. *He* was the reason for my parents' call and why I was here?

"Bartlett, thanks for letting us try out. I'm sorry it was a waste of time, but I'm not joining without Eliza. And not accepting her—that's a *huge* mistake. Also, explain the rules better next time. Have a good night." Merri smiled at him and grasped my sleeve, towing me out of the room. I hoped my silent exit seemed triumphant, but truthfully I was gobsmacked.

"I didn't make it." The freezing air snapped me out of my stupor and I shoved my arms in my coat. "I strategized that completely wrong. I was thinking total points, not the sections independently. If I'd known the scores I needed to beat—or if I hadn't skipped—I could've—"

"It's okay," Merri said.

I shook my head. No part of what just happened was okay.

"Eliza!"

Merri turned and waved to Curtis, but I refused to acknowledge his shout. Not even when he added, "Wait up! Please."

"Eliza Marie Gordon-Fergus." My best friend yanked my arm. "Do not be rude to Curtis *again*. He's our friend. It's not his fault."

"He's *your* friend. I tolerate him for your sake." But I stopped walking and turned to watch Curtis take a shortcut across the grass and splash through a slush puddle before skidding to a stop near us.

"Bartlett is an ignoramus." His breath came out in puffs that fogged in the cold air.

"Did you just want to state the obvious?" I asked. "Also, you're standing outside in twenty-degree temperatures in a school blazer, so let's maybe not cast too many aspersions on other people."

Merri kicked my shoe, but Curtis laughed. "Fair point." He shoved his hands in his blazer pockets, pulling it tight against his shoulders. They weren't broad like Lance's, but they weren't narrow either. I noticed, then decided to ignore, the way they strained against the seams of his jacket. "Listen, can we talk for a sec? You're on the team—both of you—if you want to be. I'm hoping I can convince you."

My stomach sank. "Did you tell Bartlett who my parents are?"

Merri's eyes went conflict-avoidant wide. She muttered, "Oh, geez," and then gave me a fake smile. "I'm going to... um, walk over to the headmaster's house and see if Fielding and Sera are there. I'll get him to drive me home, so...talk to you later!"

"Traitor," I said.

"Play nice," she answered.

I watched Merri scamper down the path, her satchel bumping against her leg and her purple gloves held slightly out to her sides to keep her balanced when she hit an icy patch.

"How scared should I be that that question made your best friend run away?" Curtis asked.

I gripped the straps of my backpack tighter; *12, 24, 36, 48, 60*...I reached *132* before I responded. "I don't want special treatment. I want to achieve things on my merit, not theirs."

"If Bartlett wanted you to focus only on one section, he should've told you that. You strategized based on the information given, and he's too stubborn to admit he screwed up."

"Just like that, he's cool with me being on the team? You mentioned I'm related to Nobel Prize winners, and I'm no longer redundant?" I tilted my head, daring him to lie to me. Because there was no way an ego like Bartlett's would make a one-eighty that quickly.

"No." Curtis shuffled his feet, but he didn't look away. "He's giving you a probationary offer. We've got a couple of weeks until our first competition. You can prove yourself during practices. You're not a redundancy."

But I was. I was an unnecessary repetition of my parents. A weaker copy. So redundant that I had no place in their daily lives. I'd seen each of the Campbells cry because they missed Lilly since she'd gotten married and moved across town—and she saw them daily at the store and family dinners and Sunday brunch. My parents didn't hesitate to leave me behind when they went to different continents. "I don't need your pity."

"Well, that's good, because you don't have it." Curtis reached out to cup my shoulder. "The team needs you."

I looked at his hand and raised my eyebrows. He pulled away and held it up in a gesture Merri called *I come in peace*. I stepped back. "And I'm just supposed to accept that you're secretly smart?"

Ugh. I hated the imprecision of that word, but I was too frustrated to come up with an alternative.

"Accept it or don't." He shrugged and tapped his head. "Your evaluation has no actual impact on what's up here."

I exhaled for *8, 16, 24, 32, 40.* Why would anyone choose to play ignorant? What could be the benefit? I couldn't tell if I was angrier that he was an intelligent person masquerading as a fool or that I hadn't noticed he was intelligent. Did everyone know but me? My cheeks burned. "Why should I join?"

"You tried out for a reason. I'm assuming you *want* to be on the team."

The sky was starting to darken, and my cheeks were getting cold. My fingers were too, even through my gloves, so Curtis had to be miserable. "Who's the adviser?" If he said "Gregoire," I was bailing.

"Badawi."

I grimaced. Dr. Badawi was almost as bad.

"Please?" Curtis took his hands out of his pockets and held up crossed fingers. "I saw Dr B on the way out, and when I filled her in, she looked like she'd won a Wolf Prize. Are you going to deny an old woman such happiness?"

A tension headache began to brew behind my temples. If I walked away now, there was zero chance she wouldn't email my parents to try and change my mind. There was zero chance they'd support my decision. And the longer I stood here delaying the inevitable, the less time I'd have to cram in my homework and daily log and hit the treadmill before my mandatory bedtime. "Fine."

"Excellent!" Curtis held up a palm. I arched an eyebrow, and he grinned, took his other hand, and high-fived himself. Was it any wonder I'd assumed he was vacuous?

"Don't make me regret this!"

"You won't! I won't!" He shook his head, a dazzling smear of white teeth on display. "You're going to love it. Practices are Tuesday and Thursday. If you need any help—"

"I won't." I narrowed my eyes as I palmed my car keys. "Why is this so important to you, anyway?"

"Because," he said with a happy nod. "I'm finally going to have some competition."

6

Merri called when I was midsprint. I pulled the emergency clip on the treadmill and jerked to a stop. Leaning against the control panel and breathing hard, I answered, "Hello?"

"Hi! *Sooo*, how did things go with Curtis?" Her voice was falsely chipper, and the words sounded like she'd been rehearsing them for the past hour.

"He's still breathing with limbs intact." But I'd been too keyed up to head straight home from our parking-lot encounter. Nancy wasn't observant, but she'd notice if I stomped through the kitchen while she cooked. I missed cross-country and the hills I could've pounded if I had someone to run with. Instead I'd stopped at Reading Railroad, the town book- and board games store where Merri spent the majority of her paychecks. Without her, it wasn't an hourlong browsing excursion. I'd known exactly what I wanted: a copy of *Frankenstein*.

"Are you mad?" Merri asked.

"At you? No." I unscrewed the top of my water bottle and took deep swallows. I was sixteen ounces short of my parents' daily hydration quota.

"I could've stuck around and played mediator, but I didn't want to make things worse or have you feel like I was picking his side."

I tightened my grip on the bottle. *Would* she have picked his side? "Don't you remember when he called me 'Legally Blonde' in the middle of English class?"

"Gah, if looks could kill, he'd have been a casualty. But... he's not like Brandi. He hasn't repeated it since he realized it wasn't funny to you. And he did get you a spot on the team. By the way, are we joining?"

I stepped off the treadmill; my stolen workout time was over. Pressing the phone between my sweaty shoulder and ear, I untied my shoes. "You're on the team; I'm on probation."

"So you'll take over as captain in, what, a week?" Merri laughed.

"Perhaps." I smiled, heading upstairs to dinner and homework. "I'll pick you up tomorrow."

The other thing I'd bought at Reading Railroad was sitting on the kitchen counter beside my bowl and plate. Nancy usually ate in her office. I unwrapped the plastic on the box while I picked at beet salad and carrot-and-turmeric soup.

I'd played Trivial Pursuit before—years ago at a Campbell family game night. When I'd mentioned it to my dad over a video call from New Guinea, he'd suggested that we play too—long-distance. But when I asked about it on their next call, he'd changed his mind. "We looked at the game—only the green category was interesting, and the questions were far too elementary."

Green was science and nature. I'd brush up on those as well, but I was focused on the other five categories: geography, arts and literature, entertainment, history, and sports and leisure. I had no use for the game board or the dice or any of the wedge-shaped pieces. I wanted only the cards. I flipped through them as I ate.

Which president's ghost is said to haunt the White House?

That couldn't be a real question, could it? *Who* said? Couldn't anyone offer an opinion and invalidate the question? Also, the only acceptable answer would be: "None. Ghosts aren't real."

What was the name of the car in the 1968 Disney film **The Love Bug?**

If that was the sort of question we'd be asked in quiz bowl, I might strangle someone with my buzzer's cord.

I scanned for the card's science question: *What's the best way to pick up a rabbit?*

Nope. That sounded like the setup for a bad dating joke. I pushed the box away. Maybe quiz bowl was the worst club for me—lately all I had was questions and no answers.

∞∞∞

There was an email waiting from my parents post-shower. Two emails in two days was almost an excess of communication.

Your LifeTracker alerted us to elevated heart rate twice today. The anomalies took place at 10:48 and 16:03 EST. There was also a gap in the monitoring from 17:31 to 18:44. Please account for these. If the sensor is malfunctioning, order a replacement.

I sighed and hit Reply.

I can't account for the anomalies. The first occurred in English class, and the second was during quiz bowl tryouts.

It was actually *after* the tryout, while I was bickering with Curtis in the parking lot. But mentioning a boy would result in a lecture on hormones and societal pressure to date and why they forbade it.

The gap in the data is my fault. I thought the band was on its charger while I did homework. It must not have been connected. I don't think it's malfunctioning, but if it continues, I'll replace it.

That was a half-truth. The charger part was real, but it was while I was running. In the meantime, having some must-be-the-sensor wiggle room was a bonus.

I hit Send and pulled out *Frankenstein*. A piece of paper fluttered from under its cover. I frowned as I unfolded it—I'd recycled my book list at the end of English class. A gesture meant to signal to Ms. Gregoire that my choice was final. How had a copy gotten in this book? My arms rippled with goose bumps; I blamed them on the wet hair that was soaking through my pajama shirt, not on my adrenal glands. These were a physiological response to cold, not emotion. I shoved the list in a desk drawer and grabbed a sweater.

But when the sleeve snagged on my silver wristband I wondered if it was sending yet another alert, because my pulse was definitely reacting to holding this book. Normally I'd read the introduction and historical notes, but I flipped past these to the preface. A few pages in, I frowned.

Where was the science? The lab? The enormous green monster? I'd never seen the movie, but everyone knew the gist of the book from Halloween decorations and cultural references. So far the novel consisted of a man writing letters to his sister to justify his entitlement and life choices. But wouldn't his sister already *know* his personal history? He kept telling her how, despite his lack of formal learning, he was super special.

I was over him: a newly rich boy who wanted to buy a boat and play sailor, whining because there was no one on the ship who met his snobbish friendship standards. I had zero empathy for his loneliness. Zero interest as he described his determination to find a faster route to the North Pole. Maybe his type of passion and commitment was supposed to be admirable? After all, my own parents frequently uprooted their lives and faced danger and isolation in order to follow their thirst for discovery—but I lacked that particular brand of ambition.

Finally, as I was wondering if I'd ended up with the wrong novel between these covers, a man is rescued from a dogsled floating on a piece of ice. The captain is delighted to have a friend—albeit one who's currently half-dead—and promises to transcribe the man's "strange and harrowing" story.

Something about the words made me shiver—or that could've been my damp hair. January wasn't exactly air-dry weather. Whatever the man's story was, it would have to wait. I had math and history homework...as well as a response from Mom.

Re: LifeTracker-Strange. Neither of those instances should've cause elevated heart rate. It's a given you'd make the academic bowl team, so I can't imagine any thrill in that victory. From all accounts your English class is standard.

I curled in on myself, one knee up on my desk chair and shoulders hunched down, like I could make myself as small as that email made me feel. I hated these moments when I had to stare down irrefutable proof of how little they knew about my life.

If Mom couldn't imagine a thrill in making the quiz team, how would she react if she learned I hadn't?

I was sure there'd be more anomalies for my parents to notice if they did a deep dive into my LifeTracker's data from that night. I'd gone to bed on time, but my sleep had been restless. The feeling persisted the next morning. After spilling my oatmeal, vitamins, and a bottle of dish soap, I headed to Merri's house early. Nancy had already gone to her lab. Maybe I needed company to chase away this skittishness.

I hesitated only slightly before opening the Campbells' front door. Merri's parents had been encouraging me to come in without knocking for years.

"Hey, Eliza." Mr. Campbell lifted a soapy hand from the sink and pressed the Pause button on his phone to stop whatever podcast was playing. "How are you doing, pumpkin?"

He was the only male in the world I'd allow to call me a diminutive. Maybe because it didn't seem gendered or condescending from him—I'd seen him call their male dogs "sweetheart" and refer to Lilly's husband as "sunshine." In every instance, the only emotion it conveyed was affection.

"I'm fine. Is that Merri in the shower?" If so, she was running late.

"Yup. Rory snagged it first, and then I heard her on the phone. With you?"

I shook my head. "Probably Fielding."

"Ahh. The boyfriend." He paused. "Can I ask you a favor?"

"Maybe?" But I wanted to say "Sure." While it was so hard to impress my parents, Mr. Campbell always seemed genuinely happy to see his daughters—happy to see *me*. It was probably pathetic, but the idea that I could please an adult just by showing up was foreign and enticing.

"How do you like Fielding? Merri's clearly besotted and I've had no misgivings, but after Monroe..."

"He's nothing like Monroe." Merri's ex-boyfriend had trampled every boundary she'd erected and assumed his prerogative trumped hers. I was glad he was gone—both dumped by Merri and expelled from Hero High. "Fielding's a truly decent person."

"Good. It's much easier when my girls date people we already know." Mr. Campbell smiled at his youngest daughter as she entered the kitchen and went straight for the box of teas. "So, thanks for that, baby girl."

"No problem," Rory said with a smile. "Morning, Eliza."

"Hi." I narrowed my eyes to study her. Not long ago she would've answered her dad with snark—something like, "Yeah, because that's exactly why I'm dating the boy next door, to make life easier for you." But since she'd started seeing Toby, Rory'd been less prickly. Less inclined to perceive everything as an attack. Her grades had also *improved*. She was the antithesis of my parents' anti-dating arguments. An outlier in their data set.

Rory added a mint tea bag and boiling water to her travel mug. She slid a pecan bar in her pocket, palmed an apple, and wrapped a muffin in a napkin for Toby. Her dad offered his cheek, and she kissed it before spinning back out of the kitchen. "Bye, Dad. See you at school, Eliza."

Mr. Campbell pulled off his pink, ruffled apron before taking a seat at the table. He nudged a chair out for me. "You okay? I know it's dangerous to comment on a person's appearance, but you're looking tired, Eliza-loo."

"I'm fine." But to distract myself, I picked up an apple from the paw-printed fruit bowl and spun it between my hands.

"Are you up for a science question, then?"

I sat up straight. "Always."

He beamed. "Okay, CRISPR…what is it? They've been talking about it on this podcast I listen to, but it's over my head."

"I can explain it."

"What would I do without you?" he asked. "Also, when are you starting a podcast for old duds like me?"

"You're not a dud." This was our long-standing routine—his questions, my answers, him joking about me starting a podcast called *Science for Fools*. But he wasn't one. It's just that the science community used so much specialized and exclusionary jargon. I leaned forward. "So, CRISPR stands for 'clustered regularly interspaced short palindromic repeats.' It sounds fancy, but let's break that down—"

These moments made me giddy. I wanted to clap, or laugh, or slow time. My parents talked science *at* me. My teachers recited material for tests. Merri tolerated my occasional science-journal tirades—but no one else asked. No one else wanted to hear me. I took a deep breath. "It's amazing. They're using it for gene editing and drug development—"

"Sorry, sorry! I'm the latest of the late and the worst and—Oh! Muffins!" Merri spun into the kitchen in a clatter of saddle shoes half on and books spilling out of her bag. I caught her copy of *Maria; or, The Wrongs of Woman*, a bookmark already wedged halfway through.

"Well, I won't make you girls any later. But maybe you could tell me another time, Eliza." I swallowed my disappointment as Mr. Campbell patted my shoulder and kissed Merri's cheek before she dragged me out the door.

"It's super depressing," Merri chirped as she plucked the novel from my hands. "Definitely not a romance."

"You should change books," I said. "Ms. Gregoire told me I could." Already I was wondering if I *should* pick one that didn't make me dream of icebergs and isolation. It wasn't like I needed Merri's permission to change, but if she also switched books, I'd feel less sheepish.

"Nah." Merri shrugged and climbed in my car. "It's one assignment. I'll find a way to make it work for me."

I sighed. If she could, I could too.

7

How's the future Most Likely to Succeed doing today?" Curtis dropped his lunch on the table, the metal clank of his water bottle so much louder than necessary.

"Are you talking to me?" I asked.

"Do you see anyone else who looks like they could write a self-help book at sixteen?"

That wasn't a compliment, was it? It couldn't be. Being named "Most Likely to Succeed" would be impressive only if you added "without even trying," and lately all my efforts felt transparent. "You're going to get voted 'Most Likely to Invent the Next Fidget Spinner.'"

"Awesome."

"I didn't mean it as a compliment," I clarified as he reached to fist-bump Lance, who asked me, "What's mine?"

"What's your what?" Merri scooted in next to me, grabbing a grape from the aluminum container in front of me and offering one of the hot breadsticks she'd bought from the buffet.

"Eliza's doing superlatives." Curtis filched the breadstick I'd declined.

"*You* started it," I answered.

"You escalated it to avoid answering my question."

He wasn't supposed to notice that. "I've changed my mind. Yours is 'Most Likely to Drive Someone to Murder.'"

"Do I at least get a cool getaway car?" he asked.

"What? No, not 'drive' like a chauffeur; like *you* are the cause—"

"Do me!" Merri paired her interruption with a shoulder nudge—a silent signal to stand down.

"'Future Bestselling Author,'" I said.

"'Most Likely to Accidentally Start a Cult,'" offered Curtis. When everyone head-tilted, he added, "Come on. Who hasn't followed her walking the wrong direction to class? You telling me that if Short Stack gave us Kool-Aid, we wouldn't drink it?"

"On that depressing note, you'd be 'Most Athletic,' 'Most Musical,' 'Best Dancer,' and 'Most Likely to Own a Bookstore.'" I pointed from Lance to Toby to Sera to Hannah, the last three having arrived during Curtis's cult recruitment.

"'Most Likely to Be Knighted,' 'Save Shelf Space for the EGOT,' 'Most Likely to Look Kickin' in a Tutu,' and 'Trout-Fishing Champion,'" countered Curtis.

The first and last ones didn't make sense to me, but everyone else was laughing. His were a reminder of their shared history. Mine highlighted that I'd known them only a few months. It was one-upmanship, and it was obnoxious.

The quinoa puff I'd been holding disintegrated in a fine dust beneath my fingers. The thing I was most likely to succeed at right now was murder. See, I'd been right about his.

Merri glanced over, but she didn't nudge or kick me or link her foot with mine beneath the table. My posture was rigid, my teeth ground tight, and the last thing I wanted was to be touched. She cleared her throat, and fine, maybe Curtis wasn't wrong about her potential as a future accidental cult leader, because everyone shut up and turned toward her. "Personally, I think I'm 'Most Likely to Be Covered in Dog Hair.' And Eliza's 'Most Likely to Discover a New Element.' I'd like to go on record that 'Merridium' would be an awesome name."

And just like that, she prevented lunch from ending in bloodshed. I hoped the magic held for quiz bowl practice.

Dr. Badawi was embarrassingly excited about my presence at practice, gushing, "Everyone, gather round. We have new teammates!" Only when she introduced *me* to the team, it was less an Eliza version of "This is Merrilee Campbell; she's a sophomore," and more a recitation of my parents' greatest hits with my name and "the daughter of" tacked on.

"...they're currently stationed in Antarctica, but I'm looking forward to the day we get to meet them and hear about their experiences and research."

Merri and I exchanged looks. My parents didn't do school events. They spent their rare trips home with colleagues and speaking at prestigious universities. Hero High wouldn't hit their radar. *I* barely registered on it; they always seemed slightly surprised and uncomfortable when our paths crossed in the upstairs hallway. Like they'd forgotten I existed as more than a voice on the other end of a phone line, or they didn't know how to interact with me outside of assigning work.

"...two years after receiving the Nobel Prize in medicine, they were awarded the Crafoord Prize in biosciences..."

And each time the Campbells invited them to a parents' organization meeting or class party, my parents' short trips home were suddenly shorter. Excuses given, flights booked. No, they would not be coming to talk to the team or bio classes. I shifted in my seat.

Bzzzzt!

Everyone turned to see Curtis holding a buzzer. Dr. Badawi tried to continue. "And their work on—" *Bzzzzt!* "As an undergrad, I read—" *Bzzzzt!* "Mr. Cavendish!" *Bzzzzt!*

"Sorry!" he shouted, then lowered his voice as the buzzing finally stopped. "The button was stuck. But it's fixed now. We're ready to start." He pointed to the other members of the team: a tall Black boy with a gold cross and wooden glasses; a prim white girl with pearls, but one pinky fingernail painted neon yellow; and a round Asian guy who looked up from a soccer-themed phone case and smiled. "That's André, Lynnie, and Norman. You know me and Bartlett. Let's play."

I didn't want to be beholden to Curtis and his interruption skills. I dug into my backpack, pulling out the pencil I'd carefully stowed in one of its elastic loops. "Here. Thank you for letting me borrow this."

He waved it off. "Keep it safe for me."

"I'm not your stationery security," I snapped, but I slid the pencil back in my bag. Cracking it in half and flicking the pieces at him would've been more satisfying but also a waste of wood and graphite. And maybe he read the urge in my scowl, or he was mocking my weak comeback, because he raised his eyebrows and grinned at me. Somehow, no matter how snarky I was to Curtis, it *amused* him—like my irritation was an inside joke, which only annoyed me more.

We were still staring at each other. I narrowed my eyes; he laughed.

Bartlett cleared his throat dramatically. "Today we'll be

practicing with no teams, all toss-ups. Everyone can buzz and answer. We clear?"

Merri and I glanced at each other. Mostly clear? This felt like a thing that required experiential knowledge. We nodded, accepted buzzers, and joined the others in the semicircle of lab stools that faced Dr. Badawi's podium.

She began to read from the tablet in front of her. "John Trumbull completed several oil paintings depicting the death of General Warren at this battle, the result of which was a Pyrrhic victory for the British, who suffered the highest casualty count of any battle of the Revolutionary—"

Bzzzzt! "The Battle of Bunker Hill."

"That's correct, Bartlett. Next. *Mein Leben* is the title of this famous composer's autobiography. Often associated with the use of leitmotifs—"

Bzzzzt! "Wagner."

"Yes, Lynnie."

Wait. She wasn't even finishing the questions.

"Bordered by two major rivers and named after a French king, this city is famous for being home to the world's tallest arch—"

Bzzzzt! "St. Louis."

"Yes, that's two for Bartlett. Next. The author of *Liber Abaci*, a 1202 book on numeration and place value. This Italian mathematician was also known as Leonardo Bonacci. He popularized the Hindu-Arabic numeral system, as well as a sequence of—"

Bzzzzt! "Um." Everyone turned toward Merri. "I think it's . . ."

"Do you know it?" asked Bartlett. "Don't buzz unless you do. If you don't answer within five seconds or you're wrong, we lose points and the other team gets it."

"It's Fibonacci," Merri said.

"Correct," said Dr. Badawi. "Next question. It's a science one." She looked over the top of her glasses at me before reading from her tablet. "This British baron scientist was the Nobel Laureate of 1911. Known as the father of nuclear physics, he worked on the discovery of the electron—"

I knew this one! I slid my finger onto the button, but the *Bzzzzt!* came from across the room. It was Norman's buzzer that lit up: "J. J. Thomson."

"No," said Dr. Badawi. My chin jerked up, but she'd already resumed reading. "He worked on the discovery of the electron *with* J. J. Thomson, who was both his teacher and a colleague. His work included disproving Thomson's plum pudding model of atomic structure by firing particles at—"

Bzzzzt! I felt Curtis's eyes on me as he pressed his button. "Ernest Rutherford."

"Yes." Dr. Badawi set down her tablet. "Maybe our new members aren't clear on the rules. Buzz as soon as you know. If you're wrong, the other team gets a chance to hear the whole question before answering. In this case they would've heard, 'by firing particles at thin sheets of gold, and determining that the nucleus of an atom was positively charged. Other discoveries included the concept of radioactive half-life and alpha and beta radiation. For ten points, name the scientist for whom the element with the atomic weight of one-oh-four is named.'"

"But—if they hear the whole question, it's easy," I said.

Bartlett scoffed. "That's the point. The smarter you are, the sooner you buzz. But be right, because if not, it's a freebie for the other team."

The rules made sense, but his language didn't. It wasn't about being "smart"—it was about the possession of specific pieces of knowledge. I would've guessed J. J. Thomson too—he'd fit the given information. Two questions later, Merri incorrectly answered "Allen Ginsberg," when it wasn't revealed until the end of the question that they wanted the title of one of his poems.

What was the tipping point between early and informed?

Bzzzzt! "Iran-Contra Affair."

Bzzzzt! "Chromatography."

Bzzzzt! "Kant."

Bzzzzt! "Azores."

Bzzzzt! "Caligula."

Bzzzzt! "Anne, Charlotte, and Emily."

The questions continued. Buzzers, flashes, clues, and answers. Merri nailed another few in math and most of the literature. Bartlett was all over historic battles and world leaders and geography. Lynnie knew current events and music. André and Norman covered religion and philosophy. Curtis handled science.

I sat.

I was never quick enough on the buzzer. Never a hundred percent certain.

As practice ended, Dr. Badawi distributed question packets for us to study. She gave two to Merri and said, "Pass one to Eliza." I was standing right there. It could've been for expediency, but it felt like rejection.

"Why practice old questions?" I asked. "I doubt they're reused."

"Spoken like someone who hasn't answered any."

"Shut up, Barty." Lynnie said it with a smile. Whether it was for him or me, I wasn't quite sure. But she added "Hang in there" before donning her tweed jacket and a wool cloche hat.

She headed out the classroom door, passing Fielding on his way in. His cheeks were rosy from the cold, and his eyes brightened as they landed on Merri. Her chin jerked up as she turned to him like a magnet that felt the pull of his presence. I watched them smile—his a quirk of lips, hers a full flash of teeth—as they met in the middle of the classroom. He tugged off leather gloves, then his long fingers were cupping her face.

He hadn't been a PDA person before Merri. Frankly, he'd been a teenage curmudgeon before her, but she loosened his rigidity and he reined in her wilder impulses. I doubted he'd ever participate in a sloppy public make-out session, but he did lower his mouth to hers in a quick kiss that was full of tenderness. My cheeks burned with the instinct to look away.

"You're scared of the buzzer."

I jumped. Had Curtis watched me watch them like some creepy voyeur? He held out his hand. It took me a blink to realize he wanted the black cylinder I still clutched. At least my thumb was no longer poised over the red button on top.

Not that it would've done anything had I pressed it, because he'd unplugged it and wound the cord in a neat bundle—waiting, patiently but fidgety, for me to give him the handheld part.

"I am *not* scared of the buzzer." But when I flexed my fingers, I realized how tense the tendons had become from my relentlessly tight grip.

"You hesitate." Curtis twisted an elastic band around the bundle. "When you do push the button, you flinch. You're a flincher."

I followed him as he crossed the classroom to the lab benches and tucked my torture device in a plastic bin beside the others. "I'm not a flincher. You should pay more attention to your own buzzer."

"*I* can do both. You may not have noticed, because you were too busy hesi-flinching, but I got ten questions today."

"And I got zero." I said it before he could. "I bet you regret recruiting me now."

"Nah. Though you're almost hopeless."

"How dare you!" I hated that phrase. How dare he what? State his opinion? One that was probably shared by everyone on the team? Why wouldn't he dare? Clearly there was no real consequence to his saying the words, since I couldn't even think of a decent retort.

"Kidding. But you need help."

Help was something I *gave*, not received. But my pulse was accelerating toward another anomaly, and Dr. Badawi's disapproval was veering toward a parent email. I swallowed, and it tasted of desperation. "What kind of help?"

"Come home with me. I'll show you."

started for the parking lot, but Curtis pointed in the opposite direction. "It's walkable. This way."

I kept glancing sideways, waiting for him to tap-dance, or do some parkour. I almost wanted him to, so his noise would drown out my *why-are-you-doing-this* thoughts. "This had better not be some sort of trick."

"It's not." He stopped walking. "We're here."

A short driveway led to a brick ranch. The house's trim was painted white, and the bushes in the flower bed were wrapped in burlap to protect against winter. The walkway was salted, and the stoop had a mat that read *Everyone Is Welcome.* A wreath of eucalyptus and bay leaves hung on the door.

Curtis swung it open, and we stepped directly into a family room that connected to a dine-in kitchen. There were coats hanging on a rack beside the door, and a shoe mat was set next to a bench. I took these as invitations to slide off my loafers and hang my coat. I left my book bag on the bench, hoping Curtis didn't have a dog like Merri's Gatsby, who assumed anything at snout level was his to chomp.

I checked for dog hair but concluded that even if there were a dog, I wouldn't see any; the house was immaculate. It was smaller than mine, Merri's, or most in town, but everything was organized: A basket for remotes on the coffee table beside a neat stack of coasters. Blankets folded over both arms of the couch and a trio of throw pillows lined up between. The curtains were sheer with elaborate gold embroidery. The laminate floors gleamed, and the kitchen counters sparkled beneath a wire basket of fruit and a plate covered in plastic wrap.

The bookshelves to my left displayed children's crafts and photos and cherished mementos. I wasn't sure how a human tornado like Curtis managed to come from this space, but before I could study the other people in the picture frames, he said, "So, does it pass inspection?"

"I—uh." Had he seen me swipe a finger across the windowsill to check if it was as dust-free as it looked?

"The curtains were sent from Egypt by my mom's mom—my teta."

He had. And it was.

I looked away. There was no way to explain my thoughts. Merri's house was homey but chaotic. You were welcomed, but good luck finding things where you'd left them or leaving without needing a lint roller. Mine was pristine but sterile—people hovered in the center of rooms and never felt comfortable touching anything or sitting anywhere. How did his house do both—be organized *and* inviting? Like, *go ahead and flop on the couch; here's a handy basket for the pillows if they're in your way.*

"Are we the only ones here?" I should've asked before following him home. I should've insisted on knowing what he wanted to do once we got here. I should've taken a minute to mentally prepare myself for Curtis to look so human and vulnerable when standing beside a framed handprint turkey, signed with crooked all-capital letters.

He shook his head. "Win! C'mere."

A guy who had to be his younger brother ambled out of the hallway on the left. His skin was a darker gold, his hair shorter and wavier, his jaw wider. They had the same wild eyebrows and long lashes, but his eyes were wary. Curtis's default expression, I realized, was curious.

The boy approached like each step was a decision he'd rather not be making. "What?"

Curtis shot me a grin. "Before you get cranky, I want you to—"

"Nope."

I gasped, not that he heard me. He was too busy walking away. "What was that about?" I asked.

"Eh, it's report-card season. I don't take it personally." Curtis stepped farther into the room. "Win, wait a sec. I just want to introduce you to Eliza."

Win paused and looked me up and down. "Now you're dating the hottest girl at your school. Cool story, bro. Tell me how it turns out—CliffsNotes version. You know I don't read."

"That"—Curtis tilted his head at the now-empty hallway—"was typical Win. It's not personal. He's just...angry."

"At least he didn't fawn over me." I'd take surly over lascivious any day.

Curtis laughed. "Oh, there's zero chance of that."

I wanted the beige throw rug to swallow me. Could I sound more conceited? "I didn't mean—"

"He's gay. You're not his type." Curtis flushed. So now we were a pair of awkward statues studying the ground. "I'll clarify later—you know—that we're not dating."

"Good." The word came out more emphatic than I had intended. "I take it you guys aren't close." I had no sibling experience, but when Merri and Rory fought, they weren't like that.

"Not so much." Curtis crossed to the kitchen and swiveled an empty stool. "I wish we were, but he makes everything so hard. Even when he came out last year—it was like he was expecting it to be this big deal or this fight or drama. He seemed disappointed everyone was like, 'Cool. Love you. Love whoever you decide to love.'"

"Maybe..." I fought the urge to grind my teeth, because *why was* I wading into his family dynamics? Especially with almost zero data and less than zero desire to get entangled? Perhaps because I'd been there—the one who shared with her parents, only to be not heard or appreciated? "Maybe he was disappointed because it *is* a big deal to him. And he wanted you all to treat it that way. Maybe he didn't want a fight, he just wanted acknowledgment that it was a dramatic moment for *him*."

Curtis frowned. "Maybe? I don't know. Win—I love him, but I don't get him. He's convinced everyone sees him as a screwup, and then he does self-destructive things to prove his point. For example: sabotaging his Hero High interview." He yanked off his tie and shoved it into the pocket of his blazer. "It's why he and my sister are doing their freshman year at public school."

I was unqualified and uninterested in playing family counselor. I kept my expression neutral as I took subtle steps toward the door. Whatever help Curtis planned to offer could be found baggage-free on Google.

"At least you can meet my sister without drama. She's probably got music on; I'll get her." Curtis disappeared down the hallway before I could object. I wasn't here to draw his family tree. I didn't need to meet his sister, analyze his brother's struggles, or see his report card full of As hanging beneath a green alien magnet on the fridge. I wanted him to stay the obnoxious guy from my lunch table. This—the handprint turkey, the muddy running shoes beside my loafers, the Halloween picture of gap-toothed siblings in Harry Potter costumes on the bookshelf—was making it too real.

I picked up my backpack.

"Eliza, meet Wink." The girl beside him had long, dark hair tucked beneath the white headphones looped around her neck. "Wink, this is Eliza."

She smiled as she said "Hi," so already she was friendlier than her twin. I slowly lowered my backpack to the bench.

"Win and Wink? Those have got to be Curtis nicknames."

"She's got your number." Wink laughed and poked her brother. "That's how you know if Curtis likes someone, whether or not they get a nickname. My real name's Lincoln. People shortened it to Linc, and with twins and etc.... it became Wink." She pointed at her other brother, who'd reentered the kitchen during her explanation and opened the fridge. "Win's short for Winston."

"My parents have a thing for last names as first," Curtis explained.

"How'd you escape?" I paused. "Though I guess Curtis can be a last name."

"Do you really not know about..." Win pointed his pinky like his milk glass was a posh teacup before adding "*Montgomery*" in a half-decent British accent.

"Who's Montgomery?" The question slipped out.

"Um—me." Curtis raised a hand, then held it out for me to shake. "Hi. Montgomery Curtis Cavendish, charmed to meet you."

I swatted at his hand. "Curtis isn't your name?"

"Are you feeling well, Eliza? Because this isn't a hard concept." He pointed to his chest. "Curtis is my middle name."

"Mine's Conan. He definitely got the better deal," grumbled Win, but his head was half in the fridge, so I assumed the comment was addressed to the carton of milk he was putting back and therefore required no response.

"Why not go by Montgomery?" My throat itched like I was upset or having an allergic reaction, and I didn't have a reason for either. It wasn't *my* name that had been kept secret for months. So what if I apparently didn't even know the fundamental facts about him? Like his grades or family or first name.

"Because 'Montgomery Cavendish' is a lot of letters when you're four years old and learning to spell your name. 'Curtis' is only six."

"You changed your name because you're lazy." I clutched this fact. It fit my existing schema. This afternoon had been like a carnival's fun house—full of mirrors that stretched and distorted everything I'd known to be true. I'd felt *foolish* at quiz bowl practice. Ignorant in a way that occurred only while talking with my parents. And every idea I'd compiled about this boy was warping.

"Also, neither of the twins could say it. Though I'm doing a book by a Montgomery for Gregoire's project."

"You're ridiculous."

"You've told me that before. Recycling your insults? You're slipping, Eliza."

"No, I told Curtis he was ridiculous. This time I'm telling Montgomery." My cheeks heated as soon as the words were out. I'd aimed for snarky but landed on something that sounded like a bad attempt at flirting. *Blast!* He even had a nickname for himself. Win, Wink, Short Stack, May, Sir Lance, Bookworm, Tiny Dancer...Everyone in our social circle had one. Everyone but me. And, yes, he'd called me "Legally Blonde" that one time, but that hardly counted. I crossed my arms and glowered at him.

"You guys are so cute." Wink sighed as she propped her chin on her hand. She'd joined Win at the kitchen counter, both of them eating slices of some sort of dessert loaf.

"We're not," I answered. "I should go."

"But this is better than LiveFlix." Win took an enormous bite and washed it down with gulps of milk. He wiped his milk mustache on the back of his hand. "Especially since Mom and Dad changed the password and I'm locked out."

"Stay," begged Curtis. "Win, I need your help." He'd taken off his Hero High blazer while fetching Wink, but now he reached for the buttons of his white shirt too.

I averted my face. "What are you doing?"

"Chill. I'm not stripping in my kitchen; I've got a T-shirt on underneath. But I'm spill-prone and my mom said I'm responsible for my dry-cleaning bill. So, the shirt comes off before the cranberry juice comes out. Want some? And date bread?"

I dared to glance back over. He hadn't been lying; he did have a T-shirt on. It was a white V-neck, slightly frayed on the edge of one sleeve. I guess it had to be slim-cut to fit under his dress shirt, but it skimmed his body in ways I wasn't prepared for. I followed the smooth lines of his arm muscles down to his hand, and my mouth felt dry. I had to swallow before asking, "What's on your wrist?"

The silver disk tied to two black cords. A flash of red glowed out from the metal.

"Medical-alert bracelet. I'm allergic to peanuts."

"How do I not know this?" My voice was shrill. "That's information you need to disclose to your lunch table. If I'm going to kill you, I want it to be on purpose, not because I packed veggie pad thai."

Win snorted. "I like this girl. I was going to say no, but, yeah, I'm down. What do you need help with?"

I ignored him. "What else don't I know about you, *Montgomery*?"

"A lot? You and I don't have many actual conversations." Curtis rubbed the back of his neck, and the bracelet slid along his wrist. "Mostly we fight and you tell me why I'm wrong."

"That's not—"

"Are you really going to tell me I'm wrong about you telling me I'm wrong?" He laughed.

Yes. "No." But I was still going to glower.

"Good. Win, set up the Switch. I'm thinking *Mario Kart*."

"I want to play," said Wink, and both of her brothers replied, "No."

"She's a shark," clarified Curtis as Win opened a cabinet and pulled out remotes.

"It's true," Wink admitted. "Fine, but none of you are allowed to be Peach."

"You brought me here to play video games?" My lip curled.

"We're going to get you past your buzzer phobia."

My parents would tell me this was a waste of time. They had invectives against screen time and violent games and—

"We need to get you familiar with remotes, work on your reaction times and dexterity and fine motor skills. It's a myth, you know, that games will make you addicted or violent. But they have been proven to enhance cognitive functioning."

"How so?" I demanded.

"Attention span, spatial processing, decision-making, memory, perception, and perseverance." He rattled these off.

Wink nodded. "It's true. We had to write up a rationale with sources before my parents would buy the Switch."

I couldn't include this in my daily log, but I shrugged off my blazer. "Fine. It can't hurt." I sat beside Win on the couch. "I'm warning you, I'm going to be bad at this. Pass me a remote."

I spent the next hour losing races. Sometimes losing *while* my dinosaur was driving backward and with Wink screaming suggestions. But at least I was losing by less now, and staying on the racetrack more. The remote wasn't as awkward in my hands. I didn't fumble as much or have to look down to locate the buttons.

"Mom and Dad are going to be home soon. You staying for dinner?" Wink was sitting on her hands to stop herself from grabbing our remotes.

"You should," Win added as he launched himself off a ramp. "Thursday's pizza night."

Curtis froze in surprise before he echoed his formerly prickly brother. "You should."

"I can't. I need to go after this race." I didn't do parents—at least not besides Merri's. And speaking of parents, mine had made several demands on the hours remaining before bed. There was a journal article to read and summarize; a workout; dinner to prep, eat, and record. Nancy would be expecting me... My dino's speed dropped from zoom to putter.

I was barely over the finish line when Wink stood and grabbed Win's arm. "We'll, uh...get out of here. So you have privacy or whatever."

Win said, "Come back and get your butt kicked again some-time," and Wink called over her shoulder, "Next time I'm play-ing too."

I jumped up. "I should go."

"I'll walk you to your car." Curtis's eyebrows were raised, presumably in preparation for whatever retort I'd launch. My jaw tightened, like now that the sibling and video-game buffers were gone, I needed to sharpen insults between my teeth.

It was such a contrast to three minutes earlier when his arm had reached around my back to steal his brother's remote, and the feel of his warm, bare skin through my shirt had also stolen my breath, causing me to steer off the rainbow road. Or the time five minutes before that, when I'd come in not-last and his hand had connected with mine in a high five so enthusiastic I'd dropped the controller. I needed to do some research and find an explanation for why my hand had tingled even after he removed his.

I shoved the memories out of my mind and my arms into my coat sleeves. "Thanks." While I wasn't one for chivalry, I was a fan of personal safety, so regardless of the fluke reactions I'd had to his touch, I let him walk me back to campus.

The sun had set, and outdoor lights illuminated the rem-nants of snowbanks. I was so conscious of the space between our dangling hands as we crunched down salted sidewalks. I wanted to thank him or apologize or explain. But where to start? The first time we met on campus, or the first time I saw him as a person? September? Or just a few hours ago?

I opened my mouth and got as far as "I—" before Curtis's words tumbled in, cutting mine off. "Do you think that—Oh, sorry. You were going to say something."

"It's nothing." I licked my lips. They tasted like mint balm. His probably were flavored with date bread or cranberry juice. "It's just—you have nicknames for everyone. Why not me?"

"I have one for you." He glanced sideways at me, and I felt my lips pull thin.

"Don't you dare say 'Legally Blonde.'"

"Ha." He laughed once, then turned serious. "No. That was clearly a nonstarter. What was the one you hated from your old school?"

My stomach churned—that ancient physiological signal that the body is in stress. So much stress that it stops the digestion process, and the pain is a signal to move, flee, get away from the stressor. Only I wasn't facing a saber-toothed cat or a mastodon. My body didn't need to switch from parasympathetic to sympathetic response. Running from Curtis's question wouldn't make me feel better. Sometimes evolution was slow to catch up.

I exhaled a deep breath and kept my feet planted. I'd learned a lot about him tonight. Merri was always on me about keeping people at arm's length—*You need to build gates, not fences.* Maybe it was time to follow her advice.

"The less-bad one was 'Ice Queen'—Elsa and Eliza are unfortunately close." I patted my hair self-consciously. I hadn't worn a braid since *Frozen* released. "But the one I really hated was 'Brainiac Barbie.'"

He whistled. "Why do people suck sometimes?"

"I don't know." His question was rhetorical, but my answer was earnest. My parents considered psychology to be an imprecise science, but that didn't stop me from wanting a road map of others' motivations and reactions. I took a deep breath and turned to Curtis. "What's my nickname, and why don't you call me it?"

His head dipped almost in line with his shoulders. Shoulders I shouldn't notice had gotten wider since the first day of school. Or, wait—why shouldn't I notice? That was biology. I *should* be making observations, especially about biological factors. Besides, noticing his shoulders and wanting to touch them or lean my head against them—those were totally different things.

"If you're not going to tell me, just say so."

Curtis met my eyes briefly. "Firebug."

I took a step backward. "Firebug? Like, *Pyrrhocoris apterus*? Why?"

Curtis's forehead creased. "No. Like Lampyridae. But I didn't like firefly or lightning bug—so I made a mash-up."

"A mash-up? Of course you did." Because why bother using the correct science terms or most common names when nick-naming someone after a beetle. A beetle!

He'd been watching my reaction, curiosity and concern warring on his face, but he ducked his head when he added, "'Firebug' just sounds cuter."

I blinked. "I'm not..." How to say this in a way that wasn't obnoxious? "I know I'm...attractive. But I'm not—Merri is, Hannah is, Rory's friend Clara is...but *I'm* not cute."

"Cute" was for smiles and freckles and gigglers and impulsive huggers and whisperers. People who didn't skip-count or list prime numbers to keep their expression blank. "Ice Queen" and "cute" were not compatible.

Curtis grinned. He took a step forward but then stopped and shoved his hands in his back pockets. "I think you're freaking adorable."

"What?" I felt dizzy, like my feelings had been spun in a centrifuge. *Adorable?* It hadn't been said in any infantilizing or insulting way, but *who said things like that?* And why did I want to smile, blush, and demand an explanation? But...No. He couldn't be serious, and I wasn't sticking around for the punch line. Maybe my long-ago ancestors were onto something. I speed-walked to my car, pretending not to hear his footsteps behind me.

Before I pressed the Unlock button, I spun around. The space between us felt alive, like the air was comprised entirely of charged ions. "Why are you even helping me?" I wasn't his concern. I wasn't anyone's. I was independent and self-reliant. And not cute.

He quirked an eyebrow. "Why did you let me, if you dislike me so much?"

"I don't dislike you," I snapped. "Our friends are friends. I don't have that luxury."

Curtis reached around me to open my car door. "Good luck maintaining that distance, Firebug."

9

Except for when I needed a guardian's signature on something, Nancy and I basically coexisted. Her predecessors—other female doctoral students who had been vetted by my parents as responsible and sufficiently brilliant—had been chattier. Or had at least attempted to be until they'd realized I was small talk intolerant.

So I was surprised when Nancy practically ran to meet me in the kitchen when I came in.

"Are you excited?" she asked.

"About?" She clearly was. Her eyes glowed, and her pixie cut stuck out like she'd been playing with a Van de Graaff generator.

"Your parents!" Ah. That made more sense. She'd turned the guest room into a shrine to their accomplishments. They must've added another publication or award or honorary doctorate. Nancy's hands wrung the neck of her water bottle. "I can't believe they agreed to judge. I would've been incoherent if I'd gotten to meet them as a teen. I want to drive to Delaware and see if my parents have any of my old projects."

"Judge what?" I mean, they were full of judgment, so whatever it was, they'd excel. But something about Nancy's uncharacteristic ramble tightened my throat.

"The Avery Science Competition! Your entrance forms and info packet are on the counter." Nancy paused for my reaction. When I didn't give her one, she provided her own. "You *have* to do something impressive. You can't embarrass them."

I shook my head. "You're mistaken. I'm not allowed to enter science fairs."

There'd been an incident in fourth grade. A parent had objected to my win, protesting loudly and publicly, "There's no way a child did that project. She cheated. Clearly her parents did it for her."

My parents had been on another continent, but their reaction had been definitive: Science fairs were off-limits and beneath me. They'd instructed me to return my prize—and then I'd come home to a house adorned with all of theirs.

I glanced at the plaques and trophies on the mantel as Nancy flipped open the folder. "Look." The bold star on the cover proclaimed, **JUDGING PANEL INCLUDES NOBEL PRIZE-WINNING SCIENTISTS DRS. VIOLET GORDON AND WARNER FERGUS.**

My eyes widened in shock, then narrowed in hurt. The competition was being held at Princeton—just an hour away—six weeks from now, right before spring break.

Finally, I found my voice. "They're coming home?"

Tonight's workout was supposed to be yoga. Instead I tied my sneakers. I'd explain why I'd ditched the mat for the treadmill when they explained why they hadn't told me they were coming home.

For a science competition. Not for me. And when they'd compiled their list of people to tell, I'd been left off. Dr. Badawi's comments at the start of today's practice made sense now. She *would* get to meet them. I lurched, almost tripping over. What if she told them how unimpressive my quiz bowl performance was?

I steadied myself with both hands on the treadmill's arms. I couldn't think about it, or about Nancy saying "You can't embarrass them." Or the fact that they'd be under this roof and able to see my unauthorized runs. How would they react to catching me playing an hour of video games?

I looked down at the iLive band I'd forgotten to take off; they'd know I'd disobeyed. Despite my fierce *I'll explain myself when they do* vows, I hadn't meant to get caught.

I didn't care. I nudged the speed up and opened my book. I was staying on here until I felt calmer; if that took the rest of Mary Shelley's saga, so be it. At least then I wouldn't have to live in Victor Frankenstein's morose head anymore.

A few pages later I put the book down in disgust. Victor's inner monologues felt like my parents reaching through the pages. They'd love for me to lift my chin and announce, "So much has been done…more, far more, will I achieve…I will pioneer a new way, explore unknown powers, and unfold to the world the deepest mysteries of creation." Instead I was left with the memory of being ten years old and trying not to cry as I turned in my first-prize ribbon. My chest felt tight in ways unrelated to the speed of my feet. Was I really allowed to enter? Did I want to? I had zero ideas and only six weeks.

I picked the book back up. Maybe if I couldn't find my own genius, I could borrow some of Victor's. He was the sort of child my parents should have had. They'd admire the way he dove into an obsessive study and isolated himself for months at a time with a singular purpose. They might have a slight pause about his *actual* purpose—building a body with stolen corpse pieces he intended to reanimate—but they'd praise his work ethic and ambition.

The chapter in which he succeeded was where I stopped reading and running. Because nothing about the scene felt celebratory. As his piecemeal body breathed and moved, he said, "the beauty of my dream vanished, and breathless horror and disgust filled my heart."

Victor's vocabulary changed: His "creation" became a "creature," a "wretch," a "monster." He ran shrieking into his bedroom and shut the door, then fled the apartment and stayed away all day—like that was going to magically undo what he'd done.

The monster wasn't a swarm of bees. It wasn't a skunk that got in your car, so you leave the doors open and hope he'll find his way back out. He may have been wretched, but he was Victor's responsibility. And Victor's relief when he returns to his apartment and finds his creation gone infuriated me.

People didn't get to do that—create something and then abandon it to raise itself. Be super obsessed with science to the point of losing touch with the side effects of their experiments. Victor owed the monster so much more than that. He was its parent and—*blast!*

I was sure Ms. Gregoire would've had thoughts about how much I was projecting and blaming a book for my own mother and father. She might have applauded my personal connection to what I was reading...but more likely she'd have smiled sympathetically and reminded me of her warning: *Frankenstein* was not an emotionally healthy book for me.

10

Merri was having dinner at the headmaster's house on Saturday. It wasn't the first time Fielding's dad had invited her to dine with them, but apparently the menu was "spaghetti." We spent Friday's drive home brainstorming apparel. "Would black or red hide the inevitable twirl-spatter better?"

"Do you own any black?" I asked, because her nonuniform wardrobe was an arsenal of colors and prints. Mine was the opposite: I bought clothes only in white, black, gray, or the occasional dusky purple. It made dressing efficient and uninteresting. Merri teased that I'd "had a uniform even before we went to a school that required it."

The thing was, nothing about my clothing drew attention to itself. Nothing was sparkling or short or tight or low-cut. But it shouldn't have mattered if they were *all* of those things. Harassment was a game of power—one I was constantly forced to play but could never win, since it stemmed from the harasser's belief that their prerogative about someone else's weight, religion, race, gender, sexuality, appearance, etc., trumped a person's right to that identity.

And while Merri spent Saturday night at her boyfriend's house camouflaging sauce stains with a shirt she'd stolen from

Rory's closet, I spent mine being hassled by a clerk in the grocery store.

He interrupted me while I was crouched and scanning the spice shelves. Coming closer and closer until I couldn't ignore the scuffed brown loafers that had entered my personal space. "All those groceries in your basket—are you here with your boyfriend?"

I narrowed my eyes. "I'm here with my shopping list."

The man, who was around the same age as my father, wiped his hands on his green store apron and leaned down. "Ah, single. Well, here's a tip: you can find single fellas by the frozen dinners."

I stood and propped a hand on my hip. The aisle was empty, but the store was busy enough that it felt safe to respond with anger instead of escape. "I'm shopping for groceries, not a date. Also, I'm not impressed by your heteronormative assumptions." I wanted to tell him to look up the term "amatonormativity" but decided not to waste my breath.

The clerk stroked his chin. It had a single dimple, like someone had poked him with a skewer while the doughiness of his face was still rising. The image was satisfying. "So you're looking for a girl? My neighbor's got a daughter that likes girls."

"I'm looking for turmeric. And a new grocery store." If there was ever a time to be an ice queen, this was it.

But doughface grinned like I was joking. "Top shelf. And think about smiling more—it'll make you approachable."

I didn't need "approachable." I needed the opposite of approachable. Because after the confusion I'd felt at the Cavendishes' house and in the parking lot Thursday night, I'd done my best to freeze out Curtis in school on Friday: changing direction on a path, getting engrossed in my phone, starting an impromptu conversation with a startled girl from my history class whose name I'd never learned, ducking into the bathroom.

And yet, every time I shut a door or swiveled away, I caught him grinning in my periphery. Worse, when I could do so without being seen, I couldn't help grinning back. *Blast.*

When it had been time for Friday's Convocation, I'd gathered Merri and Hannah around me like human shields, sitting between them and instigating a conversation about a book series that had them both salivating. They'd talked across me and over each other about "cliffhangers" and "world-building," and I'd leaned smugly against the bench.

Only to feel breath and words tickle the back of my neck. "Win wants a rematch—and Wink wants in. Says she'll play one-handed if we let her join. So, want to make my siblings happy?"

My lips had twitched into a smile—a safe one, since he couldn't see it. There couldn't have been more than three inches from his lips to my ear. He must've been seated on the edge of his bench and leaning forward. If I'd shifted even slightly, my blazer would've brushed where his hands gripped the back of my row. Would they have felt as warm and electric as they had on his couch? I'd meant to look up an explanation for that—but then my parents/the Avery...and *Frankenstein.*

The words *And what about you?* had withered on my lips. I'd turned my head sharply to the left, probably lashing him with my ponytail as I'd ignored him and asked Hannah, "Do you know how many books are planned for the series?"

Standing beneath the fluorescent lights of aisle six, I pressed my teeth against the memory as I tossed a canister of turmeric into my shopping basket. In my mind, it bounced out and shattered on the store's gray floor, causing an orange cloud of powder that choked the overzealous clerk.

Sometimes it felt easier to get groceries delivered; to do all shopping online, so it arrived at my door in boxes and without human interaction. Sometimes the isolation of my parents' research base sounded appealing. Frankenstein's monster would have understood this. He knew what it was like to be judged by his appearance—*only* his appearance. Like it was the sole thing that mattered or it told the observer everything they needed to know.

After I checked out, I stood beside my car—parked under a street lamp in a space close to the store—and wanted to scream. I yearned to demonstrate my understanding of the monster's growing thirst for vengeance and his frustration with people deciding they could determine the measure of his person—his morality, his intelligence, his capabilities—based on the way he looked.

I wanted a world where I could wear whatever I wanted. Go wherever I wanted. A world that was designed to keep girls safe, instead of one where we had to adapt our behavior to accommodate the gaze and insinuations of those who felt entitled to others' bodies or time or attention or smiles.

But it was dark. It was a parking lot. I was alone. So I clutched my keys between my fingers as I returned my cart and peered in the windows of my car before I got in and drove home.

11

understood why others hated Mondays, but I was relieved to reach bedtime Sunday night. Even more relieved when my alarm went off Monday morning. Merri's and my dynamic had shifted since she'd started dating Fielding. She spent a lot of weekends at his fencing tournaments and had this vocabulary and knowledge about a sport I'd never seen. I could've invited myself or accepted her invitations, but it felt like a duo activity. I was no longer the default other half of Merri's duo.

Her priorities hadn't shifted; they'd expanded. Mine hadn't. Which left days where I spent too much time in my head. Too much time alone.

But drives to school were still ours.

"How's my favorite scientist?" Mr. Campbell asked as I walked into the kitchen. He held up a finger, asking me to hold on, then flicked the switch to run the garbage disposal. I was grateful for its loud, mechanical grinding, because it gave me time to process his words. *His favorite scientist.* He meant it. Even though I wasn't as accomplished or brilliant as the doctors Gordon and Fergus.

I didn't think I was my parents' favorite anything. Nancy had known since Thursday about their upcoming trip home, but it had taken them until yesterday to acknowledge it with me.

I'd read their short email until I'd had it memorized, hoping I'd find a way to interpret their words differently. To find some hidden excitement about seeing me.

Eliza,

I trust you've heard we acquiesced to judge the Avery Science Competition. Presumably you've realized it would be a conflict of interest for us to judge your project, so we'll abstain and let the rest of the judging panel evaluate it instead. We've included some links to articles about past winners. As you know, this competition is a feeder for the International Science and Engineering Fair—that should be your end goal.

Mr. Campbell flicked the disposal off and twisted the faucet. "Sorry about that. What's new with you? Merri's on the phone, and I'd holler up or tell you to barge in, but she's talking to Senator Rhodes about how to use early feminist writings in modern political messaging. Something about showing both progress and lack thereof?" He reached for a dishcloth to wipe down the counter. "She can explain it better. Or maybe you already know—it's her project for English. What are you doing?"

Merri had already started her project—and it was an important one. I could barely make myself keep turning pages. This made *two* projects I was behind on, since I hadn't figured out anything for the Avery either. "I don't know."

"I can't say I've ever heard those words come out of your mouth." He put down the towel and faced me. "Want to talk about it?"

If I pulled up the link to past Avery winners, I knew how he'd react—with a whistle and a request I translate those long jargon-y titles "out of sciencese." That was what my parents expected from me: a project no one beyond a select circle would understand. What *I* wanted from them? To be understood.

Rory had left a sketchbook on the counter, with supplies on top. I picked up her kneaded eraser and began to twist it. "There's a scene about a hundred pages into *Frankenstein*—that's the book I'm reading—where the monster describes how he spent a winter living in a hovel and spying on a house and its inhabitants. From them he learns what a family *is*, but not how to be part of one. Sometimes I feel like that—with you all, with my classmates. That I'm an excellent observer, but not a member of anything."

I didn't tell him the rest. How the monster hadn't just observed the family but eventually tried to infiltrate them. His presence so horrified them that they'd packed up and fled in the middle of the night. He *ruined* them. And from there he begins a streak of destructive vengeance: burning houses, committing murder...

"Can I give you a hug?" I liked that he asked—both because *consent*, and also because I desperately needed one. Mr. Campbell was short and soft. He smelled like dish soap and coffee and dog. "Eliza, you know Jennifer and I consider you to be practically a Campbell. You have parents, and I don't mean them any insult, but you are the fourth daughter we would've loved to have. You *are* part of this family and our community. An important part."

"Thank you." I whispered the words into the weave of his thick sweater. He acknowledged them with a pat on my back before he let go.

"I know I've offered this a dozen times, and I don't want to make you uncomfortable or add pressure, but the invitation to move in stands. You are always welcome here. As much as it pains me to admit it, Lilly's assured me she has no post-marriage plans to move back. Though we'd take Trent too—wouldn't we, Gatsby? Wouldn't be such a bad thing to have another guy in the house." He bent to extricate Merri's dog, who was snout-deep in the trash can.

"That's kind, but..." I shrugged and flailed for a new topic. I couldn't handle one centered on my parents right now. I'd emailed them back—reminding them I wasn't *allowed* to enter science fairs.

They'd forgotten. They'd entirely forgotten about fourth-grade me being humiliated in front of the entire school. Worse, once I'd reminded them, they'd responded like it was funny.

The judges back then probably didn't understand the title of your project, never mind the content. Ha. Rest assured these judges can keep up. Even if your peers still can't.

What was so great about elitism? It was my least favorite thing about the science community—the way it found joy in using vocabulary that excluded people. Maybe we wouldn't have such problems with climate-change deniers or anti-vaxxers if people understood the science behind them. Or like the podcast Mr. Campbell had given up on—it had the opportunity to educate him on one of the greatest breakthroughs of the last hundred years, but instead he'd turned it off because it made him feel not smart enough. I didn't want a project that fell into that trap.

He might not have a Nobel Prize, but he knew *me* well enough that he'd never have written a postscript like my parents': One other thing: make sure to check the application box that denies permission to include your image in press or advertisements. Otherwise you'll likely end up on the cover of next year's brochure looking like some Barbie doll in a lab coat.

They didn't know about my charter-school nickname, how cutting those words were. But standing in this bright kitchen, my hurt was dangerously close to the surface.

"Thank you." My words were watery, but Mr. Campbell wasn't the sort to run from tears. He gave me a nod, seeming to read that I couldn't stomach another hug or the verbal equivalent. I didn't have enough practice with affection to tolerate it gracefully.

"Gah!" Merri slid into the kitchen in mismatched socks: swords on her left foot, hearts on her right. Her socks never matched, but this pairing was a tribute to Fielding. She took out a box of toaster pastries. "I hate Monday mornings. And Senator Rhodes said my idea for mandatory three-day weekends was no go." She turned to me with a smile and held out a packet of roasted chickpeas. "If you were a senator and I were a senator, you'd cosign that bill, right?"

I didn't know who I was more disappointed in: myself for nodding because it was easier than explaining why a seventy-two-hour weekend sounded nightmarish, or her for not knowing me well enough to recognize the truth. Me for not speaking up and saying I'd missed her this weekend, or her for not having missed me and called.

I couldn't remember a time I'd lied to her before, but it felt like a tipping point or a test—one we'd both failed.

12

On Tuesday I asked Merri to ride with Toby, because I was headed to school early. It wasn't just Curtis I'd avoided since last week; it was Ms. Gregoire too. I wasn't fooling her with my ducked head and lack of class participation. She'd intercepted me on the way out of class yesterday to simply say, "Remember, my door is always open."

And so Tuesday morning I stood in front of it, debating whether to knock or walk away.

"Come in, Eliza."

I blinked. The classroom door that was metaphorically "always open" was currently closed. It didn't have windows. Maybe she could see the shadow of my shoes? There had to be a logical explanation.

Ms. Gregoire was seated at her desk when I walked in. "You are *not* Frankenstein's monster. Before we begin any conversation today, I want to state that." She put down her pen and raised her eyes to meet mine. "Do you hear me? More importantly, do you believe me?"

"I—" I glanced at her desk. My response journal was on top of it.

Last night, after I'd submitted the assignment to our class drop box, I'd pulled the suggested book list—the one that somehow had ended up in my copy of *Frankenstein*—from my desk drawer. Any title on there had to be less painful than what I was reading, but there was one that stood out. And not just because it had been underlined in green pen.

"You were right. I need to switch books." The words slid out of my mouth smoother than I'd expected, but now I needed a rationale. "It's . . . is Mary Shelley worried her readers have never seen a tree or mountain or lake? There's a tedious amount of nature description."

She smiled. "I don't think this is your real issue with the book."

It wasn't.

There'd been illness and murder and innocents executed—but the monster and Victor had finally met up again. And in the middle of the monster's confessions of his deeds, he'd issued an ultimatum: *Make me a companion and I'll leave humanity alone.*

I wasn't sure if I was horrified or jealous that Victor had agreed, but either way, I needed to be done. As Ms. Gregoire had said, I was not the monster—and yet he was the one I was rooting for. That could not end well.

"May I switch books?"

"Of course." Ms. Gregoire moved the stack of papers out of the way so she could lean forward. Her rust-colored dress was printed with old-fashioned suitcases. "Would you like a suggestion?"

"No suggestions!" I blurted. "I'd like to choose."

"Let me grab a copy of the list." While Ms. Gregoire rummaged through her desk, I studied the books stacked on top of it. A bright green cover caught my eye. I spun it around to reveal its title and froze. It was the same one that had been underlined on my list. The same one I'd come here to request: *Anne of Green Gables.*

"This is set on Prince Edward Island. Does it count as Brit Lit?"

"I give it the 'Commonwealth close-enough.' PEI only became confederated the year before Lucy Maud Montgomery was born, and she was an officer of the Order of the British Empire." With a push of one finger, Ms. Gregoire slid the novel smoothly out of the middle of the stack. The other books didn't wobble. I blinked as I tried to figure out the physics behind that feat. It had to be something about force and motion—like when magicians yanked a tablecloth from beneath an elaborate dinner spread without disturbing the dishes. She flipped casually through the book, and I fought the strangest urge to yank it from her hands as she asked, "Have you read it?"

"No, but I spent a summer there when I was in elementary school. My parents were studying the prevention of parabolic dune erosion." I didn't mention that it was my best summer, because the local scientist they'd been working with had a daughter around my age. For two months I ran down beaches and splashed in waves and danced to fiddle music at cèilidhs. Dr. Rostine and his husband had brought me to the wharf where I'd chosen my own lobster from the traps being unloaded off boats, and I'd eaten it with roasted new potatoes and sweet blueberries I'd stained my fingers picking. I'd had mosquito bites and freckles and sunburns. Red clay beneath my nails, tan lines, jellyfish stings. My hair had been snarled from blowing freely and highlighted with sun streaks, and the taste of salt water had radiated from my skin.

Dr. Rostine had been a force of nature—and while he'd never managed to get my parents on a golf course, and they'd drawn a firm line in the proverbial sand about me jumping from the Basin Head bridge, they'd also taken off their shoes, rolled up their pants, and walked along the beach with me at sunset. Granted our conversation had been about dune erosion, not the golds and pinks that streaked the sky or the red clay rocks I skipped in the waves—but it was nearly perfect. I'd almost read *Anne of Green Gables* back then, but each time I picked it up, my parents had swapped it for a scientific journal.

"Could I switch to this book?" I reached across her desk, and I swore it started moving toward me too—like my fingers were magnetic and it was a metal object within their field of pull—until she stopped it with a hand on top.

"I wish I could say yes, but someone's already chosen it. No duplicates."

I stepped back like I'd been pushed, licking lips that moments ago had tasted of memories of mussels cooked in salt water.

"Buuuut..." Ms. Gregoire drew the word out.

Normally I tolerated her theatrics; this time I interrupted. "But you'll make an exception?"

She shook her head. "I can't have it look like I'm playing favorites." I recoiled from the suggestion—I already had enough accusations of nepotism. "But you could ask the other student to switch."

"I don't want to inconvenience anyone," I lied. There were so many other books I could choose from, but Anne made me think of my parents and happy times—it was an antidote to my *Frankenstein* anxiety.

"Oh, I think this classmate would be delighted to be inconvenienced by you." She drummed her fingers on the cover, right below the author's name: Lucy Maud Montgomery. "I doubt he's started yet."

"He?" I wanted to grind those two letters between my teeth, because I knew the answer before I asked, "Who is it?"

There was only one student in school who seemed genetically engineered to cause obstacles and chaos with each breath. And he'd told me "I'm doing a book by a Montgomery for Gregoire's project."

"Curtis Cavendish. Ask him, and see what he says. Regardless, let me know your new title when you've got it sorted." She opened a notebook and struck through where *Frankenstein* was written next to my name.

I didn't trust my hands not to grab for that novel, so I curled my fingers into my palms and gritted out, "I can make *Frankenstein* work. Thank you anyway."

As I turned to leave, Ms. Gregoire said, "Eliza, sometimes we don't ask for what we want because we're scared of being told yes."

I nodded like her fortune-cookie philosophy made sense, but it was absurd. People sought out affirmation—they wanted positive responses. It was "no" that caused avoidance, not "yes."

Curtis went full dance mom at quiz bowl practice. He'd sought me out while I was shedding my winter layers, folding my gloves and scarf and placing them neatly on the lab bench beside Merri's pile. I must've been more nervous than I realized, because I let him. "I've picked out a special buzzer for you. It's a little more sensitive than the others. You've got this."

I reached into my backpack and pulled out the pencil he'd loaned me. It bothered me to have it as a stowaway among my own supplies. I was aware of it all day.

He shook his head. "Keep it. And remember, the buzzer is your friend. No flinching, flincher."

"Shut it, Montgomery," I answered, placing the pencil back in my bag. But it was impossible to inject those words with barbs while trying not to smile.

"Good. I'm glad you're together." Bartlett's stocky shoulder edged Curtis's aside. He pointed a broad finger at me, but he spoke to Curtis. "You wanted her on the team, so it's your responsibility to get her up to speed. We're not a ship; we don't need a decorative figurehead."

If this were a toss-up question, I'd be hesi-flinching, because *ouch*. I wanted words as weapons and anger that made my tongue lethal, but instead I burned with embarrassment.

Curtis rolled his shoulders back and lifted his chin. I always forgot how tall he was, because he was usually so languid. Now every muscle on him looked tight and intimidating. His cheekbones sharpened as he drew in a breath, and his voice was a low rumble. "It's a good thing this *isn't* a ship, because there'd be a mutiny." Then his posture melted back to casual. He grinned as he saluted. "But, aye, aye, Captain."

The transformation had been so absolute and so temporary. I wondered if I'd imagined it, but Bartlett's cheeks were as red as his freckles. He stomped off without replying.

Curtis held his hand up for a high five, but I turned away. I wasn't his responsibility. If I couldn't prove my worth, I'd relinquish my spot. I didn't need to owe him anything else—and I wasn't asking for any more favors.

"Eliza," Merri called from across the room. When I reached her, she said, "Looked like you needed an intervention. You're welcome."

"He's so..." I wasn't sure how to end that sentence. I let it trail off and trusted Merri to fill in the blank.

She did, with laughter. "Don't ever change."

I sat stiffly, because I *had* changed, and she hadn't noticed. No one had. Even Curtis didn't know how much effort I was putting into avoiding him. How much energy it required to find rage for my glares and blades for my words. Last night I'd spent an hour googling nonsense things like "skin tingles." I'd ghost-browsed his iLive social profile—he apparently believed in aliens and UFOs, and that alone should've exiled him from my thoughts.

A few hours at his house had stolen plates from my armor and compromised my emotional force field. I didn't know how to change things back. Especially when he beamed like *he* had gotten a perfect SAT score the first time I buzzed and got an answer correct.

I wrapped my legs around my stool and ground my teeth to keep from smiling back. It didn't take much effort, because surprised silence had stretched between the moment I'd said "isobar" and when Dr. Badawi had blinked before saying, "That's—correct! Well done, Eliza."

"Next question," prompted Merri, and I readied my finger.

At the end of practice I sent Merri to fetch our packets, because Dr. Badawi's relief at my new proficiency was palpable and I didn't want to discuss it or the science fair. She'd brought the Avery up in class the past two days—"I know those of you who typically participate have been at work for months, but the registration deadline's approaching and I urge the rest of you to consider it too, if only for the opportunity to interact with such renowned judges."

Merri had shot me a *we're-going-to-talk-about-this-later* look when Dr. Badawi named them Monday morning, but we hadn't. I'd dodged, and she'd been distracted.

Bartlett sauntered over. "I guess you're not completely worthless. But keep practicing."

Lynnie rolled her eyes and offered me an exasperated smile. "Ignore him. You did well."

"Yeah," added André. "Bartman needs to chill."

I bit back a smile, because Bartlett hated "Bartman" even more than "Barty." Especially when Curtis inserted it into the *Batman* theme song. I searched the classroom for him. He was zipping up his backpack—shoving in a book that had fallen out. One with a familiar green cover.

I turned away before he could catch me and misinterpret my expression. It was the book I was studying with such longing. Not the boy.

13

The anniversary of Sera and Hannah's first date was Friday, and from the way everyone had been whispering about it all week, you'd have thought they were planning a surprise wedding—a task Merri was more than adept at, having organized her older sister's elopement at the beginning of the month. Monday through Wednesday, I'd tolerated the conversations. I hadn't *participated*, but I'd been a benign observer. But by lunch on Thursday their hearts-and-romance frenzy grated against every raw emotion left over from last night's parental call. I wanted to muzzle them all.

"Quick—Hannah's in the bathroom, and Sera's in line," Lance said. "Does everyone know their job? I've got balloons for their lockers."

"I have a question about the cupcakes," Curtis said. "Eliza, is there a version you'd actually eat? Or is getting you to ingest anything sugary a lost cause? My theory is you fear it'd sweeten your disposition."

I heard his words, but I couldn't process them. My gaze was fixated on Merri's neck. I blinked—my eyes puffy from crying and dry from lack of sleep—but it didn't change what I'd seen. Merri had stretched her arms, and the action had momentarily exposed an inch of skin normally covered by her collar—revealing a purplish-red mark that hadn't been there yesterday.

I'd called her last night. Twice. She hadn't answered. During the drive this morning she'd paused in the middle of a story about Fielding's dog to say, "Sorry I never called you back. I was busy. Everything okay?"

It wasn't. But the explanation was bigger than the remaining two minutes of our ride, so I'd brushed it off. I'd assumed she'd been busy at the store. Or with her sisters. I'm not sure why learning she'd been busy *with Fielding* was making my stomach twist, but I couldn't stop staring at her collar.

I'd *needed* her. My parents had called...and the cursed book...and I'd *needed* her.

Victor had started building the monster a companion. I'd skipped the treadmill, turning pages while curled up in a chair, because my body felt tense and tight. I'd wanted to get in my car and drive across town and ask Curtis to trade books. I'd even checked my phone to see if I had his number. I didn't. Maybe if I did, or maybe if Victor had kept his promise, my night would've gone differently. But once Victor saw the monster watching his progress in gleeful anticipation, he destroyed the female creature "on whose future existence [the monster] depended for happiness."

The monster howled. I might've too. Except that moment—when I was feeling isolated and doomed to loneliness—was when my parents had called.

Either Dad had skipped a greeting or I'd missed it while pulling my mind out of *Frankenstein*. "You didn't respond to our last email."

"I know." Their postscript still rankled. I was supposed to acquiesce, but I doubted Frankenstein's monster was going to shrug off Victor's broken vow. He'd repay that act of betrayal in blood.

"Excuse me?" Dad was nine thousand miles away, but sound waves had carried his disapproval to my ear in milliseconds.

My free hand had curled into a fist. "'Barbie doll in a lab coat'? How do you think it makes me feel when you say things like that about how I look?" I'd immediately regretted my phrasing. "Feel" wasn't in my parents' lexicon. They valued only one *f* word: "*facts.*"

"Your appearance is not your identity." I had practically heard the hand-wave Mom had executed as she'd dismissed me.

"Yes, but—"

"You'd be the same person if you were grotesque," Dad had added. "We don't want you to derive your value from the way you look."

"But I'm not grotesque," I'd protested. "And would you say the same about intellectual capabilities? Would I be the same person if I suffered brain trauma?"

"This conversation is not productive."

"This conversation is important!" I'd objected. "I'm sick of you making me feel bad. I only get one body to experience life through. This one's mine. It's not fair of you to expect me to constantly be at war with it."

"Oh. *Oh!*" Mom had sounded like she'd had a *eureka* moment, but I'd doubted her conclusion was the same as mine. She'd cleared her throat. "We understand you're maturing and your body is being flooded with hormones that lead to sexual urges."

"Sexuality is a natural thing," Dad had interjected.

"But, this is why we have rules against dating. No birth-control method is a hundred percent effective."

"And within that margin of error is the difference between a GED and a PhD." Dad had sounded particularly chuffed with this phrasing, but Mom had sighed.

"Not that there aren't young mothers who *do* go on to get PhDs or have academic and career success, but the odds are against them."

"What we're saying is, in adolescence, your limbic system—which controls emotional receptivity—is very responsive. It often overrides the prefrontal cortex's rational—"

"She knows how the parts of the brain function, Warner. What Eliza needs is advice on dealing with... *urges.*"

"No she does not!" I'd blurted out. "I haven't even kissed anyone!"

"This explains those queries in her internet search history: 'frisson,' 'what causes skin to tingle,' 'scientific explanation for skin sensation,' 'somatosensory system'—I told you they were significant."

"You monitor my web browsing?!" But they hadn't acknowledged my outrage.

"We're going to send you articles," Mom had replied. "Some of them you've read before—but clearly you need a review. You've got too much potential to get trapped in codependency. You are a capable, independent, brilliant young woman. There's so much you could achieve. The last thing you need is to lose your identity and goals in some fleeting adolescent relationship."

The call had ended without them hearing me. I'd just needed to be *heard.* And if not by them, and not by Merri...

"Eliza." Curtis's voice was insistent. He picked up my banana from the lunch table and waved it in front of my face. "Hello?"

"Give her a minute," interjected Merri. "She's having a think. You know a problem is complex if Eliza doesn't immediately have an answer."

But I *did* have an answer; it was written in the way my stomach clenched with nonsensical jealousy when Merri put a hand on Curtis's wrist to draw his arm back. Jealousy that roared irrationally when he smiled at her and said, "I'll have to keep you around. You're like an Eliza user's guide."

She was dating Fielding. The proof of that was on her neck. Curtis only wanted her to decode *me*. Yet my churning stomach rejected these facts.

"Did you break Eliza?" Toby asked him. Like Curtis was my spokesperson. Or had the power to break me. Like I was a thing that could be broken. Torn apart limb by limb like Victor's female monster, who only *almost* existed to bring the male monster happiness.

I closed my hands in fists and opened my mouth. "I don't understand why we're celebrating this. So Sera and Hannah have been coupled for a year—why are we pretending that's a good thing? Girls in serious high school relationships have higher rates of depression and anxiety, lower rates of advance degrees, a greater risk of abusive partners. But, yes, let's make cupcakes and celebrate our friends' poor life choices."

"Eliza."

I ignored Merri. Ignored Curtis when he echoed her. Didn't even stop when I looked up and saw Sera and Hannah standing at the end of the table. Sera's mouth was gaping and Hannah's eyes were wet, but their hands were linked as they walked away.

"And you." I pointed at Merri, who had stood up to follow them. "You used to be empathetic and compassionate—a good friend. Now you're so busy chasing dopamine, oxytocin, and serotonin that you don't think of anyone but your boyfriend and the next time you can make out."

"Hey!" It was Toby who'd protested, so I turned on him.

"Like you can talk. You substituted one Campbell sister for the other like they're girl-shaped cogs to serve your need for hero worship." I knew this wasn't true—knew he cared for Rory—but I *wanted* it to be. I needed them to be wrong, for *Frankenstein* to be wrong and my parents right. My words felt unforgivable, but so did their happiness. So did the fact that I wanted to join them and that my eyes had strayed toward a certain tall, dark distraction.

That direction would lead to my downfall. I had science on my side. They only had feelings. "It's ignorant. Romance? Love? They're not real. They're hormonal urges, brain chemicals, traps. Everyone would be happier and achieve more if they were just…alone."

I choked on the last word, on the poisoned silence that followed. I wanted to take it back, carve everything I'd said from their prefrontal cortexes before it could be transferred to long-term memory. I wanted to cry, or apologize, or shut my eyes so I didn't see the four of them staring at me with betrayal or remember Sera's and Hannah's expressions when they'd fled.

"You know—" Merri's lips quivered, and mine did too. "I thought I was immune to the callous things you say when your parents' opinions come out of your mouth, but that *hurt*. And I don't want to talk to you right now."

I wanted to respect that, to say, *I understand*, because logically I did. But it was the emotional part of my brain—the limbic system—that formed the words, "For how long?"

She shook her head, tears brimming in her eyes. "I don't know. But I love Fielding. And—" She stiffened and gave a laugh.

"I do. I—I *love* him. And you know what? You're not the person I need to tell that to. Excuse me."

I knew—Curtis, Lance, and Toby knew too—that she was going to march to Fielding's classroom and tell him right now. Probably not *in* the classroom—they'd already done the public-declaration thing when she'd asked him to Fall Ball—but she'd convince his teacher to excuse him and tell him in the hall. In other circumstances the moment would be charming, and Curtis would be asking, *"Anyone know what class he has so we can go watch this?"* But now the memory would be tainted. By me.

No one met my eyes as I repacked my lunch. I kept waiting for Curtis to break the silence. Instead he stared at the fork sticking out of his thermos like he couldn't remember how to lift it.

I stood, an apology stuck in my throat, my fingers shaking around my lunch bag.

Lance dropped his sandwich onto his tray and whistled as he shook his head. "I'm not even dating anyone, but the hopeless romantic part of me is offended."

I nodded. And left.

Merri didn't look in my direction all afternoon. Not even when Ms. Gregoire stopped by Media class to ask, "I didn't get your response journal last night. Did you turn one in?"

I'd answered, "No, I'll take the zero." Because that hit to my average was less painful than the book.

During Convocation, Merri sat with Toby, her sister, and Rory's friends Huck and Clara. When I paused beside their row, Toby shook his head. I kept walking. Sera and Hannah were two benches up. They pretended to be engrossed in a conversation with Lance.

I ground my teeth. I'd made it sixteen years without crying in public; I wasn't about to start.

No matter how much my throat itched or my eyes prickled.

"Firebug." I probably wouldn't have recognized Curtis's nickname—but he touched my arm. "I saved you a seat."

I was going to reject him and his pity on principle, rub off the tingles at my elbow—just as soon as I could clear my throat.

"Today's Convocation is a snooze-fest, and Lynnie printed out a practice set. C'mon."

I did, but sat on the other side of Lynnie and hid my face in the question packet so he couldn't see my wet-eyed gratitude.

Bartlett looked to me for an explanation when Merri didn't show up for quiz bowl practice, but I didn't have one. Not a text or a voicemail or any indication that she wouldn't be there. I spent the whole two hours watching the classroom door, trying to convince myself she was running late or forgot or went to the wrong classroom. Any excuse that wasn't the obvious truth: She wasn't there because I *was*.

Merri and I had fought before—but not often. Not like this. She burned through anger quickly, fast-forwarding to the part where everything was fine again. I didn't know how to handle this limbo, other than to panic that it was permanent.

I had pressed my buzzer only once. It was by accident when Dr. Badawi had been two words into a question: *"According to—"*

Everyone had turned, and I'd given the gut-wrenching "I'm *so* sorry" that had been trapped in my throat since lunch.

Lynnie had slid off her stool and patted my back. "It's okay. We've all done it."

But Curtis had nodded like he understood—so maybe one-sixth of my lunch table forgave me.

After that, I held my buzzer limply in my lap. At the end of practice, Dr. Badawi gave me advice along with questions. "Whatever you did to prepare for Tuesday's practice, do more of that."

Curtis was standing behind me. He was always right there, like some temptation-frustration combo platter. "You heard Dr. B—you need more *Mario Kart*. Want to come over?"

"I can't. I need to find Merri."

"Give her some space. You two will get past this."

I wanted to claw the sympathy off his face. "I'm sorry, but did I miss the part where *you* became an expert on *my* best friend?" I stormed out to the parking lot without waiting for an answer; but in my car, I froze.

I could go home. Do some approved workout. Homework. Brainstorm a project for the science fair. Get the required amount of sleep. Do all these things by myself, because I was "capable," "independent," and "brilliant"—but why did those sound like synonyms for "lonely"?

I could try and engage Nancy in conversation, see if she'd take the night off to go to a movie with me—but I could already picture her slow blink as she processed my invitation before turning me down. I didn't need more rejection.

If I wanted that, I'd call my parents.

Only one thing felt certain: There was no way I could continue with *Frankenstein*. I couldn't pinpoint when I'd started reading the book as a romance—one in which I was rooting for the monster and his future companion—but now that it was clear he wasn't getting a happily ever after, I was done. I was saving both my mental well-being and my GPA.

Ms. Gregoire had said, "Sometimes we don't ask for what we want because we're scared of being told yes."

If the worst that could happen was a "no," then that was a calculated risk I was willing to take.

I needed Curtis to switch books with me.

14

in answered the door, his mouth quirked in the type of joy that's never innocent. It was the face the Campbell sisters wore when they were about to tattle. The expression I probably had each time Toby presented me with an opportunity to tell him he was wrong.

"Hey, Eliza," Win said before calling over his shoulder, "Curtis, it's the girl you claim you're not dating. The one who can't be as smart as you say she is, otherwise she'd know she's way too good for you." He turned back to me. "Come in. He'll be right out."

A door flew open, and Curtis half ran, half tripped into the living room in a tangle of untied sneakers. A twisted sweatshirt engulfed his head. "Shut up and go."

"Oh." I fumbled behind me for the doorknob. "I didn't think you were still mad, but—"

"No!" He finally managed to get both arms and his head situated in the right parts of the sweatshirt, though the hood was pulled up and the drawstring was wrapped around his neck. He clawed at it as he crossed the room. "You, stay—I mean, if you want. But since you came here, I think you do?" He yanked the string free and pulled off his hood. His pointy hair was flattened. "Him—go. Win, seriously. Scram."

"And miss all this awkward entertainment?" Win chuckled and tossed a throw pillow at Curtis. "Fine, but I'm sending Wink out, and she'll tell me everything later."

Curtis threw the pillow at his brother's back. It missed and bounced off the wall. He turned to me with a sheepish expression. "So, hi? Sorry about him."

My heart was still racing from the rejection that wasn't. I touched my iLive band. More things I'd have to account for. "Are you busy?"

"I was getting ready to run. I'm training for the Carmody Half-Marathon."

"You are? When is it?" I realized I was leaning toward him and overcorrected by backing into the door. The knob dug into my spine, but I didn't spare time to wince, because I needed to know his answer.

"Not until April. I'm working my way up to thirteen miles. Wait—you ran cross-country. Want in?"

"It's probably too late to sign up." I bit the inside of my lip and hoped this was true—because if it was, then I would have to let go of how deeply I wanted to do something I'd just learned about a minute ago. *This* was probably the eager reaction my parents expected me to have to the Avery Science Competition. And because of that competition and quiz bowl and everything else, there's no way they'd sign off on the race. But I *wanted* it. In a way that defied my normal decision-making process of lists and logic and consulting schedules and calendars.

"Nope. And I could use a training buddy." He propped his foot on the bench beside the door to tie his shoe. "C'mon, let's go for a run. You can show me what you've got."

"It's not that simple." For many reasons.

"Sure it is. What size shoe do you wear? You can borrow clothes and sneakers from Wink. She's got pairs in her closet in case she ever decides to be an athlete. Let's do this."

I looked over at his sister. I wasn't sure if she'd come out of her room to act as Win's spy or if she shared her twin's opinion that watching Curtis and me interact was cringe-level entertainment—which, to be fair, might be accurate. She was resting her lean hips against the counter, eating a cup of yogurt. Her lips curved in amusement. "Do you want to tell him, or should I?"

"What's the problem?" Curtis looked between us. "What am I missing?"

"She's got boobs." His sister waved her spoon between her own flat chest and my curves.

"Oh. Right. I knew that. I mean, obviously. I mean, not that I've been looking—" His eyes were currently fixed on the ceiling. Maybe he was praying, or just absolutely determined not to glance at anything that might get him in trouble.

Something about *him* getting flustered made me less so. It's not like I expected him to know these things. Impromptu runs were for people who didn't need strap-them-down underwire-sports-bra support. Thank you, genetics. Mom was busty too—but she said lab coats were the best camouflage. School uniform shirts—not so much.

"Rain check on the run," I said. "I came here for a reason."

"Oh..." He stepped on the back of his untied sneaker, pulling it off and setting it by the door before reaching down to unknot the other. "Don't worry about lunch. Apology accepted. And you can help me make the cupcakes. If we tell Hannah and Sera 'Eliza touched sugar for you,' I'm pretty sure that grand gesture will work as an apology for them too."

He crossed to the kitchen, shooing his sister out of the way to open a tall cupboard. He pulled out an apron and set it on the counter before pivoting to turn on the oven. To Wink he said, "If you go back to your room, I'll let you have first taste test."

"Deal," she agreed. "But come get me if you guys start gaming."

This house moved too fast for me. Everyone was five steps ahead before I realized the plan. "Wait!" Wink was already behind a closed door, so I aimed my protest at Curtis. "Are your siblings going to keep coming in and out?"

"Why?" he asked, and I practically tripped over my tongue to blurt, "No reason!"

But I'd said it too quickly. And if that wasn't suspicious, my answer was. Since when did I do things for no reason? Never. But I couldn't tell him they made me feel like a sideshow, or that I was already awkward enough around him without an audience.

"Hmm." He cocked an eyebrow. "Pretty sure they won't. Win won't risk me telling Mom and Dad about the history paper he hasn't started, and Wink's pretty motivated by baked goods. Want me to lock them in so we have privacy? Or do you want a chaperone so you're not alone with me and the muffin trays? I promise to keep my oven mitts to myself."

I wanted to curse his dark eyes and pluck his long lashes. You know—if curses were real and physical violence wasn't beneath me. No one should be allowed to be that expressive. His eyes could give a look that was sleepy and disarming, then a few blinks later be wide-awake. They could narrow in mischief and go round with fake innocence. Right now they were too sharp and too curious.

I lifted my chin. "You're blowing off your run for baking? You don't sound very committed to this half-marathon."

He snorted and pulled his phone from his pocket. "I've got the iLive RunPlanner app. Look: With one click I move today's five-mile run to tomorrow. No harm done, but if you want to come over and hold me accountable, be my guest."

"Maybe I will."

"All right then." He tossed me the apron. "But first: cupcakes."

I frowned, then turned it so the *Kiss the Cook* message faced in. "Are cupcakes hard to make? Because it'd be a terrible apology if they're inedible. I'd blame you."

He laughed. "Of course you would. But, no. Baking is basic chemistry."

"Explain," I demanded.

He did, starting with, "Baking is a simple endothermic chemical reaction that changes batter into baked good," then delving deeper after I tied on the apron and we began to measure and mix. "There're two main reactions that are going to get us the light, airy texture we want. These come from the flour's proteins that are going to form gluten chains to make the batter elastic and the baking powder—our leavening agent—which will produce the CO_2 that makes the cake rise."

The more he explained, the more foolish I felt. I'd gotten eggshell in the bowl while he described how the lecithin in them acted as an emulsifier. I'd picked up the liquid measure cup while he detailed the Maillard reaction that would be produced by the sugar I was supposed to be measuring.

I didn't enjoy feeling like a novice, and I *really* didn't enjoy being told what to do.

"I got it." I swatted his arm out of the way and dumped the bowl that contained our dry ingredients into the bowl with our wet ones. I'd figured out the next steps on my own: turn mixer on, lower beaters into bowl.

The kitchen exploded into a white cloud of powder.

I choked and blinked and sputtered as he reached around me to turn the mixer off, forcing words through the flour paste coating my tongue. "Don't you dare laugh!"

His lips were pressed tight as he nodded, his eyes sparkling.

I looked down. My now-gray tights stood in the middle of a flour ring. Powder covered both of my sleeves and pooled where I'd rolled my cuffs. The part of my crossover tie that wasn't covered by the apron had changed color, and my skirt's pleats swished from navy to gray. If there was ever a moment for magic to be real—so I could reverse time or disappear or make my cheeks *not* red as bromine—this was it. "I don't know where to start."

I looked up to catch Curtis biting his lip in amusement. He swallowed and managed to say, "Maybe go outside and jump up and down?"

It sounded ridiculous, but I didn't have a better idea. "How do I get there without...shedding?" I dropped my arms, and a plume of flour rose up.

He covered a snicker with a cough. I narrowed my eyes, and he turned toward the cabinets. "Uh...trash bags. You can either step in one and hop to the door, or—"

"*Or,*" I demanded. "And it better not sound like a field-day event."

"Okay, then." He spread two bags end-to-end on the floor. "Follow the black plastic road. I'll move one while you walk on the other."

He kept his grinning face averted as I lifted my chin and stepped onto the first bag, leaving a snowy trail behind me. I sighed and set off puffs of flour from my nostrils like some smoke-breathing dragon. Curtis sounded like a choking donkey, his shoulders shaking with the effort to hold it in.

Fine—maybe it was a little funny.

"You can laugh if you want."

"Oh, thank God." He doubled over as he opened the sliding glass door to the backyard. "I was about to die."

I narrowed my eyes as I stepped onto the concrete slab patio that faced a small square of fenced-in snow. "Maybe do so *in* the house."

I took the paper towels he'd left and dusted off my tights as best I could, wiped my skirt, untied the apron, unrolled my sleeves. Shook my hair and watched my ponytail unleash a new cloud in the air, one that matched my foggy breath. And fine, I snickered a little.

The glass door slid open. "Can I come out?"

"Are you done laughing at me?"

"For now." He grinned. "I asked Wink for clean clothes. Or you can head home—"

"I need to do the cupcake apology." And switch books. "Give me those and don't look." The pants he'd brought were covered in yellow rabbits. The sweatshirt was familiar. "Hero High?"

Everyone got a personalized one with their acceptance letter—but while this one said *Cavendish* on the back, boys' sweatshirts were gray, and this was red.

"Wink got in." His voice sounded muffled, and I glanced to see that he'd turned around *and* covered his eyes. I pulled the pants on over my tights, then unzipped my skirt. "Win didn't. She wouldn't go without him. He's reapplying to transfer in the fall. We'll see."

It was too cold to take off my shirt, so I pulled her sweatshirt over the top. "I'm good. You can look."

"You've got some—" Curtis reached toward me and I took a step backward, frantically wiping my face. He stilled, his hand hovering six inches from where my cheek had been. "It's on your eyelashes. I don't want it to get in your eyes. If you stand still—"

He reached for the paper towels on the patio table. I froze and shut my eyes, feeling his approach through the soles of my feet, the movement of air molecules as his body heat came near mine, and his cranberry-juice breath on my skin as he leaned in close. His left hand brushed my cheek and tilted my chin, while his right swept the paper towel gently across each lid.

Then he stepped back, and I was free to open my eyes. But I didn't right away. Even after he cleared his throat—twice—before managing, "Th-there. That should be better."

I didn't want him to look at me anymore. Not when I was wearing confusion along with batter. I shoved my hands into the sweatshirt pocket. "Did I ruin the cupcakes?"

He shrugged. "We'll find out once they're baked."

"I'm sorry I wrecked your kitchen." I cringed as I reentered, preparing myself for the mess, but the floors and counters were clean. "You didn't have to—I would've—"

"No big deal. I've had lots of practice. Watch this." He called down the hall, "Am I allowed to cook with beets?"

The twins' answer was a simultaneous, "No!," and their follow-ups were overlapping: "I'm not helping you repaint again." "Don't make me call Mom."

"Cool your jets—I was just telling Eliza!" he yelled back. "See? This was a five-paper towel mess. That one was five gallons of paint."

"Well, thank you." I pushed the words off my tongue, because if roles were reversed, I wouldn't have been nearly as gracious.

"Sure." He popped open the baking-powder canister and added a pinch into the mixer. "Though I want a merit badge for not taking your picture post–flour bomb. It would've been great on iLive, or in the yearbook, or maybe blown up and hung in the school hallway..."

"Shut up," I said—but I said it through giggles and while finding a tiny pile of flour he'd missed and flicking it at him. His laughter, when he joined in a second later, was sweeter than any possibly ruined baked goods.

15

N ow we frost them?" I'd been anxiously watching the kitchen timer, but the muffin trays Curtis pulled from the oven looked promising. He slid a second batch in and tipped the first onto the counter. They were golden brown, and the spongy tops bounced back as he lined them right side up on a wire rack. I was still dubious about how they'd taste.

"Frosting would melt right off. *Now* we play *Mario Kart* while they cool."

"Actually..." I sucked in a breath. The past hour had been a distraction from why I was here. "There's something I need to ask you."

Curtis scanned my face, which, despite me wiping it frantically and repeatedly, still felt powdery. "Do I need to sit down for this?"

"It's just... is there another book on Ms. Gregoire's list that looks interesting to you?"

His forehead crinkled. "That's random. I'd have to look."

I crossed the room to my backpack. "I have your copy of the list."

"No you don't. It's in my notebook." He gave me a weird look before disappearing down the hall.

I spent the time he was gone preparing to prove him wrong. I had it ready, underlined side up, when he reappeared with a paper in his hand. I thrust mine toward him. "This is yours."

"No, it's not." He traded with me. His copy had bananas wearing hats doodled on it. "I don't own a green pen."

He couldn't see the goose bumps that rose beneath his sister's sweatshirt, but something must have registered in my expression, because his eyebrows drew in. "Are you okay?"

I sank onto the bench. If it wasn't his, then whose list was this? How did it get in my former book, with the title of my next book already underlined? "I need you to switch books with me."

"No."

"What?" I lifted my head. I'd been concentrating on the floor and my breathing so the feeling of disorientation would go away, but now it was back. This was supposed to be straightforward. Even Ms. Gregoire had implied as much.

"Is that why you came over? The whole baking thing was to soften me up?" Curtis's expression was chiseled from unfamiliar stone, like irritation had sharpened his bones and made him look more like his younger, angrier brother. "Not happening."

I narrowed my eyes. "Are you really going to tell me reading *Anne of Green Gables* means that much to you?"

"Yes." He put down the list that wasn't mine and wasn't his. "Not because of my author-name connection; because of *you*."

"Me?" I hadn't read more than the summary yet, but the heroine was a wildly imaginative red-haired orphan. I was none of those things.

"I messed up the first time I met you. We both know it. I'd never met anyone as... *stunning*. And, fine, I may have drooled and stared. But we've spent so much time together since then. I thought I'd proven I see you as more than that. We're friends—sort of. But if you don't get why I want *Anne of Green Gables* as my book..." He shook his head. "I've never identified with a character as much as I do with Gilbert after he called Anne 'Carrots' the first time they met."

If his goal had been to make me back off, it had backfired. Because now I was lit up with curiosity. I had no idea what any of that meant, but I couldn't wait to read and find out. "I'm over it—the way you were the first time we met."

He leaned down. "Are you?"

"I—" I had to shut my mouth and consider. I'd *hated* him in that moment. It had occurred during our first five minutes on campus. Fielding had just made a horrible impression on Merri, and Curtis had followed up by stumbling over himself to ogle me. In that instant I'd been ready to eschew fancy science labs and flee back to the all-girls school. Better the bullies I knew than guys who proved that my parents were correct—that I'd never be seen as more than my face or body. Maybe some part of me nursed a kernel of resentment toward him, but if so, I was discarding it now. "I am."

He searched my face with eyes that seemed to discern more than I wanted to reveal. "Everything you said at lunch today—is that what your parents tell you, or do you really believe it?"

"I don't know. Definitely the first, and I used to believe them, but..." I met his eyes. "I didn't mean to hurt everyone—I was angry and I wasn't thinking. And I just...I want..."

He took a step forward. His chest rising in deep breaths and his voice low as he asked, "You want *what*?"

"I want..." I licked my lips. They tasted like sugar, even though I'd turned down every spatula and spoon he'd offered to let me lick. My eyes fell to his mouth—he'd indulged in every batter-laden utensil I'd rejected, so I bet his tasted even sweeter.

Or were contaminated with salmonella. But that risk felt less risky than finishing my thought. "I want—"

The *beep-beep-beep* of the oven timer split the air. We both blinked like we were inhaling pure oxygen after having been underwater for too long. It didn't matter what I *wanted*. My life came with directions, and none of them factored my *wants* into their formulas. *Wants* were for some point after my first PhD. Right now was for laying the groundwork for future achievements.

Curtis hadn't moved. His eyes hadn't left mine, even as the intensity in them had dimmed to mirror my own emotional withdrawal. "I've got to—" He glanced over his shoulder at the beeping oven. "Hold that thought."

By the time he'd set the second tray on the counter and walked back over—oven mitt still on his hand—the moment was so far gone I couldn't even imagine what I'd been thinking.

He prompted me with, "You were saying?"

"Forget it." That part was for him; the second was for myself. "*Please*, forget it."

16

Curtis and I were still standing by the door when it opened and a woman who looked like an older version of Wink walked in.

"Hello." She hung her purse and coat on hooks, slid her feet out of black flats, then turned to us with wide, expectant eyes. She had shorter hair than her daughter and dressier clothing, but the same slim build, the same features. Her smile was pure Curtis—curiosity and mischief. "Who's this?"

"Hey, Mom." He stepped aside to give her room. "Eliza came over to help me bake the cupcakes for Sera and Hannah."

"Hi," I said. What sort of horrible impression did it give that I was wearing Wink's clothing?

"*This* is Eliza?" Mrs. Cavendish's eyebrows had risen like two graceful halves of a drawbridge, her expression underneath both intrigued and amused. "It's very nice to meet you."

Would she still think that after she'd heard about the mess I made in her kitchen? I hoped Curtis had cleaned well, because her black sweater and slacks would highlight every fleck of flour he'd missed.

"It's nice to meet you too, but I should go. I…" I couldn't think of a single excuse. The only things waiting for me were Nancy's closed door and homework and brooding over how badly I'd messed up today. Oh, and coming up with a science fair project, a new book for Gregoire's assignment, and studying quiz bowl questions. "I'll see you at school, Curtis."

His mom asked me to stay for dinner, and Curtis protested that I hadn't tried the cupcakes, but I shook my head, grabbed my backpack and floured skirt, and fled.

Maybe I didn't want to read *Anne of Green Gables*. There were other books on the list. Other books that wouldn't be half the hassle. Maybe I wouldn't like it. I downloaded an ebook sample as I reheated the dinner plate Nancy had left out for me.

It took an entire chapter before Anne Shirley appeared on my phone screen, but once she was there I was captivated. She was an orphan headed to live with a pair of elderly siblings at their house, Green Gables. Only, they'd requested a male child. And Matthew Cuthbert, the elderly brother who picked her up from the train station, was too overwhelmed by her vivacity to tell her the truth.

Anne was nothing like me. She was effusive and imaginative and outgoing. She described herself as "homely," and she wished for beauty. She coveted pretty clothing and romance. Each of Anne's meandering conversations made my chest ache, because she reminded me of Merri—who hadn't responded to my Can we talk? texts.

I'd made up my mind about the story: It needed to be mine. Anne was unlike me, and she was also *eleven*. This book felt safe. I wasn't going to overidentify; there wasn't going to be romance. It was the perfect novel for my project. Now I needed to convince Curtis.

He'd snuck into my thoughts with annoying frequency as I read. Not just because I was trying to formulate how to persuade him, but because I was impatient to find out what he meant by "Carrots" and because Anne, like him, had an unfortunate habit of giving things ridiculous nicknames: "White Way of Delight," "Lake of Shining Waters."

The sample pages ended with Matthew and Anne's arrival at Green Gables, stopping before she learned that she wasn't the male orphan they'd requested and before I got any clarity about Curtis's strange apology about vegetables and first impressions.

I wanted to buy the book and keep reading—but I couldn't. I had my own apology to plan.

On Friday morning I hit every red light on the short drive between my house and Merri's. I had an apology written and rehearsed, plus a backup plan for if she didn't want to hear it. And another backup plan for if that one failed.

Because *I* had failed. Merri loved love—she loved big and deeply, and she loved with her whole heart and imagination. My job as her best friend was to protect her from a world that delighted in smacking down those who dared to wear their heart on their sleeve. I never wanted her to lose her enthusiasm. Or to stop daydreaming and *what-if*-ing. Her optimism was often the only antidote to the cynicism that pooled in my thoughts when I spent too much time alone.

And yet...I'd attacked all of that with jealousy and anger and confusion—cloaking my accusations with science and strategic insults. I was ready to take full responsibility and also confess the *why* behind it. The things—and the boy—that had been keeping me up at night. But when I walked into their kitchen, Mr. and Mrs. Campbell blinked in surprise and lowered their coffee mugs in that eerie synchronicity old married couples develop. "Hi, Eliza," said Mrs. Campbell. "Merri's already left. She went with Rory and Toby."

"I assumed you had another early morning meeting," Mr. Campbell added.

"No." I tapped my phone screen, sending her the backup apology I'd pretyped in preparation for this scenario. "Must've been a mix-up."

"But since you're here: Merri was searching for her crossover tie all morning, and I spotted it thirty seconds after she left." Mrs. Campbell put a finger to her lips. "If I can remember where I saw it, will you bring it in?"

"Of course." I smiled; that would be the perfect excuse to initiate conversation.

"How's the book coming?" Mr. Campbell asked as his wife left to go tie-hunting.

"I changed books. Well, I'm in the process of it. Hopefully I'm doing *Anne of Green Gables*. I thought I'd find Anne insufferable and over-the-top—but she's charming. So far she reminds me a lot of Merri."

Mr. Campbell scratched Gatsby's ears. "I haven't thought of *Green Gables* in years. I read it to the girls at bedtime when they were little. I see some Merri in her—but Anne's a lot more stubborn than my pixie."

"True. Merri forgives so easily." This was wishful thinking and also subterfuge; I studied his face to see if he had any idea we were fighting, then added another truth. "I hold grudges."

"Ah, so does Anne. You also have her drive and ambition."

I shrugged. "I haven't read that far, but I'll take that as a compliment?"

"I meant it as one." He smiled over the brim of his mug. "So, do you have time to talk CRISPR, or know anything about this gravity pulse? The one from last year that made everyone momentarily taller and shorter? I'm baffled."

"Hold on to those questions—because they're perfect." I'd been rolling around an idea in my head, and the longer I considered it, the more attached I'd become. "You know how you always joke I should do a podcast?"

He nodded.

"What if we did?" I twisted my fingers together. "There's this science fair coming up..."

I paused to collect my courage, and he chuckled. "My science fair expertise taps out with baking soda volcanoes and Styrofoam models of the solar system—something tells me you're beyond that."

"That's actually the point." Science shut the door on so many people. It made them feel like they weren't qualified to learn, and so they stopped trying. What if I changed that? "You have lots of questions about science, but no accessible source of answers."

"Besides you. You're like my own personal science-Google."

"But what if that was my project?"

He nudged Gatsby away and sat up straighter. "I'm not following."

"What if I made a project out of taking complex science questions and turning them into answers the average person could understand? With examples and anecdotes from real life. Merri loves an allegory; I've picked up a thing or two."

He nodded thoughtfully. "You'd provide the answers, and I'd...what? Come up with questions?"

"Yes. You'd keep me from veering too technical." I wasn't sure if this project was "science-y" enough for the science fair. But I'd grown up in a household that weaponized science. My parents used it to make themselves feel big and others small—and somewhere along the line, I'd internalized that elitist model. I'd proved that yesterday when I'd used "science" to attack Sera and Hannah and everyone else in love. This podcast—creating something that invited people *in* instead of shutting them out—could be my atonement and so much more. My stomach fluttered as I asked, "Would you help? I can work around your schedule."

"I'd be honored. I might not understand everything, but I'll do my best to keep up. I like seeing you excited about something, kiddo. You're always working so hard to pretend you don't care. It's good to see you let yourself shine bright."

I wanted to contradict him—tell him he was wrong, but...he wasn't. I beamed. "The whole point of the project would be for me to explain so you can understand. If I don't, your job is to tell me, so I can give a better explanation."

"I can do that." He raised his mug and clinked it against my water bottle.

"Thank you!" I didn't bounce on my toes or clasp my hands together like Merri would've, but for the first time in days, I felt like I could take a full breath. At least one aspect of my life was semi-settled. "Can we start tomorrow? Anytime. I'll come to you."

"Let's do it," he said, and I may have done a subtle bounce.

"Found it!" Mrs. Campbell was a little breathless from rushing down the stairs. "I remembered Merri was using it as a bookmark, but I couldn't remember where the book was." She sighed in exasperation. "On the side of the bathtub. I hope I haven't made you late."

"No," I said. "Your timing is perfect."

After I left the Campbells', my morning went quickly downhill. I struggled to hold on to my science-project joy as I sat beside Merri in bio. She wasn't giving me the silent treatment—she'd thanked me for bringing her her school tie—but she was the least-Anne Shirley version of Merri I'd ever seen. One who didn't chatter whenever the teacher's back was turned, or wait to walk with me to our classes, and didn't meet my eye across the lunch table—not even to tease when Curtis announced I'd helped make the cupcakes.

She didn't smile when he reenacted how I'd "made it rain flour" to the amusement and apparent forgiveness from everyone else at the table. She didn't declare custody of the leftover cupcake after I'd declined mine. She looked like someone had programmed her to run at half-speed, muted her colors, or turned down her volume.

I hated every second of it. Hated that I'd been the cause, and that my text apology and the written note I'd slipped in her locker hadn't undone the damage.

I left lunch early and headed to the library, where I logged into my email and dashed off a message to my parents. One I didn't preplan or agonize over. What would it take for you to consider staying here when you come home?

There'd been a second line of text, one I was smart enough to delete before pressing Send but that I could still picture on the screen, even after I logged out. Or let me come with you—I hate being alone. I miss having a family.

17

"Eliza!" Curtis jogged across the lawn toward where I was waiting in the mass of students funneling into the Convocation Hall. People parted to let him through. "Eliza, hey!"

"How complicated is 'Don't walk on the grass'? Why do you have such a hard time following that rule?"

"Because it's a stupid rule. It's grass. Being walked on is its job." Curtis smiled, but it looked fake. His eyes were dim. "Listen, let's get out of here."

"What?"

"Let's...go to the library or my house or yours." He wrapped his long fingers around my wrist as the crowd shifted around us.

I yanked out of his grip, accidentally banging into the person behind me. I offered an automatic "I'm sorry," but didn't turn to see who'd gotten an elbow to the kidneys. "No. Absolutely not."

"C'mon, Firebug. You really don't want to—"

"Skip school? You're right, I really don't want to." I turned and aggressively wove my way through the crowd. How could he know so little about me? I thought...

I slid into the first empty row I passed. I kept my chin up, my eyes forward. Headmaster Williams stood at the podium, droning about something, but I was busy steeping in my emotions—a stew of annoyance, loneliness, and stress.

"—by the parents of one of our own."

I sat straighter. Something about his words had penetrated my introspection. The back of my neck began to sweat.

"I'm sure by now you've realized we have the science community's equivalent of royalty among us. She's rather hard to miss."

My classmates were stirring. Some were craning their necks like this was that children's book and I was Waldo. Some jerk whistled, and Headmaster Williams paused to narrow his eyes at a clump of senior boys.

"Not only are we lucky to have Ms. Gordon-Fergus in our student body—" My cheeks burned. There were snickers as I'm sure at least a half dozen students made the crude joke Headmaster Williams's comment had set up. He ignored them. "We'll also be sending a record number of students to the prestigious Avery Science Competition this year. You may be asking, how are these connected? Well, the doctors Gordon and Fergus are among this year's judges."

He paused while students clapped. My hands didn't move. "Ms. Gordon-Fergus is every bit as remarkable as the daughter of two brilliant minds should be. And since I'm sure she has insight about the Avery, I'm going to put her on the spot—"

My eyes widened. I turned to locate the nearest exit, trying to determine if I could get through it before Headmaster Williams finished his thought—

"—and invite her to share any advice her parents have given."

Was "no" an acceptable answer? He hadn't phrased his statement as a question, but my parents had drilled into me that those two letters were the most powerful in my arsenal and mine to employ if I ever felt anyone was imposing upon me.

"Come up here, Eliza."

The students in my row stood to let me pass. Headmaster Williams had done this before—cold-called on students during Convocation. Poor Rory had it happen before Christmas break. I wondered if her walk up the aisle had felt this endless. My parents' voices were in my head, lecturing me that it was *their* reputation I'd sully if I flubbed this, since I'd been asked to speak as an extension of *them*.

"I hope you don't mind that I've put you on the spot like this," Headmaster Williams said as I reached the three steps up to the podium.

I'm sure my resentment simmered in my narrowed eyes, so I didn't bother with the polite lie. "What do you want me to say?"

"Give us a taste of what they've told you about the Avery. Any tips or hints for how to wow them with a good project? There are a few days left to turn in applications. What would you tell someone to convince them to go for it?"

I ground my teeth. What would this roomful of my peers and teachers think if they knew I hadn't spoken to my parents about the Avery? That I'd learned they were judging from Nancy, and the only communication we'd exchanged about it was a few lines of email and that comment about my appearance? That every science junkie in this room knew more than I did, because they'd likely gone on the website or read the brochure?

I'd chosen my project six hours ago. My application was still incomplete—all I'd done was fill in my name and check the "no photos" box.

Headmaster Williams thrust the microphone at me, his shaved head shining beneath the bright fixtures that spotlighted us both. I scanned the room. Merri was trying to climb out of her seat; both Toby and Fielding were gently restraining her with hands on her arm and around her waist. And as much as I loved her for whatever distraction she was trying to launch, I appreciated them for not letting her. The actions of all three left me weak-kneed with relief, because it looked a lot like forgiveness.

I exhaled into the microscope as I spotted someone else. Someone who'd tried to prevent this from occurring. Skipping was never going to be my answer—but I wished I'd given him enough credit to pause and ask *why* he'd wanted me to do it. Curtis met my eyes and nodded. The same *you've got this* gesture he'd given me the first time he placed a video game remote in my hand, or when he nudged the batter scoop in my direction and pointed toward a muffin tin lined with cupcake wrappers. I nodded back.

"They haven't told me anything." I'd had a lifetime of doing parental PR. Twisting the truth to protect their reputation wasn't mentally tricky; the only toll was emotional, as I processed the difference between others' perceptions of them and my reality. "They can't." I paired this with a small smile. "That would give me an unfair advantage." Some people laughed, and others exchanged looks of disbelief. "But they're excited to be judges and see what everyone comes up with."

When Headmaster Williams didn't move to take the microphone back—clearly hoping this would prompt me to elaborate—I set it down on the podium and left the stage.

Merrilee Rose Campbell might not be tall in stature, but her figurative heart was enormous and her capacity for loyalty was astounding. My best friend shrugged off the boys she loved best and chased me down the aisle. I wasn't staying to sing the school song. I couldn't.

Merri emerged through the door carrying both our coats and bags. She dropped them onto the sidewalk and threw her arms around me. The hug was fierce and slightly suffocating. "Dang Convocation mortification. It's like a Hero High rite of passage."

I snorted, the sound nasally and wet. "I'm sorry about yesterday."

"I know." She picked up her coat and put it on. "What you said isn't okay—but I don't think you meant it, and I forgive you." She passed me my left glove, which had gotten wrapped in her hat, then added, "I'm sorry too. Because I should've known something was going on and guessed it was this whole science fair thing."

The doors to the Convocation Hall burst open to release a flood of Friday-afternoon enthusiasm. And I couldn't correct her. Not when we were about to be absorbed by a mass of students whose weekends began right there on the sidewalk. Yes, something was going on with me, but it wasn't just my parents. It wasn't even mainly them. I nodded and forced a smile, leading the way to the parking lot. "So, catch me up. I hate that I don't know what happened when you told Fielding you loved him."

"Do you think it's too soon?" Merri stopped walking and peered at me. "I can't tell if that's a judgey face."

It *hadn't* been a "judgey" face, but now it was me masking a *hurt* face. I twisted the strap on my backpack and chose my words carefully. "I think you know your feelings, and you know the timing that's right for you. I also think he's a good person, and you two complement and help each other."

"Those are some of the nicest things you've ever said to me..." Merri's eyes glistened. I braced myself for another hug ambush, but she fanned her face and sniffed. "We should fight more often."

I handed her a tissue. "Don't push it."

18

I smoothed the bottom of my sweatshirt, making sure it covered my leggings-clad butt, and shuffled my sneakers on the *Everyone Is Welcome* mat.

Curtis answered the door still in his school uniform. He said "Hey?" with such an audible question mark that my hands clenched around the clothing I'd borrowed yesterday, which was now freshly laundered.

"Do you not remember inviting me to go running less than twenty-four hours ago?" I wanted this to be an invective against his memory, but it came out as a worry.

"Of course I do." He swung the door wide and smiled. It *looked* sincere, but doubt sat itchy on my skin. "Come in. The twins can keep you company while I change."

They were sitting on the couch and didn't take their eyes off the fantasy game on the TV, saying "Hi, Eliza" and "S'up" while jamming buttons and muttering to each other. I set Wink's clothes on the bench and shut the door.

"Oh, and put your number in here, so next time we can confirm when and stuff."

I was so focused on his casual use of "next time" and trying to decide whether to be annoyed or pleased by his assumption that I fumbled the phone he tossed me before disappearing down the hall.

"Whoa. Did he just trust you with his unlocked phone?" Win paused the game and dropped his remote on the couch before spinning around and stretching his hands over the back. "Gimme."

"Don't!" said Wink.

"C'mon, you know he wants a picture of my butt as his home screen."

Wink ignored him and turned to me. "Do you have brothers?"

I shook my head and quickly entered my number, then texted myself so I'd have his. Win hopped over the back of the couch. He pulled the phone from my grasp with a triumphant "Aha!" that turned to a "Boo!" when he realized I'd relocked it.

"Lucky," said Wink. "If you ever want one, I'll sell you either of mine for cheap."

"Hey now," said Curtis, reemerging in joggers and a zip-up red running jacket. "You'd be lost without me, Lincoln Cavendish."

"Keep telling yourself that," she said as Curtis tied his sneakers and grabbed his gloves. "But meanwhile, Eliza, if you want to get him lost midrun, go for it."

I smiled. "I'll keep that in mind."

The Cavendish boys playfully scuffled over the phone. Curtis crowed, "Got it!," when he emerged triumphant, then leaned over the couch to unpause their game. The twins shouted and scrambled for their remotes.

To me he said, "Let's go," and then we were back out the door. We hadn't run yet, we hadn't even exchanged more than a few dozen words, but after five minutes with his family, I already felt better.

Not that I'd admit it.

"Just so you know, I'm only here because I miss running outside."

"Oh," Curtis said as we walked down his driveway and he adjusted the RunPlanner settings on his phone—which reminded me, I needed to take *off* my iLive band. I wrapped it around the driver's-side mirror as we passed my car. "I see. You must live in one of those neighborhoods that only has indoors."

"A: That joke doesn't make sense. B: Now that cross-country's over, I don't have a running partner. Merri refused once it got cold."

"Why not go by yourself?" He pointed to the left and we began, both of us awkward as we tried to match each other's speed and stride. I was fast, but his legs were longer. He pointed left again at the corner. "You realize we live in a safe town. I go running by myself—even after dark."

"To do that I'd have to run with my finger on pepper spray and with earbuds in so no one would talk to me, but the sound off so I could hear someone sneaking up." My feet matched the flow of my rising resentment, and he scrambled to keep up. "Which means I hear the comments about my outfits or the way my body bounces. And worry about far worse than just words."

"Yikes. I mean, I am a Brown boy—so it's not like I get a free pass. I've had stupid people blatantly cross the street or check to see if I'm running *from* something. But I never thought about… that." He shook his head. "You can always come with me. I meant it about the half-marathon—I could use a training partner."

"Thank you." My relief at being heard and understood slowed my breathing and pushed away thoughts of Brazil. "But let's see if we make it through a single run without killing each other first."

We traveled a whole block without speaking, which had to

be some sort of record for him. Pitting Curtis and Merri against each other in the quiet game would be all sorts of amusing.

"Soooo," he said thirty seconds later, and I bit back a laugh. "You know my Knight Light adoptee? Huckleberry?"

"His name is Huck, but yes."

"He's got this thing he does—on bus rides to lacrosse games or while JV's on the field and we're on the bench—he calls it 'The Question Game,' but it's not really a *game*. You just take turns asking questions and both answering."

We were stopped at a corner. It seemed like even the red hand on the **DON'T WALK** sign was signaling a million ways this scenario could go wrong. But I said, "Let's play."

"Okay!" His response was too fast, like he was trying to hide his shock at my agreement. "Um, let's start easy—I'll paraphrase our shared friend Anne Shirley: Would you rather be divinely beautiful, dazzlingly clever, or angelically good? I know you're already two of the three, but if you could only pick one."

"Clever. The others are subjective and unimportant."

"You think 'clever' isn't? By whose definition? What's an accurate measure?"

"Valid point." One that *I* usually made whenever my parents got science-elitist or failed to acknowledge the classist privilege of educational opportunities. "But if those are my choices, it's my answer."

"I'd choose good. I mean, it's never going to happen. I was king of the time-out throne. Anyway, your question."

I pushed away the visual of a tiny, pouting Curtis in time-out. "Why a half-marathon? What do you like about running?"

"Sometimes it feels like the only way to slow down my thoughts is to speed up my body—if that makes sense. And a half-marathon because I never have and why not. You?"

I kept my eyes focused straight ahead. If I didn't look at him, I could pretend he wasn't there and that I was confessing things to myself. "I feel like I finally fit within my body when I'm running. Like we're not at war. I'm connected to it in a way that doesn't happen often. Like this body is *mine* and not everyone else's, and I'm putting it to use for something I want to do."

"I'm not asking this next question to make you mad; I want to preface that so maybe you'll hear it differently. But..." He inhaled audibly, and even his footsteps hesitated; I had to slow my own to hear him ask, "You're beautiful—like, objectively so. Why do you hate that?"

I curled my hands into fists, turning each swing of my arms into a punch at an invisible foe. "It's DNA. I'm not a better person because some combination of nucleotides dictated my face is symmetrical or created an aesthetic that's socially conditioned as attractive. I *know* I sound like I'm complaining about the stupidest thing, but..." I slammed my thumb against the crosswalk button, refusing to look and see if he understood or was judging me. I hit the button again. And again.

"People take pictures of me sometimes. What do I do with that? I'm pumping gas, and it's okay to take my picture? If I acknowledge it, they ask if I'm a model. Then feel like they have permission to tell me I should be one. If I'm quiet, I'm stuck-up. If I'm polite, I'm flirting. If I turn down a date... it doesn't end well."

The signal changed, and I flew across the street. If he wanted to hear the rest of my answer, he'd have to catch up, because I couldn't slow down. Not with the specter of so many bad memories chasing me. "I just want to know what response would be acceptable. How do I live in this body that so many people have opinions about? I mean, Fielding is classically handsome; would you ask *him* this? Do you realize that both your questions have centered on my appearance—is that what you think is most interesting about me?" I stopped short and held my breath as I waited for his answer, hope and fear clustered among the carbon dioxide in my lungs.

"No. I wouldn't have asked him." Curtis looked sheepish. "And *no,* definitely not. I'm trying to figure you out. I know I hurt you in the past; I'm trying to understand the why of it, so I don't do it again."

"It's just..." I threaded my hands together and stretched them above my head, reaching for the words to explain. "Stories are about *obtaining* the beautiful ones; Helen of Troy, Guinevere— those women don't get to be the hero. They don't get agency. I don't want to be remembered because of my face. I want to be recognized for my achievements. Just once without someone saying, 'the lovely Eliza,' or naming my parents, or adding 'brains *and* beauty,' like these are mutually exclusive."

"But..." He sighed and let that ellipsis dangle in the air as he resumed running.

This time I was the one catching up and prompting. "But, what?"

"You keep saying you didn't earn your appearance and it's genetic...but aren't mental capabilities also partially genetics and privilege? I'm not saying you don't put in a ton of effort, but you've got genius genes and your parents are paying for private school—your achievements aren't a fluke." He paused to catch his breath. "I know I'm oversimplifying, but I wish you could be as comfortable and confident with who you are physically as you are about who you are intellectually."

I didn't know if that was a criticism or a compliment, but it made my face flush. "Yeah, well...you've never met my parents." I shook off the topic with a lash of my ponytail. "It's my question.

Is there anything I can do to get you to switch books so I can read *Anne of Green Gables*?"

We had reached the middle of the largest hill in town. The creatively named Hillcrest Road wound around it in switchbacks that stole my breath, so I assumed he was quiet for oxygen-deprivation reasons. But as we neared the top, he spoke: "I'll switch books with you under one condition."

"What is it?" My voice was wary, but my pulse fluttered with hope.

"Beat me at the science competition and it's yours."

"The Avery? You're entering?"

"Yeah. Are you? Dr. B's been coaching a few of us all year. I kept waiting for you to show up."

"All year?" My project was coachless *and* last minute. Fantastic. But at least I'd picked one. I'd stolen moments all day to brainstorm my first script.

We'd reached the top of the hill. There was a little free library and a bench on the edge of the sidewalk. I veered toward these out of habit. Merri always browsed when we came here.

Curtis leaned against the bench and caught his breath. "You're entering, right? Can you, with your parents judging?"

I nodded. "They won't judge my project." My eyes were glued to a bright green cover with dirt-red lettering that sat in the precise middle of the library's second shelf. It was the exact same version Ms. Gregoire had had on her desk.

"Good," he panted. "Anyway, if you beat me, you do *Anne of Green Gables*. If I win, I do."

I pulled my gaze away from the book to meet his. "And what if neither of us does?"

"That's a bit insulting, Firebug. You clearly don't know what my project is."

It was only the fourth time he'd called me that, but it made my cheeks light up like they were bioluminescent. "You don't know mine either." And I hadn't technically started it or even read the rules. "But on the off chance we don't win, what's our backup plan? And you do realize the competition is the week before our projects are due. So, you'll have to prep a whole other book for when you lose."

"*If* I lose, I'll do whatever book you picked that you now want to ditch. So winner gets *Anne* and loser does..." He raised an eyebrow and gestured for me to fill in the blank.

"*Frankenstein.*"

"Cool. And if neither of us wins and that's not a sign of the end-times, then we'll flip a coin for *Anne.*"

I wrinkled my nose. "That's chance, not merit." But unless I could talk my parents into disclosing our raw scores, I didn't have a better idea.

"So I guess one of us better win, then." He paused. "And let's not tell each other our projects. We'll find out day of, when we see which of us gets custody of Anne and who's stuck with Frank. Deal?"

"Deal." I reached out to shake on it. My hand was painfully cold. I thought I wouldn't even register the touch of my bare fingers against his thin gloves. Instead it was an electric jolt of frissons that stole my breath more effectively than the hill had. I dropped his hand and stepped back, stumbling against the little lending library, which sent another shock through my skin. The book begged me to pluck it from the shelf and brandish it as part of our pact. I turned away.

And began to run again. Faster than we'd come up—faster than was safe on a slope this steep. But I needed space from that moment, those sensations, and the new stakes I'd added to the Avery.

Maybe Curtis felt it too, because when he caught up, he was still clenching and unclenching the hand I had shaken. "My question. You said that stuff from lunch the other day was partially because of your parents. Why?"

"They're anti-teens dating. At least *this* teen; they don't care about any others. It's a science thing." I hunched against the wind, angry that they were far away and absent but also suffocatingly omnipresent. How would they react to my emo email? "I don't want to talk about it. That's enough questions." We had a mile left, but it could be silent. I was done covering pavement while uncovering my deepest vulnerabilities. Especially since Curtis didn't seem to have any.

"S'okay," he said. "How do you feel about quiz bowl questions? I have an app—it'll read them to us."

"Fine."

We paused while he fished his phone from his pocket and tapped the screen. "Let me hear your buzzer noise. Mine is *eee-yu, eee-yu.*"

"Absolutely not. You do that again, I push you into traffic."

"Okay, I'll make a note that Buzzkill Gordon-Fergus is vetoing buzzer noises." He glanced at me. "And, I'm making another mental note that that nickname is DOA."

"Good call."

He gestured down the sidewalk, and I fell in stride beside him. Somewhere in the past few miles our paces had synched.

I beat him on eleven of the nineteen questions it took to reach his house. But we didn't go inside. We huddled on the driveway next to my car. Me blowing on my hands, him stomping his feet. The outside lights came on from either sensors or timers, lighting up our stalling tactics. I asked, "What's this app called?"

"Um, Quiz Me, Baby, One More Time."

I groaned. "That sounds like something you'd make up. Where can I download it?"

"You can't." He shoved the phone back in his pocket. "Wink helped me code it—but I can't distribute it because it uses questions from online databases. I don't own those."

It annoyed me that I was still surprised every time he proved he was smarter than I'd expected. It probably annoyed him too. "Let's play again next run. Don't peek ahead."

He leaned against my car as he stretched his quad. "Please. I don't need to cheat to win."

"Says the guy who *lost* today."

"Touché. But I have one last question—not a quiz bowl one." He lowered his foot and met my eyes. "If you were allowed to date—would you?"

I'm sure I'd been sweating since a few minutes into our run, but that was the moment when I was suddenly aware of the perspiration sliding down the flushed skin of my neck, pooling in the small of my back. I bent over, pressing my nose toward my knees and wishing I could untangle my confused thoughts as easily as the knotted muscles of my calves. He'd asked as a hypothetical, hadn't attached any names or pronouns—it should be easy to reject an abstract, but...

"Me," he clarified, and I turned my head toward him. From upside down, I couldn't decipher his expression, but I doubted any part of this would be clearer if I straightened. "I mean, 'Would you date *me*?' You don't have to answer now, but think about it."

19

Sometimes I stood under the shower and planned arguments I'd never initiate. I crafted the perfect rebuttals,
designed to bring my opponent to their knees. I imagined being triumphant, smug with facts and rhetoric,
while their ego lay smashed at my feet.

But then I turned the water off and left those daydreams
behind the shower's glass door.

Because some arguments you lose by winning. There were
fights where I could've proven I was right, but what did that
matter if the end cost was greater than the gain? Just look at last
week's lunch debacle.

I'd first learned that lesson at eight when things in Brazil had
ended...badly. Our flight back to the United States had been
booked last minute, and we were seated separately. My parents,
shaken by the events that led to our departure, had checked on
me relentlessly, regardless of whether the seat belt sign was on
or off. I'd spent the flight drafting a position paper about why
traveling so much was detrimental.

I'd won. They'd agreed and bought the house I now lived
in. The one they jokingly referred to as "home base" or "our
domicile-slash-storage-locker." My victory was short and bitter

though, because they hadn't stayed put. It was just that the next time they'd boarded a plane, they'd left me behind.

I'd gained stability and a best friend but had lost my family.

As I showered off the perspiration and chill of my run, I crafted imaginary debates I'd never have with my parents. These twisted in my mind with Curtis's unanswered question—and both topics swirled unresolved down the drain with my soap and sweat.

I tried to push them from my thoughts all night, through some historical movie of indeterminate time period Merri invited me to watch with her and Rory and Lilly. And I refused to think about them the next morning while I finalized the script for my first podcast episodes, then drove back up Hillcrest Road to retrieve that copy of *Anne of Green Gables* on my way to Merri's parents' store.

For expediency, Mr. Campbell and I were recording our first podcast in Haute Dog. The store was busy when I arrived, so I pulled out the book and read. It was annotated with someone else's thoughts. Whoever had read it first had an eerie knack for knowing lines that would resonate with me. Their green-pen underlines and margin notes echoed my thoughts. And when I reached a page where they'd drawn a heart around a character's name, my own chest constricted with affection. I put the novel down and approached the checkout counter as Mr. Campbell finished with a customer.

"How's the book?" he asked. "If you give me a minute to grab a roll of quarters for the register, we can get started."

"I think you might be my Matthew Cuthbert," I blurted, then fought through a blush to add, "I don't know if you remember him, but he's Anne's person. The adult who hears and appreciates her, and..."

"I remember." He reached across the counter and squeezed my shoulder, then pulled his hand back to swipe at his eyes. "That's among the nicest things that've ever been said to me. Thank you for letting me be your Matthew Cuthbert."

I nodded. He nodded. That was about all the sentimentality we could handle. He nodded again and said, "Okay, I'll get those quarters. You go ahead and set up the microphones."

I'd gotten them from Toby. Since Christmas—since Rory—he'd become serious about his music and composing and had gone all in on fancy recording gear. I'd borrowed the bare minimum, because despite the embarrassing number of hours I'd spent planning my script, I hadn't yet researched the technical aspects of podcasting.

Rory and Merri showed up for their shift an hour into recording. Merri happily took over customer interactions and Rory handled stockroom stuff, then sat down to draw a "pup portrait" of an English cocker spaniel named Mochi.

Two minutes later, Rory banished Merri to our side of the store for "being a distraction" to her and the dog.

"I can't help it," Merri whined. "He's my current favorite doggo. Did you see him carrying around that stick? Don't you just want to skritch his ears? He's such a pretty boy." She turned and called across the store, "You're such a pretty boy, Mochi."

"Merrilee, dangit!" Rory yelled. "Sit, Mochi!"

Merri shrugged. "It's not my fault he likes me better than her."

Mr. Campbell laughed and asked me, "Do we have enough recorded? Because I'm guessing there's about to be a Merri-Rory rumble, and we're not going to get anything usable while that's going down."

"Yeah." I could've kept going all night, but we had plenty. I disconnected the microphones and stacked my notes. We'd covered both CRISPR and quarks, and not only had I made him understand them, I'd made him *laugh*. I was giddy with the thrill of it. "We have enough to cut into two episodes. Thank you."

"Sure." He stood and immediately repositioned a dog toy that had been hung in the wrong spot. He and Lilly were fastidious, and I bet it had been bothering him the whole time we'd been talking. "That was fun. Let me know when you want to do another one."

"I will. Keep me posted on your science questions." I'd expected to feel awkward or self-conscious with a mic in my face, to be too embarrassed to ever want to listen to the playback. But it was heady, this feeling of having created something. I didn't know if the final product would be *good*, but the project already felt *important*.

Merri hovered while I packed up equipment. Conveniently, I could leave it with Rory to return to Toby. "What are you up to tonight?" she asked. "Curtis, Lance, Hannah, and Sera are going to that new sci-fi movie, but I know how you feel about 'fake science,' so if you want to come bowling with Fielding and me—"

"Thanks, but that's okay." I appreciated her offer, but I was more interested in the first part of her statement. "What movie is it?"

"Something about aliens? Apparently Curtis is a huge fan, which by default means you'd hate it, am I right?"

No. She wasn't. It should've been the perfect opportunity to tell her so, but I couldn't find the words. How could I explain to her what I didn't understand myself?

I felt my post-podcast smile slip as I forced out the answer she expected. "I'd totally hate it. His taste is the worst."

✕◇◯◇◯◇✕

It wasn't until chapter fifteen of *Green Gables* that Curtis's comments about identifying with Gilbert Blythe made sense. The first time he meets Anne, Gilbert mockingly calls her "Carrots." I was delighted to read that she retaliated—by cracking her school slate over his head.

I put the book down and picked up my phone. Scrolling through my contacts to a certain double-C name, I sent him a text message of a single emoji: 🥕.

Since he was at the movies, I put the phone down and picked the book back up—wincing as I read about Anne's humiliating punishment and stubborn vow to never forgive Gilbert. It seemed a pretty safe assumption that these two were not headed down a quick path to being what Anne called "kindred spirits."

My phone beeped. "Carrots" wouldn't be a bad nickname for you—you eat so many.

Since he wasn't there to hear me laugh at his joke, I didn't hesitate to do so. Then I responded with a different emoji.

My phone beeped again before I'd picked up the book. Wait. Do you want ME to call YOU "Cupcake"?

It kept beeping.

Or is that what you're calling me?

I'm going with you calling me. Since you won't even eat them.

Cupcake Cavendish. I like it.

If you're giving me a sweet nickname, I guess you deserve better than a vegetable.

He'd typed five messages almost faster than I could read them. I dropped the phone onto my bedspread and pushed it away. It was *one* emoji. I hadn't meant to inspire such a large response.

My phone beeped again. I poked at it with a finger before flipping it over to reveal the latest messages. Two emojis: a flame and a beetle. *Firebug.*

Which still made no sense, but I couldn't handle an explanation right now.

I knew how Merri would reply—the smiley face with heart eyes. It was her favorite emoji. If *I* used it, Curtis would probably assume someone had stolen my phone. Anne Shirley didn't know how lucky she'd had it, living in a time before text messages and rebus puzzle communication. I wished I could break my phone the way she'd broken her slate, so I'd have an excuse to escape this conversation.

My phone began to ring, and Curtis's name appeared on the screen. I held it gingerly to my ear. "Aren't you supposed to be at the movies? It's rude to talk or text."

"I stepped into the lobby when I got your message," he answered. "Do you like the book?"

"I do." I smiled down at the cover. "And I've been thinking about your question."

"Oh!"

There was a fist pump attached to those two letters, I would've bet my favorite microscope on it. So I felt guilty when I clarified, "I don't have an answer yet."

"Oh." This version was flatter, like a balloon that's been taken from a warm room to a freezer.

"I just wanted you to know I didn't forget. Also...I don't think I'd be good at it." I sank down on my bed, curling myself around that confession.

"Dating me?" he asked. "I'm making sure we're on the same page. I asked lots of questions yesterday—I really don't want us to be talking about *Anne of Green Gables* or the science fair right now."

"Yeah. Just...any of it. I don't know..." I swallowed, because those words burned. I'd been taught never to say them, or to show any ignorance. "I don't know how to flirt. It's playful talking. I don't play. I never learned how."

"Eliza..." He sighed.

"Don't say my name like that!" I wound a loose piece of string from my pillowcase around my pointer finger until the tip turned purple. It was a foolish thing to do, much like participating in this conversation. "I had a good childhood. Not everyone needs to be wild and cause a ruckus."

"Okay," he said, but his voice was soft. I shut my eyes to picture the sleepy expression that would go with it. "But you've come to the right person. I'm playful enough for eight people. I'm great at wild and ruckuses. You've said so yourself, only you used words like 'grow up' and 'indoor voice' and 'don't you ever take things seriously?'"

I laughed, but he didn't. "I'm being serious now, Firebug. I may tease you...but I won't judge you."

I didn't have an answer to that. Maybe he thought that if he waited, I'd formulate one. Or maybe, like me, he was happy to sit silently with his head pressed against the phone, thinking about the person on the other end of the line.

"Cavendish!" Lance's shout in the background made me jump. "What are you doing out here? Who are you talking to?"

"Don't tell him!"

"Umm," said Curtis. "Wink?"

I hadn't known he was a bad liar. The idea made me smile. "I'll talk to you later," I said.

"Yeah. Keep thinking about that question."

Seconds after I'd hung up—while I was sprawled on my back on my bed, fighting the urge to kick my feet in the air and squeal—my phone beeped again. Sunday, run day. Think you're up for 6?

A second message came on its heels. 6 miles, not 6am. Let's meet at 9.

I sent him one last emoji: a thumbs-up.

yawned into the collar of my sweatshirt. If you asked my parents, they'd say I'd slept for eight hours and twenty minutes. Actigraphy wasn't very accurate, and neither was the iLive band's accelerometer that recorded my steps and activity—but it was the best product on the market. What my parents didn't know was that some nights I lay in bed without moving so the band would be tricked into thinking I was asleep. While I hated the idea of skewing data, avoiding the sleep-disturbance questionnaire my parents required each time I didn't hit eight hours was sometimes worth the deception.

They called unexpectedly while I'd been counting down the minutes until I'd meet Curtis for our nine o'clock run. The conversation had been brief and specific—and they hadn't acknowledged the emotional email I'd sent them from school on Friday.

"The Avery board says they haven't received your registration. Are you having problems with your project?" Mom asked.

"No."

"Then what's the holdup?" prompted Dad.

I took a deep breath to explain about Saturday's first recording and how I still needed an adviser, then paused. Regardless of whether or not it could win, the podcast wasn't going to impress them. They'd disapprove of my plans for the Avery as much as they'd disapprove of my plans for the day. They wouldn't tell me—like Mr. Campbell had—that a half-marathon was "an impressive goal. Tell me when and where—I'll be there to cheer the loudest." Or, "You should consider doing something with this podcast beyond the science fair. It'd be a shame if I'm the only one benefitting from your brains and patience."

No one had ever called me "patient." My parents didn't consider it to be a virtue—at least not one they admired. Patience was for people whose time wasn't valuable. My vague evasions during the phone call had dangerously tested theirs.

Finally, I'd come up with a tactic that worked. "I'm worried about the ethics of it—with you as judges. I've already heard whispers that I'll get an unfair advantage. I don't want even the perception of nepotism."

"But there's a plan in place," Dad insisted. "We'll abstain from judging you."

"In the meantime"—I tightened my fingers around the phone, dreading Mom's caveat—"I'd like to see some more investment in your daily logs. I hope you're not losing focus—Nancy reports that you've been out more."

"Quiz bowl and school and my science project." There was panic in my voice, but maybe it wasn't apparent nine thousand miles away, because they accepted that explanation and ended the call.

It was early, but I fled like their words were chasing me. When I passed Nancy in the kitchen, she said, "You're going out."

It was a statement, not a question, but I stammered excuses anyway, only to have her shrug. "I'm washing sheets and towels today. I'll grab yours."

My "thanks" was a squeak. Doubts and panic crowded my thoughts on the drive to Curtis's house and poured out of my mouth when he opened the front door. "I don't want to play the question game today."

He smiled and said "Good morning," but I talked right over his greeting, slipping inside the door he held open. "But we should talk about your dating question."

"Eliza—" He lowered his voice and stepped closer.

I raised mine and backed up. "My answer is no. I'm not interested. Dating is..."

A clink of metal against ceramic pulled my attention away from his frozen expression and over his right shoulder. His family was seated around the table. The chair he'd vacated was still pushed out, while the occupants of the other four seats stared with cups and utensils and napkins suspended in horror. Well, three occupants looked horrified. Win was cutting a wedge out of a stack of pancakes.

"I—I—" If the door were still open, I would've backed out and kept going. I sucked in a gasping breath, and the scent of maple syrup made my stomach clench.

"Okay, you don't want to date me, but do you want to join us for breakfast?" Curtis's eyes were bright with mischief. "Also, Dad, meet Eliza."

As I walked past Curtis to greet his father, I mouthed, "I hate you."

He mouthed back, "No, you don't."

Mr. Cavendish stood, napkin in one hand as he extended the other. He was tall and thin like Curtis. Gray haired and smile lined—and fighting back his grin as we traded "nice to meet yous." And even though Curtis didn't seem fazed by my dramatic entrance, everyone else was swinging their glances between us.

"I didn't know breakfast came with a show." Win swallowed a mouthful and pointed his fork at me. "A little feedback though: You need more rehearsal if you want your acting to be convincing."

"Shut up." Wink must've kicked him under the table, because he jumped and winced. She glared at me.

"We should let you two talk." Mr. Cavendish picked up his plate, gesturing for the others to follow him…where? To eat in their bedrooms? Win pretended not to see, helping himself to more eggs.

"Please don't interrupt your meal," I said. "We're—it's fine."

"We've got six miles to talk." Curtis turned to me. "If you still want to run?"

I nodded. Far away from here, as fast as possible.

"Be back in an hour-ish. Save me a scone."

"You already had two!" Wink and Curtis both dove for the last one on the plate.

He got there first and licked the top. "I'm a growing boy who's running six miles. I get three." He led us out to his driveway, where I covered my face with both hands.

"You should've stopped me."

"You were pretty unstoppable." He chuckled. "Far be it from me to prevent you from speaking your mind. And rejecting me."

"I—" I had no words. They'd evaporated from the heat of my humiliation. "Does it help if I say it's not personal? Not about *you*?"

"So, your answer is no. Why not? You don't have to tell me—but Wink will ask."

"I told you: science. There are…studies." I could've offered citations, but it wasn't a moment for dry data and statistical significance. "People get distracted. I can't afford that. I need to stay focused on my goals. School."

"But those studies, your observations—they're based on *other* people." He shuffled his feet as he pulled on his gloves. "Probably very *average* people. You're not the average person."

"No, but—"

"Are you going to draw a conclusion without representative data? That's not very scientific of you."

My lips twitched. "I don't need to play with radioactive elements to confirm they're dangerous."

"I'm just saying, there are a lot of variables that haven't been factored in—you, me, our collective amazingness. There's no control group that could account for us."

I looked away. Nothing he said changed anything. "I couldn't even if I wanted to. Which I don't." I clenched my hands. "You're not half as tempting as you think you are."

"But I'm twice as tempting as you pretend I'm not." Curtis stepped closer, and I backed off the driveway and onto the lawn.

"That's fake math," I sputtered.

"*You're* fake math," he teased. "Come on, let's go running."

"What?" I blinked at him, not wanting to ask *that's it?* But... that was it? "My answer is still no."

Curtis shrugged. "Mine is still no pressure. You stated your position and I heard you. If you change your mind, you know where to find me, but I'm not going to be that guy."

I frowned. Obviously I wanted him to respect me—to hear my words and give them credence—but was I so easy to shrug off? Shouldn't he look a little disappointed?

I was.

I fussed with the cuffs of my gloves. "I hope you like waiting."

He grinned and tapped my iLive band—a reminder to remove it, though I hadn't explained why I needed to. "Look, I worked too hard to get you to tolerate me. If you want to be friends, I'm happy with that. If you want something different, you know where I stand. I'm not going to wreck this."

"I never said we were friends." But, *blast*, that was such a good answer. I had to twist away in a stretch so he didn't see my smile. "Our friends are friends."

"Which was such a convenient way for us to get to know each other and bond. Aren't you glad we did?"

"When exactly did I say we'd 'bonded'?" I made air quotes and rolled my eyes, but I wasn't hiding my smile anymore.

"I don't hear you denying it."

"Shut up and tie your shoes."

He grinned. "See, that's what I like about you—your constant concern for my well-being."

"I swear I will push you into traffic."

"There's the level of motivation I need in a training partner. Run fast or—" But the rest of his comeback fizzled into laughter when I did give him a shove—a gentle one—before draping my iLive band on my car's side mirror and heading down the driveway. I was pretty sure he'd follow me. More sure that I wanted him to.

It was easier to match our paces on this run. There were moments I pulled ahead, or when he did, but mostly we were side by side. Six miles of cold pavement passed much faster than six miles of solitary treadmill, and when Curtis invited me in for post-run water, I double-checked that the Cavendishes' cars weren't parked in the driveway, pretended I didn't have a full bottle waiting in mine, and accepted.

Curtis downed a glass in quick swallows before he picked up his scone from a plate on the kitchen island. "Want half?"

"Of the scone you *licked*? No thanks." The thought of chewing something dry and doughy post-run made me thirstier. "It's not healthy, the way you eat."

Curtis grinned. "I'm touched you care."

"I didn't say that."

"Isn't it nice how we communicate without words." He took a bite. "Rest assured, I do eat vegetables. I had a carrot and zucchini omelet this morning for breakfast. Egg whites even."

"You had two blueberry scones, and there was a muffin wrapper on your plate." His grin grew larger as I revealed way too much knowledge of his eating habits. "I can't help that I'm observant. I notice everything. You're not special."

"First, I am so special, I have stickers from elementary school that agree. Second, only one was blueberry, the other was cinnamon apple. Third, that was breakfast number three. First was a smoothie, then the omelet..."

My eyes went wide. "That's a lot of breakfast."

"You should see my dinners." He laughed. "But seriously, when I'm no longer sixteen and hitting growth spurts like pants shopping is my favorite hobby, then I'll worry. Right now I need to keep weight on or I'll be flattened on the lacrosse field."

This was the point where I backed down—I knew nothing about the nutritional needs of a growing teenage boy. I could barely manage my own and had gotten in over my head this fall when my workouts had ramped up faster than my caloric intake. I would've self-corrected if I'd had time to catch it, but my parents had quickly pounced on the slight quiver in my BMI. It had led to increased oversight of my food log and lots of articles about disordered eating and exercise.

They had made me feel small and stupid. Was that what I'd done to Curtis?

"I shouldn't have judged you," I said. "It's not my place, and I don't know all the facts."

He shrugged. "Hey, it's not like I don't judge your lunches, Captain Cruciferous. I don't think the way you eat is healthy either."

I bristled. "Excuse me?"

"Nutritional, sure. But is it mentally or spiritually healthy to be that regimented? You wouldn't even try the cupcakes you helped bake."

"Just so you know, Merri and I get doughnuts on the first day of school every year."

"A whole *one time* every year? How indulgent."

"My parents have rules." And I *liked* them. Usually. There were so many ways to disappoint my parents—clear rules were a way to get things right. Each obedient log entry was a sign I was doing daughterhood correctly.

"But when do you get to make your own rules?" He pointed the remaining corner of his scone at me. "Let me ask you this: Which of us is more controlled by food—the girl who lets someone else dictate what she eats, or the guy who has an occasional treat and makes sure to enjoy it?"

My retorts crumbled like the scone mess Curtis was making on the floor. Seriously, his plate was *right* there. But, mess-making aside, was he right? The question rumbled in my empty stomach. I intercepted the last piece of scone on its way to his mouth and popped it in my own.

It was flakey and appley, with a hint of cinnamon. One bite wasn't enough...but it was one bite more than I'd include in my log. And how long would I be keeping a log? Until I was eighteen? Twenty? Rules felt safe—but his question resonated: When did I get to make my own?

I raised an eyebrow, and he gave me a slow clap. "By the way, I figured out a solution to your dilemma."

I swallowed, the last morsels suddenly gritty in my mouth. "I didn't realize I had one."

"Your whole snafu about dating." He waved an arm, scattering crumbs. "I like you, you pretend to hate me. Regardless of *Anne* or the Avery or your 'rules,' that's still true. Let's make plans—but let's not-date."

"Plans?" I looked at him. "Like, plans to go running? Not date plans?"

"Isn't that what I said?" He grinned. "And if we're working out, of course it's not a date. No one gets purposely sweaty and stinky on a date."

It was verbal gymnastics, but it relieved the pressure in my chest. I could picture myself repeating those same words to Nancy, to my parents. *"No, of course it's not a date. It's a workout. I needed a faster running partner than Merri."*

"Fine," I gritted out. "But I'm expecting seven miles and a challenging route. Can you do that?"

"Sure. Can you keep up?" Curtis licked his finger and pressed it to the crumbs on his plate—it was like he was trying to draw attention to his mouth. Whatever, I wasn't going to look. I studied his chest instead. "Also, it doesn't matter if *this* is a not-date, because we've already had several."

My eyes flew up from mapping his muscles. "What are you talking about?"

"We went together to Fall Ball."

"We—" I sputtered. "We did not *go* together."

"We absolutely did. It was you, me, Merri, and Fielding in that car."

"Arriving at the dance in the same vehicle is not a date."

He shrugged. "What about these past couple of weeks?"

"Playing video games with your younger siblings?" It irritated me that he was calmly joking while my skin was flushing. "That's not a date, it's babysitting."

He laughed. "Please tell Win that; I'd like to see his reaction."

"It's still true." I pointed at his mouth. "Before you say it, baking was not a date."

"Exactly." He pretended to bite my finger, then grasped my hand and spun me around. "So let's have more not-dates. Lots of them."

I was dizzier than I should have been from one rotation. "What are you going to tell people?"

"If anyone asks, the truth." I sucked in a breath, because I didn't know what the truth *was* anymore. But I was perpetually aware of the untruths I was balancing—the things I was omitting from my log and keeping off my iLive band, the edited stories I told Merri. Curtis dropped my arm. "I'll tell them we're not dating. Isn't that what we just agreed?"

I exhaled my relief and let myself return his impish grin. "Yes, that is one hundred percent accurate."

21

As Merri and I drove to the Knight Lights' Martin Luther King Day service project on Monday, I was on high alert. Like her parents' dog before thunder, my ears were figuratively perked in anticipation of the storm. I was waiting for Merri to *know* something was up with me, or for Curtis to slip and make some joking-not-joking comment about us dating-not-dating.

We entered the Knight Light lounge and approached the table where our group of mentors and adoptees were getting ready to fill bags with toiletries for a homeless shelter. Everyone greeted us with smiles, so at least Friday's Convocation humiliation had erased any lingering anger about my lunch tirade.

I glanced suspiciously at Curtis as I sat, but he was busy telling Sera about an iLive vid channel devoted to melting objects.

"Eliza, can I ask you a question?" Lance was Curtis's best friend. The fact that he needed permission for whatever he was asking had me reaching my foot under the table to stomp on Curtis's.

"Ow!" squeaked Rory.

"Oh, sorry!" I winced, then turned to Lance. "What is it?"

"Not to sound stupid..." He paused. Lance was the least academic among us, and in any other Hero High group, the wary expression on his face might be warranted. Not here. We waited for him to finish. This group, this "Lunch Bunch" or whatever—they were the best part of Hero High.

Lance fiddled with a stack of toothbrushes. The table in front of us was piled with toothpaste, soap, socks, granola bars, playing cards, and more. Our task was assembly-line style: Curtis opened a baggie and passed it to Huck, who put in deodorant and passed it to Rory for soap. We continued around the table: Toby, me, Merri, Hannah, Sera, and Lance, each adding something before Lance's adoptee, Dante, sealed the full bags and stacked them in a box.

Lance finally asked, "Are your parents really in Antarctica? I didn't know anyone but polar bears lived there."

Polar bears only lived at the North Pole, but that wasn't relevant and I could be sensitive too. I choked back that correction. "It's not many people—especially during the winter—but yes, my parents are there."

"I looked it up," Curtis said. "We've got a couple active research stations down there—but there are, like, forty other countries with their own stations too." I tilted my head at Curtis, but he matched my curiosity with his own. "Are your parents at McMurdo or Amundsen-Scott?"

"Amundsen-Scott—the South Pole Station—mostly. But they travel between there and McMurdo while it's still summer."

Lance held up a finger. "Uh, it's January twenty-first."

"Southern hemisphere's summer," clarified Curtis—and I was glad he had, because I never managed to correct people without it sounding like an insult. "It's different at the pole. They get twenty-four hours of sunlight for months, then months of no sun."

The bags moved between us as quickly as the questions. Sera was next. "How cold *is* it?"

"In austral summer, the average temperature is negative eighteen degrees at the pole." I'd jumped to answer before Curtis could. Not because I was competitive—fine, I was—but because it had to be suspicious that he knew so much about me-related topics. I scanned the table, but everyone's interest seemed benign. Maybe his knowledge *wasn't* me-based? Maybe I was just egotistical and the last to realize he knew smart things because he was smart.

"Have they been there in the winter?" Curtis asked. "I don't know if I could do months of no sun."

I nodded. "They wintered over last year. They've got about another two months until they do it again. The sun sets March twenty-third."

"Wow." His curiosity felt like ordinary curiosity. It wasn't salacious. It wasn't fanboy or like he was looking for anything from me. I slid my foot across the space beneath the table again. This time my aim was better and my action gentler. As my shoe made contact with his, sliding along his inseam, Curtis dropped the baggie he was holding. We both looked down to hide our grins. Maybe not-dating was possible—maybe it was perfect.

"Hey, Cavendish, you need some help with the bags? You're holding up the line." I'd always thought Huck was the ideal adoptee for Curtis—that he was basically a white, dimpled freshman version of his Knight Light mentor. I was wrong. Clearly Huck was a menace. Curtis and I yanked our legs back beneath our own chairs. I slid closer to Merri for good measure.

Huck snickered and shot me a probing look. "I saw you two on my street the other day. Eliza, what were you doing with this goofball?"

Those were the questions I feared: *Why are you with him? Why do you put up with her?* The ones where we were categorized and evaluated on some superficial scale of looks or popularity. Where we were called upon to justify and explain compatibility.

"You must be mistaken." No one else had been paying attention—at least not until I went into panic-denial mode.

Rory snorted. "Doubtful. Huck's superpower is extreme observational skills. He's located Merri's house keys five times this month."

Merri pinched my arm—a reminder to breathe—then aimed an exaggerated glare at her sister. "The last time *my* keys were in *your* hand because you think hiding them is some sort of funny trick. Spoiler: It's not."

Their bickering drew in Toby and then Hannah and Sera as spectators. Lance and Dante were looking at something on Lance's phone. So we were likely out of the woods—even if Huck said, "Sorry, I must've been wrong," in a tone that made it clear he knew he wasn't.

>∞∞∞<

In English class on Tuesday Ms. Gregoire stopped by my desk. "Have you figured out your dilemma with Curtis yet?"

I gaped. "What? It's not a dilemma. It's not—we're not—we're not-*not*. I mean..."

"About your book?" Ms. Gregoire's eyebrows lifted. "Did you decide which of you will read *Anne of Green Gables*?"

I was too nervous to look across the circle, because if he was watching this, I'd trip him the next time we went running. Perhaps strangle him with his shoelaces if he was laughing. "We're working that out."

"Ah, so you're both still staking your claim." Her mouth twisted into a knowing smile. "Keep me up*dated*."

Maybe she hadn't emphasized the second half of that word, but it was how my ears processed it. My mouth went too dry to speak, so I nodded and nodded until Curtis caught my eye across the room and gestured to stop.

22

As if waiting for this thing with Curtis to blow up and spending hours poring over podcast forums and drafting my next script weren't enough to keep me busy, there was also quiz bowl. It's not that I'd forgotten it was more than hanging out with buzzers in the bio room; I just hadn't thought about the *competitions* until Dr. Badawi went through logistics at the end of Tuesday's practice.

"We'll meet on campus at seven thirty Saturday morning and drive in the van to Princeton. If you have family coming to watch, the competition starts at nine, though we won't know the order of teams until check-in."

The family part didn't pertain to me. I'd never had parents clapping in the audience, or chaperoning field trips, or helping run the book fair, bake fair, any sort of fair. I'd known since elementary school to recycle any handouts that asked for classroom volunteers, because if they were home, my parents reacted to them with a dizzying recitation of commitments and excuses, or a sudden need to depart.

I was used to it. I had not-reacting down. I'd casually look at my lap—find a piece of fuzz to pick off my skirt or a smudge on my shoe that needed inspecting.

My phone buzzed in my blazer pocket as Dr. Badawi droned on about letting her know if we were driving home with family versus returning in the van. I stopped searching for Catoby hair on my tights and read the text from Merri: Mom and Rory are manning the store so Dad, Lilly, and Trent can come watch US.

It was supposed to make me feel better. And it did...but it also made me feel worse. It was one more kindness I couldn't repay. What was the tipping point when the Campbells had given more favors than I was worth? I sent Merri an emoji smile, since I couldn't manage a real one.

Curtis was looking at me. I ignored him and turned to watch Lynnie greet her boyfriend, Penn, who'd come to pick her up from practice.

Their kiss was nothing like Fielding and Merri's. It was unbalanced—him leaning in too far, her standing rigid. His eyes shut, hers open. I would've thought that after dating for years, they'd have figured out the mechanisms.

But then again, what did I know? I had zero experience. I'd probably be worse than that. Curtis would—no. No, he wouldn't, because we wouldn't. And the fact that he was crossing the bio room toward me meant I needed to leave.

I dodged by him, making Merri practically run to keep up on the walk to my car.

Because the other option—the one that was way more tempting—was turning to him, asking him to come over, telling him how I felt about being the kid without parents. How in fifth grade a new student had assumed I was an orphan, since I'd been the only one at the school's move-up ceremony without people in the audience. My guardian at the time, Judith, had decided to wait in her car.

I wanted Curtis to make me laugh, to make me forget with questions from his app or video games beneath my fingers—but not racing ones, the kind where I could blow things up, because everything inside me was explosive.

That felt like more than not-dating. That felt dangerous.

Merri talked for both of us on the drive. I didn't register the route back to my house or pay attention to where I put my bag or keys when I walked in the door. Nancy called a greeting from her room—I think I answered her—but my whole focus was on getting to my laptop and pulling up the studies my parents had sent me. The ones they'd cited for why I couldn't date. I'd read the abstracts but had never bothered with more. Why would I need reasons not to do something I had no interest in doing?

But now I wanted to know.

I finished scrolling and sat back in my desk chair, stunned. My mouth was raw; I'd chewed off a coat of lip balm and the top few layers of skin. My left hand was cramped, and the portion of skirt I'd clutched within it was hopelessly wrinkled.

Normally I took notes while reading, digitally annotating facts I wanted to remember or things I wanted to look up. There was no need tonight. My conclusion was straightforward: The studies were flawed.

They weren't controlled for predisposing factors. The sample sizes were small. The generalizations sweeping and vague. Even the authors seemed to realize they couldn't draw definitive conclusions and couched their results in imprecise and ambiguous phrasing.

Granted my own sample size was also flawed and limited, but nothing I'd observed about relationships seemed generalizable. Sera and Hannah's long-term relationship differed from Penn and Lynnie's. Rory and Merri had common DNA and were raised in the same environment, but their relationships with their respective boyfriends were unique. Hannah gave Sera confidence to speak up, Sera brought logic to Hannah's disorganization. Rory inspired Toby's music, he helped her in math. Fielding curbed Merri's wilder impulses and she his overly serious ones. It was about *this* specific person partnered with that *specific* one. It wasn't possible to pair two undefined variables and predict a precise outcome.

I glanced again at my parents' "evidence." They would never have let me use this sort of study as proof of anything. They'd have mercilessly mocked any colleague who cited these in their own research.

Yet, their sending these to me wasn't some accident or oversight. It wasn't that there were other, better studies that drew the same conclusions. I'd looked. The only valid studies I'd located had findings that directly contradicted these. I placed both elbows on the desk and leaned into my hands. What did I do with this deception?

When Rory and Merri fought like wildebeests, their mom said, "You can be right or you can be friends—which matters more?"

My parents were *wrong*. I could compile a whole email of proof. But this wasn't them making a mistake; this was them deliberately misleading me. So what was the point in pointing it out?

Except, maybe this was a moment when being right was more important than being obedient. Especially since they hadn't responded or acknowledged my last lonely email. I clicked on the mail icon, words bristling on the tips of my fingers: *How dare you?* and *What sort of scientist employs flawed data to control someone's behavior?* Most importantly, *Why?*

But there was no need to draft a new email, because waiting in my inbox was one from them. It was only two sentences long—short enough that I could read it three times without taking a breath, but sharp enough to leave me gasping.

Purchase a new iLive band. It's malfunctioning again.

I laughed aloud. My parents worried only about trauma they could quantify. Had I gained or lost weight? Had there been a tremor in my GPA? Was I getting their prescribed amount of sleep or drinking enough to reach peak hydration levels?

If none of my data markers changed, they assumed I hadn't either.

Though it didn't surprise me that my iLive band was malfunctioning. I'd forgotten to take it off my side mirror after Sunday's run. It had fallen onto the driveway and cracked.

I glanced at the browser icon at the bottom of my computer screen, at the evidence I had waiting in internet tabs, and thought about the explosive fallout that would result from confronting them. What if I just... *didn't?*

I clicked to my word processor, and my fingers flew. Not on this week's response journal for English; this was a new podcast script. One on how to verify an experiment's validity, on how *not* to be duped when someone cites "science" to prove their point.

Once I'd finished a draft, I flipped back to their email. Will do. And I just want to say: you've been so inspirational for my Avery project.

I closed my laptop lid and picked up my car keys.

My parents thought they were so smart, and yet deceiving them was turning out to be the simplest game in the world.

23

called Curtis from the parking lot of the electronics store-slash-café the next town over. Bytes and Bites also had a location in the same plaza as Haute Dog, but I couldn't risk any of the Campbells seeing me.

"Hello?"

"It's me." I added "Eliza" because this new number wouldn't show up on his phone, and I couldn't presume I was the only girl who called him. Wait—did others? If we were "not-dating," did that mean he could "yes-date" other people? I'd need that clarified at some point.

"Hey."

"You don't sound happy to hear from me." I frowned. "Also, I know we're not-dating, but are we doing so exclusively?" *Some point* was apparently right then.

He sighed. "You've been avoiding me. I assume this is where you change your mind again."

"No." I climbed into my car and turned the heat on—it was too cold to have this conversation outside, and I was done making myself uncomfortable for no reason. "This is where I tell you I bought a burner phone so we can talk whenever I want without my parents having a record of it."

It had been easy to do. Phones were one row over from the iLive LifeTracker wristbands. And this—dialing his number and asking for what I wanted—was easier still. I was going to do it more often. Starting now. "Can I come over?"

"Yeah, of course. But...catch me up here, Firebug. I'm all for a good rebellion, but what does this mean?"

"It means I told Nancy I'd be out late practicing for quiz bowl, and I'll be there in twenty minutes."

"Are we going to practice?"

"Probably not." There was smugness in my voice—take that, Mom and Dad! "Though that's a good backup plan if you're boring me."

"I can safely say that no one has ever called me boring."

The laughter in his voice warmed my skin faster than the air rushing from my car's vents. I shifted into reverse, saying three more letters before I hung up: "Yet."

It was a word saturated with possibilities. I couldn't wait to explore all sorts of *yets*.

Curtis must have been watching for my headlights, because he opened the door before I knocked.

"Were you busy?" I was a person who liked schedules, and I'd inserted myself into his night at the last minute.

"No, I was baking—well, frosting. Come in."

The main section of the Cavendishes' house was empty. The TV off, the rooms dark except for pendant lights over the kitchen island. They illuminated the plate Curtis was pointing to.

"More cupcakes?" I hung my coat on a hook, slid my shoes beside his, then blinked at how familiar those actions had become. "You didn't have enough last week when I destroyed your kitchen?"

"There's no such thing as 'enough' cupcakes." His smile was too bright in the dim room.

I looked away. "These ones are probably better since half the dry ingredients didn't end up on the floor."

"Eh, we didn't get any complaints. But those ones were vanilla." I followed him as he wandered into the kitchen. "Tonight I've got all of your favorite flavors, as long as they're chocolate and as long as they're not peanut butter, because I've got a strange attachment to breathing."

"I don't eat chocolate. Or cupcakes." My words were soft and slightly wounded. "I thought you'd noticed this by now."

"Right." He spun the plate as he added, "Your parents' rules."

"I probably wouldn't eat them anyway." The mention of my parents made me want to grind my teeth. "I don't need rules to tell me if food is nutritious or not. It's not a value judgment; it's fact."

"Interesting." He spun the plate again. "So you're saying it's either good for you, or it's bad?"

I exhaled. "Exactly!"

He froze, and the cupcakes wobbled. "How is that not a value judgment?"

I opened my mouth, then shut it. He was right.

His fingers began to move again, and the cupcake plate became a hypnotic blur of frosting. "For me, it's not a coping method. Or a reward. Or a punishment. I don't feel guilty or like I 'earned' it. It's food. It's fuel. I want it. I eat it. Not every day, but definitely today. It's not a trap—it's a cupcake."

My eyes felt huge, and his felt too perceptive, like he could see his words shredding the beliefs I'd threaded through my parents' rules and had used to hang a curtain between myself and my peers.

"Plus, I didn't ask you to eat them—I wouldn't pressure you like that," he said. "I asked what your favorite flavor was."

"You didn't actually *ask* anything. You told a factually inaccurate statement." There was a word for the fast and shallow way I was breathing: "tachypnea." But knowing that label did nothing to relieve the anxiety causing it. Just like knowing Curtis was right did nothing to change my parents' rules.

I put a hand on the plate to stop his relentless spinning. We didn't need a demonstration of centrifugal force, with cupcakes flying off like chocolate bombs. Though at least that mess wouldn't be *my* fault.

Curtis stepped closer. He dragged a finger through the blob of frosting that had ended up on the back of my hand when a cupcake tipped over from the abrupt halt. "Is this how every conversation with you ends? It turns into an intellectual debate about the precision of word choice?" He stuck his finger in his mouth and sucked off the frosting.

My nod was sharp and short, because the emotions behind it were jagged.

"That's—" I waited for him to fill in the blank with "exhausting" or "obnoxious" or some other word I'd heard before. So many versions of *Can't you chill out? Why is everything an argument with you? Don't you ever let anything slide?* But I couldn't. Unless I addressed them, inaccuracies sat in my head and fermented—like Lance's comment about polar bears at the South Pole. Like my parents' lies about adolescent relationships.

"—intellectually stimulating," finished Curtis. "I dig it."

"You *dig* it?" The edges of the words were barbed, because

they were my last layer of defense against his statement. "Good for you, but I don't choose my language for your pleasure."

"Didn't think you did. But it still makes me happy."

"Where is everyone?" I didn't want a twin audience of snark and suspicion, and who knew what his parents thought of me after my Sunday-morning spectacle.

"Mom and Dad and Win are meeting with his history teacher. Wink's over her friend Reese's house. It's just me, you, and the guinea pig."

"You have a guinea pig?"

"Win does. His name is Hudson. Want to meet him?"

"No." I wasn't a fan of rodents. Not after having seen them in cages for experimental testing. If I thought of them as pets, then I couldn't think about them as "a necessary part of scientific advancement" or whatever wording my parents had used to explain it to me when I was barely out of toddlerhood.

I wasn't supposed to be thinking about my parents tonight. That was the whole point. "Fine. Maybe I'll try a bite. This one touched my hand, so I might as well..."

My words trailed off as I picked up the cupcake by its silver foil wrapper. The frosting was dented, and I had a smudge of chocolate on the back of my hand. The smell of cocoa made my mouth water. When was the last time I'd had cake?

I peeled back the wrapper and bit—teeth sinking through the slick frosting and dense cake. I swallowed, and my tongue slid out to lick my lips, chasing any crumbs or dabs of rogue frosting. I turned to Curtis with wide eyes, speechless as I tried to pass him the rest.

"You've tainted it with your germs—you might as well finish it."

I didn't need any more encouragement than that. He laughed as I jerked the cupcake away from him and took another bite.

Curtis reached past me to get a cupcake of his own. One with sprinkles on top. Did sprinkles make the frosting better? Add a contrasting gritty texture? Maybe next time I'd try sprinkles. Or cookie crumbs. Or whatever those small silver balls were. I tore my gaze away from the plate and pinned it on the boy baker beside me. "Stop watching me eat—it makes this weird."

He laughed. "Because this whole not-dating thing we've got going on, that's definitely not weird. No, it's me looking at your mouth that pushes this into the 'weird' category."

I swallowed my last bite and rinsed my hands in the sink. He was holding out a towel when I turned back around, his own last bit of cupcake disappearing between his lips. And now I couldn't stop looking at *his* mouth. Did he kiss like Fielding, or Penn? Or Toby, who seemed to forget the rest of the world when he was with Rory? They'd been dating the shortest amount of time, but you wouldn't know it from the way they fit like puzzle pieces.

I blamed it on the sugar rush, my body not knowing how to process the sudden spike in blood glucose. Because what other reason could there be for my asking, "Do you think kissing is something that can be learned?"

"Is this a hypothetical?" The laughter dissolved from his voice, and I watched his throat as he swallowed.

"What if I'm bad at it?" I focused on the towel in my hands, on methodically drying each of my fingers. "We both know I'm not good at flirting."

The pendant lights behind Curtis cast his shadow on the kitchen floor. It was touching me, though he wasn't. I kept my eyes on the distance between our shoes as I waited for him to answer. "Hasn't anyone ever told you it's okay to be bad at things?"

I laughed. Then realized he was serious and lifted my chin. "No."

"Everyone is bad at things in the beginning. walking, talking, biking, reading—you practice and you get better. Same is true for kissing."

I let this theory sink in. It started with the presumption of being unskilled. I'd trusted him to see me flail at video games, to watch me eat a cupcake, to keep whatever we were doing here to himself—but did I trust him, or myself, enough to be vulnerable *and* inept? I pressed my back more firmly against the counter. "There's a scene only a few pages from the end of the book where Anne says—"

"You finished the whole book?" Curtis snorted. "Of course you have. Anyway, continue with your spoilers, because you're going to tell me anyway, right? I might as well give you permission."

I ignored him. "Anne says, 'We've been good enemies'—she's describing Gilbert and herself to Marilla."

"But you missed the part before that," Curtis interrupted. "What Gilbert says first is more important. He says they're going to be the best of friends—that they were *born* to be. He tells her, 'You've thwarted destiny enough.'"

"Destiny's not real." My words were automatic, and while I spoke, I processed what he'd revealed. "Wait! If you know that, you've read the whole book too. I didn't spoil anything."

"Nope." He grinned.

I took a deep breath. "We've been good enemies, you and I. I've held on to the pettiest things for far too long."

"Yup."

He was trying to bait me. But I refused to snap, even though I could've offered a sequel's worth of spoilers, because not only had I finished *Green Gables* last night, but *Anne of Avonlea* as well. Ms. Gregoire's comment about "staking our claim" had been eerily accurate. Like finishing first increased my right to the novel. The whole series was eight books long—I hadn't read them all yet, but I knew more than Curtis. Holding on to that kernel helped me tell him the truth I'd been cradling. "I don't think we'll ever stop fighting—"

"Because you like fighting with me." He pushed off the opposite counter, his shadow climbing up my body as he approached.

"You're the most infuriating and frustrating and exasperating person I know."

"But you like it," he insisted.

I wouldn't make this easy—he wouldn't want me to. I lifted my chin and waited.

"You know," he said, "Anne rejects Gilbert the first time he proposes."

I scowled. There was no proposal in *Anne of Avonlea*. What book was *he* on? I should leave so I could catch up and pass him. Instead I gripped the counter and snorted. "So now you're *proposing*?" But maybe the more direct parallel was how I'd rejected Curtis's offer to date. I bit my lip to stop myself from demanding if Gilbert had asked Anne again.

"Nah. You'd get too much satisfaction out of turning me down. I'll settle for beating you at the Avery." He stepped closer and reached out to drum his fingers beside my hip. "Climb up here."

"That's a counter," I sputtered. "I don't sit on counters. They make perfectly good chairs for sitting."

"Yeah, but this is the perfect height."

"Perfect height for what?" As I asked, I braced both hands and boosted myself up. We were eye-to-eye. My knees would touch his hips if he stepped an inch closer. My toes were already brushing his red flannel pajama pants.

"For this—" Curtis kept his gaze on mine as he leaned in. My eyes widened as my breath caught. I was capable of explaining the biology behind why his pupils dilated; I'm sure mine had too. But when his nose brushed against mine, I hid my pupils behind my eyelids and let out a shuddery breath, my mouth pursing in anticipation of his.

Instead it was our foreheads that touched. Then he was pulling away, and I was opening my eyes, my mouth too—gaping at him in confusion, frustration, annoyance.

"You have to tell me you want this," Curtis said. "I won't kiss you unless we're on the same page."

I nodded. That would have to be good enough, because I wasn't going to beg.

"Then let go. I've got you." Curtis tapped the hands I had clenched around the counter.

"This is not the *Titanic*, DiCaprio," I quipped.

"No, it's not, because both of us are smart enough to calculate how both Rose and Jack could fit on that door. C'mon. Let go. Hold on to me." His hands were warm on mine—not tugging or prying, just resting there like an invitation it was my job to accept.

"Curtis—" I slammed my mouth shut. His name had come out in a breathless, desperate whisper. It was a voice I wouldn't have recognized as mine. One I never wanted to hear again. I was better than this. I was stronger.

Except, *blast!* Who had cranked up the sensitivity of my nerve endings? I shivered as he trailed his hands up my arms. "What, Firebug? What do you want?"

When a person is nervous, their amygdala is activated. It pumps the blood in their body away from their brain and stomach and toward their arms and legs. It's an ancient instinct—part of the fight-or-flight-or-freeze mechanism. But it makes you stupid. So incredibly stupid. My stupid prehistoric instincts were counter to what I would've done if there'd been adequate blood or oxygen levels in my brain. If I'd been able to think clearly, I never would have used my feet to pull him closer, my arms to reach up and steady myself on his broad shoulders.

"Kiss me." I shut my eyes, leaned in—

And jumped, bashing my forehead against the bridge of his nose when my blazer pocket began to buzz.

It was a splash of cold water. A redirection of adrenaline. Now my fingers were shoving him away, even as my mouth was forming the words, "I'm so sorry, are you okay?"

He waved off my concern with a short laugh, but winced as he reached up to touch his nose. "Maybe you should get that, in case it's important."

My eyes were on him as I pulled out the phone. My distracted "Hello?" would've been cause for interrogation from my parents, but Merri's chipper voice responded, "Hey pal, what are you up to?"

I looked at Curtis. His cheeks were flushed, his eyes dazed. At least he wasn't wincing or hadn't gotten out an ice pack. Maybe I hadn't hit him that hard? My forehead barely hurt.

But did I look that starry-eyed? I felt it. So forcing myself to answer, "Nothing," and watching the smile fall from his face scraped me raw.

I hopped down from the counter, turning my back on Curtis and the cupcakes. "I'm sorry, what did you say?"

"Math homework," Merri repeated, a hint of exasperation in her voice. "I need you to settle a bet."

"Math homework?" My voice pitched up—because I didn't even remember we'd had any.

"Toby and I are arguing about the answer to number seventeen." I heard his voice in the background, and she laughed. "Prove me right. What'd you get?"

"Problem seventeen?"

"Eliza, you okay?" Merri's voice was concerned, and she shushed Toby. "You sound funny."

"I'm fine." The words were automatic, but flat. Their deception burned the sweetness off my tongue. Fingers softly touched my hand, and I jumped. Curtis grinned at my overreaction, but it didn't reach his eyes. He held out a notebook, tapped a thumb next to problem seventeen. I scanned his calculations. "The answer is negative thirty-seven."

"Yes!" Merri shrieked so shrilly that even Curtis flinched. He stepped back to toss his notebook onto the counter. I'm not sure if he purposely put it where I'd been sitting when we almost... but it made my cheeks burn. "In your face, Mayday. You owe me a doughnut or a cookie or a cupcake. I should make you owe Eliza one too."

"Cupcake?" I repeated.

Curtis tilted his head at that word. He pointed to himself and mouthed, "Talking about me?"

A watery laugh escaped my lips, because I wished I had been. I wished I was the type of girl who could use pet names or tell my best friend what I was doing.

"Don't worry," Merri was saying in my ear. "I don't expect you to eat it. More for me."

Right. No one would expect that of me. My parents weren't the only ones who had me pigeonholed. "I've got to go." My words were for both of them, and I crossed the room to get my coat with the phone still pressed to my ear like a shield. "I'll see you tomorrow."

24

'd texted Merri to tell her to ride to school with Toby—added that they could stop and pick up her math-problem prize.

She'd responded, Sure. But why?

I hadn't answered.

The truth was I'd beat Ms. Gregoire to campus Wednesday morning. I was pacing outside her door before she walked down the hallway, coat on, classroom keys in her hand.

"Good morning, Eliza." She smiled. "Give me a second to get this unlocked."

"Are you sure we can't do the same book?" I asked as the door swung open. The lights flickered on, triggered by motion detectors.

"Very."

I groaned. "I know it sounds silly, but I feel like I *have* to do this book."

"That doesn't sound silly at all. You've found your story." She nodded sagely. "But it might not be *only* yours, and rules are rules. You'll have to sort this out with Curtis."

Something about her words made me shiver. "We have a bet." I took a gulp from the cardboard cup in my hand. "Curtis and I—we bet. Whichever of us wins the Avery Science Competition gets to do their project on *Anne of Green Gables*. The loser does *Frankenstein*."

"I see." Ms. Gregoire placed her bag and coffee mug on her desk, then crossed to the closet in the back of the classroom and hung up her coat.

"But I can't do the science fair without a faculty adviser..." I'd finally filled out the application last night, and that requirement was in bold.

"You're asking me?" She laughed. "Well, then—I have a few questions. One: Are you using any materials that are radioactive, banned by arms treaties, or illegal?"

"No. I'm not really using—"

"Two: Any dead bodies? I've read *Frankenstein* too, you know."

"No. My project is—"

"Don't tell me. I want to be surprised." She laughed at my shocked face. "Eliza, you and I both know you want a signature on a piece of paper, not science advice. If you'd needed that, you wouldn't be seeking an adviser in the humanities building."

True. I pulled out the application. "Here's the form to sign. Thank you."

"So you need to beat Mr. Cavendish." She straightened a few desks as she crossed the room, patting the back of one to indicate I should take a seat. She *hmm*'d as she scanned the document. "He's a formidable opponent. But then again, so are you. How are you coping?"

"I'm overwhelmed by—" I laughed. "Everything. It feels like everything is a competition lately—quiz bowl, science fair, half-marathons, now this book—"

"Competition isn't always a bad thing." Her signature was all poetry and flourish. And green. I stared at her pen. "Sometimes it's what we need to get out of our comfort zones and help us grow. Take Anne and Gilbert—"

I winced and took another sip. I'd been thinking of almost nothing *but* Anne and Gilbert. Except for all the moments I'd been thinking of Curtis and me—and how annoyed he must have been after I'd left like that last night.

"Sometimes the people we compete and conflict with are those who challenge our way of thinking and push us to be better." Ms. Gregoire handed back the application. "Sometimes—like Anne—we're too stubborn to see it. I don't know where you are in the book, so I hope I'm not spoiling anything."

I shook my head. "Anne hates Gilbert—*hated*. Past tense. I didn't realize at first that it was going to change. But in the later books of the series—they don't conflict. They start supporting each other. They need each other to get through college. And when he decides to be a doctor—"

"Whoa, let me cut you off there, Eliza. Did you read the whole series last night?"

I shook my head. Wisps from my ponytail were escaping and brushing my neck. I'd need to fix that before class started. Neat, high, tight. There were only so many deviations from the norm I could tolerate. "I'd already read *Green Gables* and *Avonlea*. I read *of the Island* and *House of Dreams* last night. I skipped *of Windy Poplars*—I know it comes fourth chronologically, but it was published later, and from what I saw online, it doesn't advance the plot. Maybe I'll come back to it, but I'm not much for epistolary novels. And then I wasn't sure what to read next: *of Ingleside* or *Rainbow Valley*—the message boards were split about whether to go chronologically or by publishing date. What do you think?"

"Eliza." Ms. Gregoire's voice was concerned. "Did you sleep at all?"

Another headshake. More strands escaping. "But it's okay, because my parents know I bought a new iLive band and I emailed them that I didn't have time to set it up. As long as I get it calibrated before bedtime tonight—but not until after our run—might as well get another one in before I need to find excuses..." I trailed off and looked up at Ms. Gregoire.

She nudged the Cool Beans cup away from my hand. "I'm guessing that's not your usual herbal tea?"

"Quad shot espresso." It promised a high concentration of caffeine—but maybe jumping straight into the deep end of the coffee pool wasn't the smartest decision. My fingers trembled on the desk without the warm cup to steady them.

"You should head home," suggested Ms. Gregoire. "Things will look calmer once you've gotten some sleep."

"Can't." Nancy would have to excuse the absence, and what explanation could I give that wouldn't set off parental alarms? "It's fine—I'm fine. But... could I do a later *Anne* book and Curtis could do *Green Gables*? Would that work?"

Ms. Gregoire shook her head. "I don't think you actually want me to say yes. I know you're amped up on caffeine and lack of sleep right now, but you—like Anne—are a fan of the chase."

25

un today? I wrote the note on the tiniest scrap of paper I could tear from my biology notebook. The letters were shaky, written with nervous and caffeine-jittery hands. It was several minutes before Curtis looked my way. The first time he did, he gave me the barest flicker of a grin before turning back to Dr. Badawi's titration demonstration at the front of the lab. I wrapped my legs around my stool and stared at him—willing him to look. When he did, I nodded at the scrap—no bigger than my pinky nail *before* I'd folded it in half—and placed it on the far side of the lab table's sink.

His eyes narrowed, then widened in comprehension. He reached upward in a dramatic stretch, and I wanted to groan. But then again, Curtis was *always* dramatic. It would've been *more* obvious if he'd attempted subtlety. On the downward arc, his hand rested briefly on the front of our table. When he brought it back to his lap, the scrap was gone.

I didn't see him unfold or read it, but he nodded. Then, feigning a yawn, he popped the paper in his mouth and swallowed like some ridiculous cartoon spy. Next time our glances clashed, he winked.

I bit my lip. Curtis was having way too much fun with the stealth part of whatever it was we'd been doing. Ms. Gregoire had been wrong—he might like the chase, but *I* did not. She'd been right that I should've gone home though. By the time we reached English class, I was swaying on my feet and my yawns were nearly contiguous.

"You okay?" Merri tugged me out of the path of a bank of lockers.

"Eliza." Ms. Gregoire saved me from another lie by beckoning me to her desk. "I need you to run an errand for me in the library. It might take all class, so bring your things." She dropped her voice and added, "There are study corrals in the back corner that can't be seen from the circulation desk. Set a timer so you don't sleep through lunch, and go take a power nap."

I nodded. I wasn't ready to agree with Merri that our teacher was magic, but she *was* intuitive and perceptive—and compassionate. Compassion was a trait my parents considered as useless as patience, but I was grateful for it and for the Hero High blanket that was folded and waiting in one of the corrals. It smelled of laundry soap and had a chocolate on top of it, like a pillow at a fancy hotel. It was good Ms. Gregoire had reminded me to set a timer; otherwise I would've flopped face-first onto the blanket and woken up tomorrow.

As it was, I barely limped through lunch and my afternoon classes. On the drive home I waved off Merri's concern by blaming my lethargy on a headache, then felt guilty when she turned off the radio and sat quietly, whispering, "Feel better," as she got out at her house.

I felt even guiltier when pointing my car in Curtis's direction provided a caffeine-free jolt. The anticipation was its own stimulant, and I had to take a steadying breath as I pulled into his driveway and grabbed my gym bag.

"Hey." Win let me in and asked with a wry smile, "So what's today's accomplishment? Colossal feats heroic, academic, or athletic? Or all of the above?"

"Somewhere between five and seven miles," I said as Curtis emerged from the hallway. I expected a smile, but my answer made him cringe. Puzzled, I turned back to Win. "Do you run?"

"Not unless I'm being chased." His words were sharper than usual, less humored and more...harsh. I cast about for a response.

"My best friend's sister Rory is anti-running too. She's pretty intense with yoga. Have you tried that?"

"Do I look Zen?"

He looked...angry, but I couldn't help it; when I opened my mouth, a correction slipped out. "That's a common misconception. Zen isn't a physical trait. It's—"

"Enough, Eliza," interjected Curtis, and I winced.

"I like you better when you're picking on Curtis, not me." Win rolled his eyes and stormed down the hallway.

"Despite...*that*, he must actually like you, because Win's at anger level nine and you're not crying, so he didn't give *you* a level-nine performance."

"I'm formidable." The words were automatic, and my real question lurked behind them. "What did I say wrong?"

"I'll tell you on our run."

"Fine." I toed off my loafers and took off my coat. "So this science competition where you think you're going to beat—"

"Shh." Curtis swiveled to look down the hallway. "Don't—"

"I'm not asking you to tell me your secret project—"

"Firebug, I swear, for once, shut it." He pantomimed zipping his lips. "Just until we're out of the house. Please."

"But— He reached out and pressed a finger to my mouth. The sensation was so startling, I swallowed the rest of my question—*But why do you call me "Firebug"?*—and leaned into his touch.

Curtis pulled his hand back, looking sheepish. "Sorry. Go get changed. Then I'll tell you where we're running today."

Instead of heading down his driveway, Curtis climbed in my car and directed me to a local park.

Standing beside the park's wooden map, I blinked at him as my sneakers both crunched on frozen mud and sank into less-frozen mud. "You want to run trails?"

"Yup." He blew on his gloved hands and bounced on his toes, making the ground squelch. "You said you wanted a challenging route. This hill kicks my butt at least once a week."

I gave him a dubious look as we headed into the woods. In only a few strides the path narrowed and the parking lot was no longer visible. "This looks like the setting for a crime show. The opening where someone stumbles over a body."

He laughed. "If we run into a trail-dwelling murderer, I promise to volunteer as tribute."

I scoffed. "I'm a blond virgin—do you really think they'll kill you first? I've seen a horror movie."

"True, but I'm a Brown dude. My chances aren't any better."

I ducked under the branch he was holding out of the way and used the opportunity to pass him. "Maybe we should just agree that those tropes are problematic and focus on not being killed."

"Or tripping," added Curtis. "I've left a fair amount of skin and blood on these roots."

"Another reason I prefer treadmills." It was a lie. The roots and rocks meant I had to pay attention to where I placed my feet. Rather than tuning out and getting the run over with, I was experiencing it.

"The treadmill won't give you my stellar company or these views."

"Fine, the view's not awful." But I wasn't looking at mossy rocks and the layers of decomposing leaves that gave the air such an alive smell. He'd passed me, and for a moment I let him have the lead so I could admire the spread of his shoulders, the way they tapered to his waist, the spot of sweat at the small of his back that darkened the blue fabric of his running shirt.

His foot landed with a *squelch*. I laughed and breezed by him as he extricated his sneaker, now invisible beneath a thick coat of mud. "You think that's funny? Oh, you better run faster, Firebug."

The trail was serpentine—winding back on itself as it progressed uphill. Conversation became harder as the route steepened, but despite this, Curtis kept his promise and explained his brother's attitude. "Basically, if Win *can* interpret something as an insult—he will."

"So me asking if he was a runner? And yoga?"

"Yup. But it could've been anything. He's in a mood. Last night's meeting with his teacher didn't go well."

"And the science fair?"

Curtis paused to wipe his face—with the hem of his shirt! I was so thrown by the unexpected flash of skin and abdominal muscle that I almost ran into him. "Careful, there." He dropped his shirt to steady me, but I dodged his hands.

"I'm fine." Of course I was. It was just skin. Just a stomach. I had one. So did every one of our classmates. I didn't spend time thinking about any of theirs. But I also hadn't expected his to be so—as Merri would say—"cut."

Not that muscles mattered; I was aware of culturally conditioned beauty standards. It was good that he was fit—apparently *very* fit—but that was the start and end of my interest in his abs. I was so busy telling myself this that I stumbled over a root and had to catch myself on a tree.

"Still fine," I called out. "Did you answer me about the science fair?"

"Take the left path up ahead, it's got fewer tripping hazards." Curtis laughed, and I caught myself before I gritted my teeth. "According to Win, I'm only entering the Avery to make him look bad. Same reason I play sports and do quiz bowl and get good grades. The less he knows, the less it hurts him."

"Oh." My pace faltered, because that was the missing variable in my Curtis equations: the *why* of him downplaying his intelligence and using humor to hide his insights. If I'd had a sibling, would I have been willing to make similar sacrifices? I doubted it.

"We share a room. Before I started at Hero High, we were at the same school. Even at my stealthiest, he's nosy. It's hard to keep things from him."

I paused where the trail forked to face him. "I'm sorry you need to. No one should have to hide who they are to make someone else happy." Curtis gave me such a wry look that I replayed my comments. "Shut up."

But in the silent—and steep—stretch that followed, I wondered why I had immediately mentally rejected sacrificing for imaginary siblings but was willing to do it for my parents. The longer I thought about this, the faster I ran. Curtis didn't say a word but matched his strides to mine until we emerged, gasping, in a clearing at the top of the hill.

"Oh," I breathed out. "This is amazing."

"Told you the view was better than a treadmill."

I laughed, the sound bubbling up from deep in my stomach and echoing off the open space. I shoved him playfully, yelping when my gentle push seemed to send him careening. Only to realize he was doing it on purpose—arms out wide as he cut a path back and forth across the sloping field. His face was lit up in a grin when he turned back toward me. "C'mon, Firebug. Airplane with me."

My toes curled around the edge of a flat rock. "You sound like Merri."

"So? You like Merri. You like me. Maybe this means you should try it?"

I swung my head left, my ponytail flipping over my right shoulder. But I couldn't complete the headshake. My instinct was to contradict him. To state emphatically that I *didn't* like him. But I did. He knew it. Whether or not I admitted it, I did too.

His chest was still heaving from the run, but as my silence stretched, his shoulders slumped. His grin faltered. I'd disappointed him. I'd disappointed *me*. I was sick of letting everyone down.

He shrugged and turned back around, throwing his arms out and whooping his glee as he ran. His happiness was independent of my decision not to participate. And, *blast*, why was that so attractive?

I pushed off my toes, leaping upward and letting gravity snatch at my feet, pulling me back down from the feeling of flying. It took me a second to lift my own arms, but when I did, I laughed. The steepness of the decline made running in switch-backs necessary and exhilarating. My whoops harmonized with Curtis's, and for the space of that hundred yards, I was as care-free as Anne. The scope of my imagination was as large as hers, my zest for living beating wildly within my chest, escaping in plumes of laughter and gasping breaths.

Curtis turned at the bottom of the hill to watch me, his arms still out. Maybe it wasn't an invitation for a hug, but I was done hesitating.

It's possible I underestimated the difference between our inertias. He had the mass, but I had momentum—my velocity overcoming the discrepancy between our weights and causing him to stagger back two steps until we were braced against the papery bark of a birch tree.

His smile glowed brighter than the sunset that was settling around us, filtering through tree branches like the segmented frame of a stained glass window. "You never stop surprising me."

"Then this is going to shock you—" I pulled off my gloves and dropped them to the ground, threaded my fingers around the back of his neck, pushed up on my toes, and brushed my lips against his.

Curtis's arms had folded around me mid-collision, but now they tightened. There was a difference between a hug and an embrace. This was the latter, and the difference should be quan-tifiable, but it required a language I didn't yet know.

My mouth was rather preoccupied learning something else at that moment—a brush turning into a graze. His lips moving against mine, sending shivers down my spine, forcing a choked growl from between his teeth.

I lowered my feet, pulling back to check that I was accu-rately interpreting his reactions as positive. Curtis blew out a breath, his eyes slow to open and dazed once they did. He was still clenching the back of my sweatshirt in his fist. "That was either some beginner's luck, or, like with most other things, you're a prodigy at this."

My lips twitched, but I fought a smile—he didn't need to know I'd worried. "Of course it's the latter. 'Prodigy' is practically my middle name."

"Prove it," he challenged.

So I did.

26

hadn't quite forgiven Curtis for being the one to end our kissing session in the woods yesterday. Granted he'd sounded like it pained him to say, "We have to stop," and he'd had valid reasons. "It's almost dark, and we're a half mile from the trailhead. Not only does the park close, but roots are much less fun when you can't see them."

Still, I'd wanted him to be as lost in that moment as I'd been—location, weather, and time of day had ceased to exist while my lips had been exploring his. I'd gotten home and stared in the mirror at my swollen mouth and bright eyes. And for once I hadn't been caught up in resenting my reflection.

My lips weren't puffy on Thursday, but I was still aware of them. I felt that awareness every time Curtis glanced in my direction, and also the moment Ms. Gregoire caught him doing so in English and raised her eyebrows. "Eliza, you're looking happier today."

I jerked back in my seat, banging my elbow and scattering a stack of SAT flash cards. "What? I'm—I don't—"

Where were the words about defining my own self-satisfaction and not being dependent on others? But vaguer ones, so Merri wasn't tipped off? She'd already narrowed her eyes and called me "unusually chipper" on the morning drive.

"You look less tired," Ms. Gregoire clarified. "I notice your iLive band is back. I assume you got some sleep?"

I'd expected to be up all night reliving those moments on the hill, second-guessing and scrutinizing my actions until the memories were tarnished with doubt. Instead I'd fallen asleep quickly and woken in the same position nine hours later.

I gave a polite nod. "Yes, thank you."

"Good!" She clasped her hands together. "You'll need your wits about you—I hear from Dr. Badawi that today's the show-down for spots at Saturday's quiz bowl competition."

Even though I knew this, my stomach clenched. It stayed queasy through afternoon classes, and my face felt tight, like I'd left on one of those hardening masks Lilly loved. I'm not sure what my expression looked like as I said goodbye to Hannah and Lance after Convocation, but he paused and asked, "You okay? If your headache's back, I can run to the nurse and get some Tylenol."

"No, I'm fine." I forced my shoulders down and the corners of my mouth up. "But thanks."

Merri was flirting with Fielding—her hands tucked in his blazer pockets, her face lighting up when she pulled out a rose-bud he must have strategically planted there for her to discover. I grinned and turned to give them privacy. She'd meet me at practice.

"Gotta admit, that's a pretty baller move." Curtis was a step behind me, fractionally closer than two constantly bicker-ing acquaintances might stand, but the difference was subtle enough that I doubted anyone would notice. "Fielding's setting the bar pretty high."

"There is no bar."

He winced, and I wished I could take the words back. "Right, because we're not-dating."

I hadn't meant it that way. I'd meant I didn't compare him to others or believe in some set standard for romance. That flower-pocket thing might be swoony for Merri, but I became breathless over muddy trail runs.

"Fielding—" We'd reached the science building. I looked around to make sure we were alone, then grabbed Curtis's hand and pulled him into the doorway of the next classroom. "Fielding has never made me laugh."

Curtis's forehead creased. "At him?"

"*With* him." Knowing what I did about Curtis's motives for clowning, this was such an important distinction. "And at myself—I've never done that before."

Curtis chuckled. "You can be unintentionally hilarious with your science talk and rules."

I scowled. "Don't take it too far."

He squeezed the fingers we had linked. "You're not nervous about practice, are you?"

"A little." Did he realize what a concession that was? The type of trust I was showing him? I didn't get nervous. I wasn't *supposed* to get nervous.

"You've got this, Firebug." He punctuated this statement by leaning in, then pausing, his eyes darting around the hallway to make sure we were still alone.

Forget Fielding and all the flowers in the world; a guy who respected my need for privacy—*that* was romance. So I kissed him. And learned I didn't need exercise endorphins to make my head spin. Yesterday hadn't been a fluke, and this guy—this infuriating, insightful, intelligent guy—made me dream of impossibilities.

The science building's door banged open, and we sprang apart as Merri barreled in. "Gah, Eliza! Did you see what Fielding did?" She waved the flower and beamed.

"I did." I took another step away from Curtis. "You guys are the cutest."

She blinked, surprised by my endorsement, then bounced on her toes. "Thank you."

It was a calculated risk to use that word, but I wanted her to reclaim it. And it was true. Merri and Fielding were cute in a way that was accessible. Even if Curtis and I weren't *not*-dating, "cute" wouldn't be a category we'd compete in. I wasn't threatened by that. I wouldn't expect everyone to understand our dynamic. I didn't need them to.

Merri tilted her head. "What are you two doing out here?"

Curtis cleared his throat. "Eliza was telling me how I might as well—what was it again? I want to get the exact phrasing right."

He turned to me with laughter in his eyes, and I fought the urge to stomp his foot. "Yes, um—he might as well...hand in his buzzer now!" I smiled triumphantly at having completed his Mad Libs with snark. "Because he's not going to need it."

Merri rolled her eyes. "Should've known. Let me point out, there's room for *both* of you on the team. Or none of us, if we miss practice." She led the way, oblivious to the intense looks we exchanged above her head. Mine said, *You'll pay for that.* And his was, *I can't wait.*

Curtis did in fact need his buzzer. It got quite the workout. Mine did too. Merri and André and—unfortunately—Bartlett also made the cutoff.

Lynnie seemed happy to be the designated alternate, and Norman shrugged off his last-place finish. "Cool. Now I can sleep in. Good luck, guys."

Merri elbowed me; a warning not to say, "Luck's not real," but I hadn't planned to correct him. I was too busy feeling smug. A few weeks ago Bartlett had told me I was "redundant," and now I'd easily out-performed him. Take that, hours I'd spent studying old packets and stolen minutes I'd spent talking to Curtis on my burner phone while his app asked us questions.

"Don't be late," Bartlett was lecturing. "We're not waiting—I don't care if you thought you'd have time and the line at the Cool Beans drive-through was super slow.'" He shot a look at Lynnie. "Newbies, we're representing Hero High, so we wear our uniforms. And press your tie this time, Cavendish."

Curtis saluted him, and Barty droned on. But not even his ego-driven condescension could curb the thrill of my victory. Nothing could.

Nothing but the email from my parents that was waiting in my inbox. One I was glad I hadn't read *before* today's practice.

Eliza,

Thank you for the log-in information for your new iLive band. It seems to be functioning.

A note: The Williamses—not the headmaster's family; your father's college roommate and his wife—will be at your academic bowl competition this weekend. Their daughter, Emma, is on one of the opposing teams. We look forward to boasting about your triumphs when you beat her.

They're rather insufferable with their constant iLive posts about their two children and three dogs. Pets should never outnumber offspring. Fair warning: Both Stacey and Brooke were always "social," I bet their daughter is too . . .

In a few lines they'd managed to make me regret qualifying and dread the upcoming competition. I wanted to be a person—their daughter—not ammunition in a ridiculous, one-sided feud that stemmed from Dad's roommate daring to have a life beyond the labs or be publicly proud of his family.

Their expectations were so...so *cloying*. Sticking to me like invisible wisps of a spider web I'd blundered through. But I wasn't allowed to scream or flail. I had to silently permit them to tickle the skin beneath my shirt, wrap around my arms like itchy manacles.

I typed up a short reply, then left the cursor blinking after the final word.

I won't let you down.

It was such a blatant lie, I couldn't press Send.

Most of my friends had Friday-night dates, but my plans involved one of my favorite males, a lot of science—and recording equipment. This time in the Campbells' kitchen. Toby was setting up the microphones and computer before he and Rory headed to an art show. While he opened the recording program, Mr. Campbell put the teakettle on, and Rory spoke test sentences into the mics.

I reviewed my notes. I was absurdly glad about spending time with someone who cared more about my happiness than my GPA.

"I get to study paintings to my heart's content," Rory told us as Toby fiddled with settings. "He'll be busy—the gallery owner hired him to play background music on the piano."

"That's awesome," I said, and Toby nodded. Whether it was to acknowledge the meaning of my words or the way they'd registered on the recording, I wasn't sure. But then he turned to me. "Do you have a title yet? It needs one."

"Oh, um." This was the sort of thing Curtis would've been perfect for—if it weren't for the bet. "I was thinking *Science Party*? Because the point of the podcast is everyone's invited and can understand." Six eyes blinked at me. Eight if you included Gatsby's. "That bad?"

"No," said Toby. "That good. Say that whole thing again into the mic. I'll record it and add it to the episodes."

"You're sure?" Since when did I need Toby's validation? Still, I held my breath.

"Yeah. I've listened to each episode a few times while editing." I was glad he turned back to the computer so I had space to react when he added, "They're good. You're really creative."

"Creative?" I laughed and pointed to Rory. "She's creative. And Merri."

Toby didn't look up from the screen. "Apparently you are too. Deal with it."

Rory crossed to stand behind him, resting a hand on his shoulder. "I want to listen. When can I?"

"After the Avery?" I said. "I might put them up in case anyone else wants to hear them."

"Hello?" Rory waved her hand. "I *just* said I did."

Mr. Campbell chuckled. "I'm going to want to hear them again too. Lots of people will."

Their reaction matched the overwhelmingly positive feedback I'd been getting from the podcasting forum where I posted—anonymously—asking for advice. But I shrugged. "It's not a typical project."

Toby stood from his crouch. "I know nothing about science fairs, but like we're all saying, these are good. Besides, can't you win this sort of thing in your sleep?"

I blinked slowly—his expectations weren't that different from my parents', but they diverged on discernment. I swallowed down my growing uncertainty—was this project good enough to win the bet? Could I handle *Frankenstein* if it didn't?

It felt important—it *was* important—but would the judges agree?

"I guess we'll see," I mumbled.

Toby reached for Rory's hand. "Click here when you start and again when you're done. Then I'll splice it down."

"Thank you." I was still astounded that he and I were at a place where I could ask him for favors and he'd say yes without any coercion from Rory or Merri.

When the door shut behind them, Mr. Campbell set two mugs on the table. "Ready? Because I've got a question for you."

I pointed to the mic. "Go for it." If I didn't know the answer, we could address it on the next episode. In the meantime, I was excited about what I'd prepared for today—having a frank conversation about the ways "science" was used to shut down debates or exclude people. I had tips for discriminating between serious studies and pseudoscience. Advice on how to ask for clarification when being railroaded with "facts." Mr. Campbell would love it.

Next week I wanted to talk about the opposite: how to use true scientific facts to disprove false beliefs—e.g., "the earth is flat" or "vaccines cause autism." I already knew what my conclusions would be: You can have all the data in the world and explain it calmly and clearly, but there's no magic trick for making people listen or be logical.

Mr. Campbell cleared his throat. "How do I explain to a customer that global warming *is* a real thing? Just because this January the snow reached their Marshmallow's knees and last year it only covered his paws doesn't mean it's 'fake news.'"

I grinned and leaned toward my mic. "'Global warming' is just one aspect of climate change. Those terms are often used as synonyms—but they're not the same. It's like—say climate change is 'pasta,' then global warming is 'manicotti.' If a store temporarily runs out of manicotti, it doesn't mean they don't have pasta. Let's break this down..."

27

'm nervous. Typing those words on Saturday morning felt reckless. I was creating a permanent record of my vulnerability. I could scarcely look at the screen as I added, And I'm scared Merri will guess.

Telling her meant saying I was wrong about romance, admitting I was scared. It meant this thing with Curtis was real. But not telling her felt like a betrayal. I left the message unsent as I began the short drive to her house.

She'd seemed plenty suspicious last night when she came back from hanging out with Sera and Hannah and Fielding—crashing my podcast party as we were packing up, then going into interrogation mode. "Something is up with you—I just can't figure out what. You'd tell me, right—if something was going on?"

I'd stared at her, willing her to guess. When she didn't, I'd told her "of course"—lie number two. It weighed on my conscience as I pulled into her driveway. But if I didn't *tell* her, I needed to warn Curtis to be wary *of* her. So I pressed Send. Merri bounced out of the house, her uniform skirt floating over red and navy plaid tights, her eyes on her phone and her expression confused.

"Hey." I pointed to the two pink Cool Beans cups I'd picked up as penance. Hers was a mocha-sugar-whipped something. I'd said, "It's for Merri," and they'd known what to make. Mine was a small half-caff with almond milk. I was trying this coffee thing again—but easing in.

"Thanks." She buckled her seat belt, then waved her phone at me. "But what are you scared I'll guess?"

I slammed my foot on the brake. Since we were still in her driveway, still in reverse, the only consequences were the coffees splashing out their sip holes and Merri's bewildered "Are you okay?"

I grabbed my phone. The text hadn't gone to Curtis—I'd sent it to *her*. And judging by the arch of her eyebrow, my explanation needed to be bulletproof.

Blast! This was why I'd bought the freaking burner phone. It worked great for whispered late-night calls where Curtis and I quizzed each other and bickered and found our own strange form of flirting, but since I was spending the day *with* Merri and Curtis, I'd left it home.

I eased my foot off the brake and offered Merri an eye roll that would've made Win proud. "That's the last time I use the AI text function. It was supposed to say, '*"Are you scared?" send Merri this text.*'"

She laughed. "Gah, I guess 'guess' and 'text' sound alike to a robot." She picked up her coffee and I exhaled, though the muscles of my shoulders stayed tight. "And, no—I'm not scared about anything but you and Curtis."

"What?" The traffic light was newly yellow, but I braked abruptly.

"That you two might kill each other midcompetition?" She patted my arm. "You're really jumpy. Want me to drive?"

"You don't have your license." Otherwise, I might've. "And you're not wrong about the chances of murder." Because I was suddenly angry with him for putting me in a position where I had to lie to her. Yes, the lies were my idea, and yes, this was a trap of my own making...but *he* was the one who'd made them necessary. Him and his stupid feelings and flirting. Life was simpler back when I actually hated him instead of pretending to.

"He's not a bad guy. He's smart and nice and kinda cute." Merri's voice was a hesitant mouse squeak.

"Excuse me?"

Her face pinched as she tried to figure out which statement had offended. "He's not classically gorgeous like you or Fielding, but he's not unattractive—"

"Curtis has good bone structure and strong features. He'll be undeniably handsome once he grows into them. He's already attractive. People overlook that with his behavior." I huffed. "Not that it matters to me."

"Right, of course." She was saying the correct words, but her expression turned suspicious. "But maybe let's talk about this when you're not driving. Did you notice the car behind us is beeping? Because the light just turned yellow again—we missed an entire green."

"There's nothing to talk about," I said, jerkily accelerating to get through the intersection before it went red.

Merri's "Uh-huh. Sure." was definitely knowing. If I'd been looking at her and not the road, I'm sure she'd have paired it with a wink.

We were early—a full four minutes before seven thirty. Just because we were the last to arrive didn't make us "late," no matter how much Bartlett wanted to pretend it did.

Dr. Badawi was behind the wheel of the white minivan with "Hero High" emblazoned on the side above our school emblem. Curtis, Lynnie, and André were crammed in the back row.

"Get in," Bartlett ordered. "So we can leave."

I followed Merri to the van. She climbed into the middle row behind Bartlett. That left me with shotgun, and it quickly became clear why the veteran team members had chosen seats as far from Dr. Badawi as possible. Despite the map on her phone screen *and* the volume of the navigational system being turned up high, she didn't seem capable of following directions.

Each time it said, "Recalculating," she sputtered, "Oh dear, was that the turn?"

By the time we arrived, my fingers were cramped from gripping the armrest, and Merri was clutching her stomach and had turned an alarming shade of carsick green. After checking in at the lobby, Dr. Badawi herded us into the auditorium, but then everyone scattered: bathroom breaks, coffee cart, off to greet parents or friends from other teams. I was fairly confident Merri had dashed off to vomit. She wouldn't want an audience but would feel better afterward. I fished a mint out of my bag for when she returned.

I turned to inspect the stage. It was set with two tables, each with five chairs, five microphones, five buzzers. Both tables were angled at the audience so they resembled a *V*, with a podium and smaller table at the point—presumably for the moderator and judges.

Around me people were talking in groups. Normally Merri would be with me, chatting and introducing me to every living being in the room, two- or four-legged. But she hadn't returned from the bathroom, and I felt conspicuous.

Why had I worn my hair down today? Blow-dried and brushed it and stood in front of the mirror, feeling ridiculous when I told myself, "You're allowed to feel pretty." Pretty foolish. Ugh, this wasn't as dramatic a mistake as when Anne Shirley had accidentally dyed her hair green—but I understood her regret. I hadn't even let myself bring a hair band. Past me hadn't planned for present me's cowardice.

I ground my teeth and scanned the auditorium for Merri. The rear door opened, and a familiar face appeared within the frame. His eyes met mine, and my expression transformed to match his wide smile. For the first time since I'd stepped into this room, I felt my chest relax.

I didn't run to him. It wasn't necessary. Curtis made his way over to me. "Hey, ace navigator."

"I don't know how to use those buzzers." I pointed at the stage. They weren't the type you held in your hand. They were small black boxes that sat on the table. On the top was a green light and a red button. Presumably the first lit up when you pressed the second, but what was optimal hand positioning? How sensitive were they?

"Breathe, Eliza." He touched my hand quickly, lightly, but it was enough to distract me from the tightening of my throat. "That's better. Now I want you to picture everyone in here with their IQ tattooed on their forehead."

"Isn't it supposed to be 'in their underwear'?"

"Eh, that's always creeped me out." His hand skated across mine again. "Plus, the point is to make you feel better. Wouldn't seeing their IQs make you realize how much you don't need to be worried about this?"

I rolled my eyes. "The only thing an IQ test measures is your ability to take an IQ test." Granted my ability was astounding, but still.

"There's my firebug." He grinned. "You're ready."

28

Our match wasn't first. Or second. I sat in the audience pressing an imaginary button on my knee as I listened to other teams' questions, keeping a mental tally of the ones I could've answered. When the match before ours ended, Dr. Badawi said, "You're prepared and capable. Now go take your seats."

I wanted to pause the moment, nominate Curtis to give a real pep talk. One that ended with us laughing. But Bartlett was already herding him up the steps and to the far end of the table. No! I'd been counting on him sitting next to me so he could squeeze my hand or bump my knee beneath the table. Instead I was sandwiched between André and Merri.

The team across from ours wasn't wearing uniforms. They were from the public school Win and Wink attended. Emma Williams was on it. She had a bright smile that I caught in flashes as she pivoted from the teammate on her left to the one on her right. Her whole team seemed relaxed, jocular. They were chatting and sharing lip balm. Wasn't that distracting? Shouldn't they be focused and silent like our side of the stage? I wiped my hands on my horribly unabsorbent skirt and only realized it was my turn to introduce myself when Merri stepped on my foot.

The moderator went over the same rules as before both prior matches. It was a good thing I'd listened then, because all I could hear was the pencil Merri was rolling across the green tablecloth and André taking deep, meditation-style breaths.

I leaned forward and looked down the table. Curtis was already turned in my direction. He nodded. One chin tilt up, chin tilt down—but it was enough. I sat back, exhaled, then poised my hand on the buzzer, just in time for the moderator to announce, "Here's our first question—"

Eleven toss-ups and eleven bonus questions later we had a four-minute break before the second half. "After this, how do they decide which winners play against which other teams?" Merri asked.

"You're kidding, right?" Bartlett was angry we'd hesitated when the moderator asked us to name our team captain—the *only* player allowed to buzz and answer bonus questions. "This is a single-stage tournament. After this, we're done. So keep it together."

I glowered at him. We were doing fine. We'd taken possession of six of the eleven toss-ups and also captured the one they'd missed. We'd gotten most of our bonuses correct. As long as we didn't flub it, we could use the second half to expand our lead.

"Time," said the moderator.

Except we *did* flub it. André got a toss-up wrong. Bartlett didn't buzz in fast enough on two bonuses. Merri exceeded the time limit to answer a computation problem, though she'd had it right on her notepad. I hesitated on a question I knew. We also had questions correct, but our lead went from comfortable to nonexistent. And with only one question left, all ten players were sitting forward, hands trembling over buzzers.

"This author of twenty novels and more than five hundred short stories was the first Canadian female to be made a fellow

of the Royal Society of the Arts. Though not an orphan herself, Lucy Maud Montgomery"—my eyes shot to Curtis, but his
were already on me, his mouth set in concentration, his eyes
bright—"is best known for her series of novels about a red-haired
orphan girl, set in the Canadian provin—"

Bzzzzt!

I wasn't sure if Curtis had delayed because he had expected
me to take it, or if I'd hesitated waiting for him to buzz in. But
despite both our thumbs being smashed on red buttons, the
light that lit up wasn't either of ours.

The moderator pointed to a boy on the other team with
dark skin, clear-rimmed glasses, and a popped collar. He cleared
his throat into the microphone. "That would be Prince Edward
Island."

I couldn't hear the applause because blood was pounding
in my ears. But I didn't need to hear the moderator tell him he
was correct or see the points awarded. I dropped my chin, not
wanting to watch the bonus. I'd already done the math. We *were*
ahead prior to this question. Now we'd lost.

The others pushed back their chairs. They were standing
to cross the stage and shake hands. Doing what Bartlett had
referred to as "The losers' walk of shame." I'd told him that was
rude—but smugly, because I'd never expected to be doing it.

I couldn't move. I couldn't unbend my finger, and it wasn't
until I heard the low chime and saw everyone turn toward me
that I realized I was still jamming down the button. The moderator must have reset them after the last answer—the one I
should've gotten.

"Hey." Curtis's voice was quiet. He unplugged the buzzer's
cord before gently prying my finger from the button and setting it
on the table. The noise stopped, and chatter and congratulations

rushed in to fill the silence. "You've got to get up. Go shake some hands. Fake a smile. You can do this."

I followed his instructions. Crossed the stage. Forced the corners of my mouth up. Extended my hand for shaking.

"Eliza Gordon-Fergus, right? Our parents are friends." Superficially Emma resembled me—blond, blue eyes—although her hair was short and her eyes were warm and inviting. I'd bet my parents' Nobel that she'd never been called "Ice Queen." "I'm Em. It's so nice to meet you."

They flashed the auditorium lights in a five-minute warning, and I blinked—claustrophobic on a stage that was filling up with people getting settled for the next match. I needed my hair up off my neck, because it was suffocating me, slipping over my shoulders as I nodded. It wanted me to shake my head—deny my name, reject her words—so it could fly outward in wild strands.

"My parents are here. They'd love to meet you. I've heard so many fun stories about your dad—like the time he tried to use my dad's DJ turntable as a centrifuge." Emma laughed, but I had no idea what she was talking about.

Her parents showed up to things. They told her stories. They'd probably post proudly on iLive later about Emma's victory—but if I'd won, mine would never have done that. Instead they'd demand ratios: Questions answered versus questions asked. My ranking on the team. They'd find ways for me to improve, because it was never enough. *I* was never enough.

Emma stepped out of the way of the players taking their seats for the next match. "We were going to go out for a victory meal. Er, sorry—um, a post-match meal. Want to come? Who doesn't like spaghetti Bolognese?"

Curtis approached, subtly holding out his hand for mine. Merri appeared with a water bottle. Emma asked, "So, lunch? You In?"

I rejected all of their offerings, and instead turned toward the wings of the stage. Then, I ran.

29

My lung capacity hadn't changed. The molecular makeup of the air hadn't altered to include less oxygen. Yet my chest felt tight and my breaths were shallow as I pushed out the auditorium's doors. It had started to snow. The flakes were fat and lackadaisical as they drifted in the cold air. Two guys were laughing, holding hands, tilting open mouths at the sky. A girl rushed past me, phone to her ear. "Definitely cocoa weather. Meet you there. Five minutes? Save me a seat."

I glared at their good moods and frivolity. Didn't they need to be shut up somewhere studying? They were at an Ivy League school—did they really have time to waste on cocoa or ingesting pollution-laced snowflakes?

Even when I made it here or MIT or Stanford or Harvard or Cambridge, I wouldn't get to frolic. My parents would know my professors by name. They'd hear about my progress or lack thereof. They'd be the standard I was measured against.

I paused outside a large stone building, hiccupped, then sank onto the snow-dusted steps. Even when I was a toddler, my parents hadn't tolerated crying. *Use your words, Eliza. Throwing fits accomplishes nothing.*

What would they say if they could see me now? Sitting in snow and salt and cinders, sobbing so hard my breath caught. *Use your words*—I should've. It only would've taken three: "Prince Edward Island."

Footsteps crunched up the sidewalk. I didn't look up, not even when my jacket was draped across my shoulders. I'd known Merri would find me, so when she settled beside me, I leaned into her for the hug that would be waiting.

It was...*not* the hug I'd been expecting. This embrace dwarfed my shoulder and drew me into a firm chest. A big hand offered me a crumpled napkin. "It's only the first match. We'll get them next time."

"You don't understand." The words were thick and gummy. I scrubbed the napkin across my face. "We lost. I knew that answer—I...*failed*."

Curtis threaded my hands through my sleeves like the toddler I probably resembled, gathering my hair out of the way before zipping my coat. "I did too. I knew that answer. It's okay to fail every once in a while."

My laugh was wet and bitter. "In what world is failure acceptable?"

"This one." Snowflakes were catching on his eyelashes, melting in his blinks as he studied me earnestly. "You don't have to be perfect. No one is going to love you less if you make an occasional mistake."

I shifted, feeling the grit of salt snag on my damp tights. "No. No one expects *you* to be perfect. They won't love *you* less." I meant for it to come out as critical, but it sounded wistful. His parents had been in the audience, cheering so loud that he should've been as embarrassed as his twin siblings sitting next to them, but he'd grinned and waved. "You don't get it. That girl from the other team? My parents know hers. I disappointed them. I embarrassed them."

Curtis picked up the fist I'd been pounding on the step. He brushed off the debris and cradled it in his hands. "So? That's their problem."

"They're all I have!" The words were a gasp, coming on the crest of a new wave of sobs. I never should've asked to switch novels, not when *Frankenstein* was so accurate. I never should've joined a team—because then I couldn't have let them down. I was meant to be a solitary creature. *Doesn't work well with others*, my elementary school teachers had indicated on all my report cards. My parents had asked, "Why should she if they're intellectually inferior?" But it was more than that; I didn't fit with my parents—*or* my peers. Like Frankenstein's monster, I didn't fit anywhere.

"Come with me." Curtis stood and opened the door of the science building. It was so warm inside that I nearly cried again as the coldness of my fingers and nose and thighs began to register. In the lobby, he dragged two overstuffed chairs so we were practically knee-to-knee, then draped his coat over me like a blanket. "Okay, now that you're not an Eliza-sicle, let's talk. Your parents are *not* all you have. You have Merri and the rest of the Campbells and Fielding and Sera and Hannah and Lance. I know you and Toby fight, but I also know you'd step into traffic for each other. You have me."

I bit down on my lip to stop it from quivering, wishing I could stop the spill of tears from my eyes. "That's just ridiculous. Why would stepping into traffic ever help?"

"I don't know, but there's not one of us who wouldn't do it. Missing a question on quiz bowl isn't going to change that. You're stuck with us."

For now. Until I said the wrong thing at lunch again. Or messed up during a bigger competition and was cut. Or beat him in the science fair. Or he got fed up with my mixed signals and awkwardness and realized I wasn't worth it. I bet I was a lot less attractive with snot in my snarly hair and my face all blotchy.

"We both knew the answer," I whispered. "I never should've let you talk me into this not-dating farce. I said it'd be a distraction and destroy my focus. I was right."

"One quiz bowl competition isn't going to keep you out of the Ivy Leagues."

What had Mom said? *"Patterns start with one anomaly."* I dropped my chin. "It starts here. First it's one question, then it's one test, one class... No. This isn't working."

"Then we review and revise." My hands were fists and he pried them open, sliding his thumbs inside. "We form a different process. You don't throw out the whole experiment."

I flinched back against the seat, pulling away from him.

"What?" he asked. "What did I say?"

"I don't want to be an experiment. Not with you."

Comprehension settled across his lowered lashes. His mouth thinned. "Is that how you think your parents see you?"

"They—they just *leave* me. After Brazil—they just *left*. If I don't follow their rules, if I don't live up to their standards..." I was grateful for his coat across my lap, because I tucked my feet up, pulling my knees to my chest, like that could stop it from feeling hollow, cover up everything raw and vulnerable that was leaching into my words and leaking out my eyes. "In Brazil—I almost got abducted. I broke the rules. I wasn't supposed to leave the lab. They brought me back to the US. And left..." I hiccupped and finished in a wet whisper. "What if they don't come back?"

Curtis swore under his breath and passed a hand over his eyes. "We're circling back to the Brazil thing. But first, do they know you feel this way? Because if they don't..."

In spite of tears, blotchiness, and a runny nose, I made myself meet his eyes. "I'm their daughter. Shouldn't they miss me? Why don't they miss me? Why am I so easy to leave?"

"Oh, Firebug." He was out of his chair and in mine, sliding my legs across his lap so we were hip to hip. He put a hand on each of my shoulders and met my eyes. "In case you haven't noticed, I don't scare off so easily. And Merri isn't going anywhere. It's their loss. You're amazing and it's—as Anne would say—'tragical' that they're cheating themselves out of the chance to know you."

I lowered my head to his chest, and he patted my back with one hand. The other clutched my shoulder like I might disappear. We were a graceless tangle of limbs and furniture. Nothing like I'd seen in any of Merri's favorite movies. I was dripping on his blazer, there were runs in my tights, one sleeve of his coat was dangling into the puddle our shoes had left on the floor. The chair smelled faintly of cleaning products.

It didn't match any definition of romance I'd seen. But it was *ours*, and the grip I had on him was as tight as his on me. "I know I'm bad at this, but please don't give up on me."

His breath was warm against my hair. "We've already had this conversation, and you're not bad...But I also never wanted perfection. I want *you*. I have since the first time—"

I shut my eyes. The obvious ending to that sentence was the absolute wrong one. —*I saw you on campus.* Saw me, and wanted me, because I was a thing to obtain.

"—you told me off at our lunch table."

I laughed. That answer was the exact right one. The absolutely Curtis one. I pressed my cheek harder against his chest, feeling the hammer of his heart.

"I want you covered in sweat after a run. With frosting on your nose that I put there. Doused in flour because I dared to tell you what to do. Right now, when you're letting me know how you're feeling—I want you more than—"

"Kiss me," I whispered, my voice strange and breathless, but I didn't care. "Please? Kiss me."

"Anytime," he answered, lowering his mouth to mine. "All the time."

30

It could've been two or twenty minutes later—time ceased to function in a linear fashion when I was engrossed in discovering how Curtis's mouth moved against mine and how his skin felt beneath my hands—but when I heard someone whisper-shout "Oh—*Oh!*" I reluctantly disengaged my lips from his neck.

"Uh. Hey, Merri." Curtis's voice was deep and startled but not embarrassed.

It's possible I nipped his neck—accidentally—before whirling to see my best friend taking backward steps with her hands over her eyes. "Um, don't mind me. Carry on. But heads-up, the van leaves in ten minutes." She bumped into a chair, then almost sprawled over a table.

"Merri, uncover your eyes before you end up in the ER," I said.

"Is it, um, safe?" she asked. "Are all hands where I can see them?"

I tugged mine out from under his shirt. I'm not sure when they'd gotten there, but I was going to go ahead and blame that on needing his body heat to warm up my fingers. Curtis untangled his from my hair and folded them in his lap.

"All clear," he said.

Merri lowered her hands. Her eyes were enormous, her smile bigger. "I didn't mean to interrupt. We can talk later. Like, I'll give you five more minutes to...whatever, then I'll still have five minutes to interrogate Eliza before the van!"

Curtis looked between my beet-red face and Merri's happy dance. He grinned. "We can 'whatever' another time—why don't you take the whole ten minutes." He squeezed my hand. "That okay?"

I nodded and sat up, straightening my skirt so I could return his coat without flashing my torn tights.

He stood. "I guess I'll go find my family so Win can mock me about his school beating mine." He looked at me. Looked at Merri. He patted her shoulder, then squeezed mine. "Uh, good luck?"

"Goodbye, Curtis." Merri's wave looked more like a shooing motion as she plopped onto his chair.

When he and I had been knee-to-knee it had been comforting and sweet—but Merri in that same spot made me claustrophobic. The strategic move would be to go on the offensive—take control of the conversation before she could—but my mind was a whirl of panic.

Merri crossed her arms and tried to look stern. "Just so you know, I'm reserving the right to be angry at some future date—but we only have ten minutes! So let's skip the part where I yell at you for lying to me and get to the part where you tell me all the heart-squish swoony details."

I laughed. If there was a better person on this planet than Merrilee Rose Campbell, I'd never met them and had no interest in doing so. No one could ever replace my best friend.

"Wait!" She held up a hand. "But maybe first just explain *why* you didn't tell me?"

My laughter choked to a halt and I studied my hands. "You know how you always say we have friendship ESP?"

She stuck out her tongue. "And you always tell me it's not a real thing."

"I know—but I've been wishing it was. Hoping-slash-dreading you'd guess what was going on with Curtis. Almost resenting that you didn't, because I couldn't figure out how to *tell* you. I know it's not fair."

My words and emotions were so contradictory, but Merri didn't seem fazed. She nodded thoughtfully. "I have five magic—yes, *magic*—words for next time." She smirked, I chuckled.

"Go ahead."

"*Merri, I need to talk.*" She shrugged. "I'm sorry I didn't guess—but I would've listened."

My eyes filled again. "I know."

She handed me a tissue printed with bulldogs from a pocket pack and waited for me to wipe my eyes. "Okay, there's only six minutes left. Start with the good stuff."

"I guess it's maybe, slightly possible I rushed to judgment when it comes to Curtis and what you just saw." I was mumbling, and I hated mumblers. "Or something like that."

"I believe that's what we call"—Merri did an offbeat drumroll on her lap—"being chicken-lickin' wrong."

"No. We absolutely don't call it that." I scrunched up my nose. "Don't use the phrase 'chicken-lickin'' ever again. It sounds like a revolting way to catch salmonella."

"Fine, but how long have you two been secretly dating? That's so romantic! I wish Fielding and I had secretly dated before telling everyone. Does it make things extra steamy?"

She was starry-eyed and clasping her hands beneath her chin. I was shaking my head and pressing back against my chair. "We're not dating. And you can't tell anyone."

Merri dropped her hands. "Of course I won't if you don't want me to—but why not? And what *are* you doing?"

"We're..." I shrugged, because the whole "not-dating" thing was going to get lost in translation. "I don't know what I want. I'm still figuring that out."

"You need to trust your instincts."

I stared at the dregs melting off of Merri's shoes, puddling on the floor. Curtis and I were like those snowflakes—we'd hold together only under perfect conditions. Alter the temperature even one or two degrees and we'd phase-change—go from solid to liquid, from not-dating to not-anything. I wasn't allowed to date, and secrets could stay secret for only so long. Like ice crystals when they reached zero degrees Celsius, we were doomed. I looked away. "I trust science."

"But *you* are more than science."

I stood, melted snow dripping off my coat as if to prove my point. "I am precisely science. Everything I am from the sub-cellular level is science. I know what you're saying, but there's science to emotion, and it often contaminates rational thought."

"You don't always have to be rational." Merri stood too. "What you were doing in here *wasn't* rational—and that's okay. You can be angry and disappointed and frustrated and happy and silly and besotted—you don't have to analyze the facts behind your feelings and decide if you're permitted to feel them."

"Maybe *you* don't." But the last time I'd dared to raise my voice at my parents was in the airport leaving Brazil, and it turned out to be the last trip they'd taken me on. And when I'd used the word "feel" on the phone ten days ago, they'd shot me down.

"Eliza—" The timer on Merri's phone went off, and she grimaced as she mashed the button. "We need to get to the van, but seriously—there's so much you're going to miss if you don't let yourself take risks. If you don't let yourself *feel*."

But risks meant risking failure. Today, I'd failed…and while I didn't yet know the fallout with my parents, failure had brought me *here*, to the building I was exiting where I'd had the most captivating who-knows-how-many minutes of my life. It had brought me to honesty with Merri about my *something* with Curtis and her impossible and wise advice. It was even a failure on a math test—fine, technically a B plus—that had brought me to the quiz bowl team and thus to Curtis and cupcakes and half-marathons and not-dating.

Merri linked her mittened hand through my arm while Ms. Gregoire's words from a week and a half ago replayed in my head: *Sometimes we don't ask for what we want because we're scared of being told yes.*

I think Anne Shirley would agree with my conclusion: Some risks were worth it.

31

Exhausted with relief that Merri *knew* and accepted me-plus-Curtis—even if she didn't quite understand the secrecy—I slept during the van ride back to school. It was a good thing too, because I spent the drive to her house fending off a barrage of Curtis questions. I let her hug me before she got out of the car, and I held on to that loved feeling as I entered my sterile, silent house.

Nancy wasn't home. I could've sprawled on the floor or eaten cookies on the taupe couch—not that there were any cookies in the pantry. I could've cranked the volume of the TV and danced around. Called Curtis on speakerphone and practiced my flirting while he walked me through some baking project.

Instead I turned off the kitchen lights and headed to my bedroom. Merri and Curtis had both said the obvious: If I wanted my parents to know how I was feeling, I needed to tell them. How they responded—that wasn't my choice or responsibility.

Hi Mom and Dad,

I had my first quiz bowl competition today. We were paired against Emma Williams's team.

I gritted my teeth and forced my fingers to keep typing.

Unfortunately the match came down to one question and the other team answered faster. Though now I have a better sense of what to expect in a competition; I'm confident we would beat them if we face off again.

Sorry.

I hesitated, then deleted those five letters. Replaced them with:

I'm glad you'll be home in three weeks. I miss you. I miss being part of a family. It gets lonely in this house.

Before I could second-guess or go too far—if I hadn't already—I hit Send.

The time difference was plus eighteen hours—my five thirty p.m. Saturday would be their eleven thirty a.m. Sunday—but that didn't signify anything. They tended to work and rest at odd intervals, exacerbated by the ever-present or ever-absent sunlight at the base station. I spent five minutes staring at the screen, willing an answer to appear. When one didn't, I took a shower—then returned to stare. I made dinner and ate it at my desk, then picked up my laptop and walked downstairs.

My parents' lab was behind double doors just past Nancy's office and the kitchen. Technically they called it "our lab"—but I hadn't been in there since they were home at Christmas. They hadn't assigned me any experiments since then—probably because they assumed I was working on my own for the Avery.

Despite that, the epoxy resin of the lab table was gleaming and there wasn't any dust in the sink or any crevices of the gas valve. My lab coat and safety goggles were on their hook, along with protective gloves and apron. There was the locked, fire-resistant cabinet for the more volatile chemicals, and regular cabinets for stable compounds. I opened one door—containers all in neat rows, labeled with contents and expiration dates.

Nancy had taken meticulous care of the lab. She invested way more effort here than she ever had in me. But it felt eerie without my parents. Lonelier. Being in here, however, was a necessary first step in my plan to get them back. To stay.

I opened all the cabinets and the lid of my laptop. I didn't lack for resources: materials, equipment—if it wasn't here, I could order it or call any of my parents' colleagues to get access to it. What I lacked was *time*. There were three weeks until the Avery. I *had* to impress them. I couldn't do that with quiz bowl losses or Bs on math tests. As much as I hated to admit it, I couldn't do that with the podcast.

It was like that scene in *Anne of Green Gables* where she needs to apologize to the gossipy Rachel Lynde. Anne doesn't want to, but since she has to, she makes it grandiose. I needed a new project—one so advanced and erudite that even my parents would be pleased. I might loathe every second of it, but like Anne said, "I'll try to do and be anything you want me, if you'll only keep me."

I had three weeks to pull off something amazing. Something that would win first prize, win *Anne of Green Gables*, win over my parents and convince them I was impressive, worth it. Convince them to stay.

I spent the next two hours analyzing the projects of past winners, looking for commonalities. By the time I'd settled on my own, I felt slightly ill. It went beyond ambitious, to a point where I was questioning my sanity. Could I do months of work in twenty-one days? Did I have a choice?

I'd gone back to where this all started, with Mr. Campbell's question about CRISPR. But instead of explaining it, I'd be using it.

I hit Refresh one last time before shutting down my laptop— the action more reflex than expectation. But at the top of my inbox was a response. Or rather, a *word*—since the whole email was just one.

Noted.

My parents had a strict rule about no eating in the lab. I obviously understood why—especially since I'd be working with bacteria—but this meant I had to leave the room three times on Sunday to eat, drink, and use the bathroom. Technically there was a fourth time when Nancy knocked on the door, but I'd just leaned into the hall and chugged the tea she'd made me without stepping fully out.

I still had school and homework. Still had quiz bowl practice and trying to squeeze in runs with Curtis—runs where I often prioritized kissing over training—but it felt like every second I wasn't bent over bacteria cultures working on DNA extraction was one I'd regret later.

I wasted many, many futile moments refreshing my inbox, looking for an addendum to their one-word email. It didn't come. And more than once I fell asleep on the lab bench while working late into the night—but I didn't bother filling out sleep-disturbance paperwork when I woke up, or even trying to rig my iLive band so it looked like I was getting the right number of hours.

Those lab-bench dreams were always nightmares. Ones where I transformed back and forth between Frankenstein's monster, waiting to see if Victor would accept my heartfelt request for a companion, and Anne sitting anxiously in her bedroom at Green Gables, fretting about whether Marilla and Matthew would keep me. I blamed it on the fumes from the disinfectants I was using to maintain sterility or the white noise of the fan in the lab hood, but my waking worries weren't that different. If I could pull this off, I'd definitely win custody of Anne's book—and hopefully borrow the outcome of her story too.

I managed to isolate the DNA of my targeted gene, but in doing so, I'd isolated myself as well. A week into my Avery sequester, Merri texted me: My best friend is missing. I need you to send me proof of life.

I took off my latex gloves and snapped a quick picture of myself next to the thermocycler before I started the next round of polymerase chain reactions. I sent it with a brief explanation of the science fair bet and why I had to win to get *Anne* and escape *Frankenstein*.

She'd written back, Totally get it. How can I help?

I wished I could come up with any other answer but the truth. Be patient. It'll all be over soon.

Too soon. Because through all this and across two weeks, my experiment grew—both literally and figuratively—and the doctors Gordon and Fergus didn't call or email. I'd gone back to the book I'd skipped, reading *Anne of Windy Poplars* on the bus ride to our next quiz bowl competition—which we'd won. But despite spending those hours reading Anne's letters to everyone in Avonlea, I got zero inspiration from its epistolary format. If my parents weren't writing to me, I wasn't writing to them.

I'd managed to insert the isolated genes into the DNA plasmid of the agrobacterium and then swab it across the shallow score marks I'd cut into my plants' stems, but I hadn't yet managed to tell Mr. Campbell about the project change. When he asked about our next recording session, I kept my answers vague. And when Toby sent me the final edited versions of the first four episodes of *Science Party*, I wouldn't let myself listen.

Mr. Campbell would forgive me—he'd be way more understanding than my own mom and dad, which almost made the betrayal worse. I started waiting in my car for Merri on school mornings, pulling out my laptop and working on my Avery abstract if she was running late.

I was waiting—for a response from my parents, for the other shoe to drop with Curtis, for the agrobacterium to infect my plants and insert the foreign gene into their cells.

For the first time in forever, I was looking forward to the weekend. Not because of fun plans—though Curtis and I had seven miles mapped out for Saturday afternoon—but because I needed the lab time. Friday night, as I was eating my dinner in big gulps while standing at the island, Nancy wandered into the kitchen. "You should probably slow down and chew. I don't know if I remember the Heimlich maneuver from my seventh-grade health class."

I wasn't sure if she was joking or not—I could never quite tell. Still, I swallowed. "Have you heard from my parents lately?"

She blinked at me. "Of course."

I was unsurprised that she didn't ask "Why?" Dad had told me privately that Nancy's lack of curiosity would be her undoing as a scientist. She excelled at recording facts and compiling data, but there was a next step missing from her work—the step that came from questions and looking for *more*.

But her lack of curiosity or interest meant I could drop my dishes in the sink and answer, "I'm headed into the lab."

She nodded. "I'll bring you tea later if I make some."

I wanted to make a joke—something about tea not being a choking hazard or such—but my brain was too tired, so I nodded. "Thanks."

Somehow by the time I looked up from my plant trays, it was already eleven p.m. The tea was long cold. I leaned against the doorframe and rubbed my eyes. Pulling my phone from my pocket, I scrolled through the dozen texts Curtis had sent. They were all different versions of the same message.

I made cupcakes if you want to take a break and come over.

The twins want to play Mario Kart with you.

Fine, just Win and me. Wink's still pissed at you for rejecting me.

But she might get over it if you come over?

Never mind, she's headed to her friend Reese's house.

All the more reason to come.

I scrolled to the last one: I miss you.

I missed him too. I missed everything about life outside this lab and resented every second I was spending bent over my laptop and under grow lights. But it didn't change anything.

One more week. After the Avery was done I'd have my prize, have my book, and hopefully have my parents' attention and approval.

One. More. Week.

32

By Saturday afternoon I was claustrophobic and restless from being trapped in the lab. It had warmed up to a balmy forty-eight degrees, which meant the ground had thawed to cold mud and our trail run had been a slippery mess. This hadn't stopped us from revisiting the site of our first kiss and reenacting it.

"Have you heard from your parents yet?" Curtis asked.

In that post-kiss moment, I didn't mind answering. "No. I'm not sure if I should be angry or scared."

"Be both?" Curtis suggested, his hand slipping around my waist. "What would you miss most if you were in Antarctica?"

"Sunrises and sunsets." I kept my gaze latched on the pink sky in front of me, because it was easier to be vulnerable when not facing him. "My dad missed the sunrise in September. He was in the middle of something and didn't take a break. It had been dark for so many months, how could he not take a break?"

"Wow." Curtis was quiet. I assumed he was admiring the vista and the profoundness of my words, until he added, "I was expecting you to say *me*, but I'll accept that answer."

I snorted. "People are a given. Merri's not going anywhere, even if either of us do. I mean, geographically we may separate, but I'm not worried about that hurting our friendship."

"She's your ride or die."

"I have no idea what that means, but it doesn't sound pleasant."

"Would you rather 'kindred spirit'?" he asked.

"Yes. Anne had Diana Barry, I have Merri Campbell. Personally, I think I got the better deal." I narrowed my eyes, daring him to disagree with me. He wisely didn't. "Maybe I'll write my *Anne of Green Gables* paper on that—after *I* win the science competition." I gave him a shove and headed down the trail, his feet and laughter chasing me back to my car, where we panted, muddy and breathless.

"So, we've done a seven-mile run. We've quiz-bowled. According to you we've 'babysat' my siblings—though if Win ever hears you say that, be prepared to go witness protection." He paused for me to laugh, then added, "I've got an idea for what we should do next."

"More baking?" I'd noticed that our cupcake misadventures hadn't made his list.

"No, but hang on to that thought, because there's a vegan bakery on our way home that Toby told me about; Rory's a fan."

"I'm in." I'd thought a lot about Curtis's words regarding my attitudes toward food and what it was and wasn't. This wasn't a rebellion. It was a choice. I was choosing to make my own choices. I was choosing cupcakes. And Curtis.

Even though I didn't say any of this aloud, he smiled. "Good, but hear me a second. I think we should go on a date." He watched me stiffen. "A real one—where we're not in uniforms or running clothes. I don't care if we have to go to a different town—we can go to a different state if you want—but can't we have a night where we admit we're real?"

It'd been two and a half weeks since we first kissed. It'd be three weeks and one day on Thursday—Valentine's Day. Was that the motive behind this? What if he did something thoughtful and sweet and I didn't know how to reciprocate? I'd been hoping we could ignore it—smile politely and change the subject when our couple friends shared their plans.

"You're not happy with what we're doing?" Those were the words I'd spoken, but the hidden question was, *you're not happy with me?*

"That's not what I'm saying." Curtis fiddled with the zipper on his sweatshirt, then shoved his hands in his pockets. "I want to go somewhere with you—on purpose, just us—without worrying you'll flip out if anyone sees us together."

"I don't flip out." Except I totally had. "Do you think Huck suspects?"

Curtis opened the passenger door. My car's interior lights made me blink, and they illuminated rare impatience in his expression. Right. I guess we didn't need to have this conversation in the rapidly darkening parking lot. I slid behind the wheel and admitted, "Fine, I might have slightly panicked when Huck said he saw us running."

"Much like you're doing now?" grumbled Curtis.

I glared at him as I fiddled with the heat vents. I wanted to be flirting, practicing quiz bowl questions—even discussing my parents' silent treatment or answering more of his questions about Brazil would be better than talking about romance. I got enough of that at school, where the hallways had exploded with heart-shaped posters announcing MAKE YOUR VALENTINE FEEL SPECIAL— BUY THEM A CARNATION & SUPPORT THE PROM COMMITTEE!

He was asking for more than I could give him. I'd been crystal clear from the beginning that we were *not*-dating, which included the words "not" and "dating"—and should make the answer to his date-request pretty obvious. He'd asked anyway and was waiting for me to give him an answer—one that would only upset us both. "I don't know what you want me to say."

"'Heck, yes!'?" he suggested. "I'd even settle for an 'I guess so.'" He sighed. "But you're not going to, are you?"

I studied the tiny flecks of mud that stood out against my white-knuckled grip on the steering wheel and shook my head.

The dashboard clock counted up two minutes before he spoke, quietly, slowly—the type of voice a person would use with a wild animal they were trying not to spook. It didn't fully mask the hurt in his voice. "Fine. I rescind the offer—for now. Real date is temporarily off the table." He reached over and touched my cheek—he might've been wiping off mud, but it felt like a caress. Either way it was achingly gentle. I searched his face, trying to decode which emotion was beneath his weak smile as he added, "But you'd better believe I'm going to be coming in hot about stopping for cupcakes."

I couldn't give him a date, but I could handle baked goods. "Then let's get you some."

Curtis seemed fine on the drive to the bakery. He joked with the baker as he picked out cupcakes. "You know, I could make the flavors punnier. If you're ever looking for a cupcake titler, give me a call." My mouth twitched as I tried to imagine what he'd come up with. He was still pointing in the display case. "And let's take another half dozen. How about one of each of your gluten-free flavors."

Did he notice the paper hearts taped beside where his fingers rested? Or the streamers and cupids dangling from the ceiling? The cozy couples seated at the tiny café tables? It made me conscious of how far apart we were standing. Of the fact that our hands weren't clasped. We didn't have a song, or a couple name. He'd given himself a pet name—but I'd never called him "cupcake."

The bakery air was hot and sweet, but it made my stomach turn. I shoved my credit card into the chip reader. "My treat. Hit the buttons when it asks. I'm going to wait outside."

His forehead creased. "Sure, okay. I'll be right there." He turned back to the baker. "I guess pack them to go."

That he'd even considered staying made my forehead prickle with sweat. We didn't belong in there. We'd be imposters in a sea of authentic couples. Couples who knew what they were doing and were allowed to date...and not terrified of it. Because if I was honest, it was equal parts rules *and* fear that had made me reject Curtis's offer of a "real date."

He caught up with me in the parking lot. I was leaning against my car, my hands pressed against the cool metal as I breathed in deep gulps of cold air. He handed me my credit card and the receipt. "Thanks. Are you okay?"

"It was hot in there," I lied. "Maybe I'm having low blood sugar."

"Luckily we have plenty to replenish you with." He lifted the bright blue bakery bag. "Want to head to my house for a *Mario Kart* and nosh? We've got enough to share with Win and Wink."

I shook my head. Since the brunch debacle where I'd rejected her brother, Wink had stopped being friendly. Curtis must have forbidden her from interrogating me, but I could hear the unasked questions in her suspicious glances. It made me so aware of the answers I didn't know. *Mario Kart* would become *Mario Massacre.*

As long as we didn't go into the lab, as long I didn't have to even think about the work waiting behind those double doors... "We could go to my house. No one is home." I hit the Unlock button on my car, then paused. Those words might imply something different coming from any of the coupled-up people in the bakery. "I don't mean that how it sounds. I *do* mean no one is home—Nancy's looking at apartments for her old roommate—but I'm not implying anything. There's no subtext."

"Relax, Firebug." Curtis tugged my ponytail. "I'd love to see your house, but whatever makes you comfortable. We can eat these in your driveway if you want."

I normally loathed when people told me to relax, but normally it was laced with impatience or annoyance as the person speaking tried to police my reactions. Curtis meant every word he'd said—and I could picture that cold-pavement picnic he'd offered.

Inside my house might not be cozier…but at least it'd be warmer. I exhaled slowly and leaned toward him. "Let's go to my house."

33

Standing in my kitchen watching Curtis take in the stainless-steel appliances, neutral, empty countertops, and drab, utilitarian furniture was torture. It must've been how he'd felt the day I'd scrutinized his home. But his had personality—photos and knickknacks to analyze and help me learn more about him. We had the bland furnishings that came with the house. The only thing that made my house unique was down a hall and behind a set of double glass doors. Most families had a living room where they watched TV and lounged; we had Bunsen burners, an emergency eye-wash station, and acids and elements my parents needed special permission to keep in a private home.

"Wow." He gave a low whistle.

"'Wow,' what?" I demanded. "Context, please."

"Wow, my house must seem very small and loud to you." He opened the fridge and looked at the organized shelves of produce and glass storage containers. "I feel like I'm in an appliance showroom. Or a health spa."

"The most impersonal, boring spa ever?"

He laughed and set the bakery bag on the counter. "But, hey, at least the spa now has cupcakes." He took off his sweatshirt and slung it onto the back of a kitchen chair. Two minutes here and the house already looked brighter and more lived-in from his presence.

I got us each a glass of water, since the only other thing in my fridge was almond milk, and according to him, calling it "milk" was sacrilegious. "Can I ask you something?"

He clinked his glass against mine. "Sure."

"Why me? I—I believe you, that you like *me*, not just the way I look." Those words were harder to say than I'd expected, but the freedom I felt on the other side of them was emboldening. "But what do you get out of skulking around with someone who makes everything so difficult?"

He didn't hesitate. "I like that you challenge me. And you're smart. I like that *I* can be smart around you. Don't get me wrong, I'm a goof—"

I poked his arm and smiled. "That's one word for it."

He winked. "But...you're a place I don't have to *be*. Around you I can be brainy and understood, and no one feels threatened by it."

Win's words from a few weeks back flashed in my mind. "Feats heroic, academic, or athletic," I whispered.

"Yeah." He drained half his water. "Hero High is my... haven. Dr. B lets me spend extra time in the bio lab. Last year's chem teacher does too. I try not to bug them—but it's a place I can talk science without anyone feeling like I'm targeting or insulting them. My parents try, but they're busy and it's not interesting to them. So I've got Hero High...and I've got you."

I turned away, looking for something to clean or fiddle with. An excuse to hide how flattered I was by his words. I settled on paper towels, tearing off two in case we needed them. "And next year the twins might be at Hero High."

"Yeah, *if* they get in and we can somehow afford it." He groaned. "Does it make me a bad person if I don't want them to come? At least not Win. But that's worse, because he'd be crushed if Wink left him behind."

I didn't have solutions for sibling dynamics, but the idea of sanctuary resonated like an electric current. I reached for his hand. "How about, no matter what happens with the twins and school, I'll be your 'smart' space—if you'll be my 'wild.'" His face lit up so brightly that it set off warning bells, and I dropped his fingers and picked up my glass. "Just don't take it too far— I'm talking cupcakes and trail runs, not turning into an adrenaline addict."

"But—" His grin grew impossibly larger. "You realize you're talking about *next* September. As in, seven months from now?"

I hadn't. My skin itched at the permanence that suggested. There was no way we could be stealthy until them—but how long was too long? And when I thought of the alternative—ending this—my stomach soured.

"Stop overthinking it, Firebug," he said. "Let's eat some cupcakes."

"Explain that nickname first," I countered.

He dragged a hand across his face. "I knew you were going to ask eventually. Here goes: You light up when you talk about things you're passionate about—science and causes and social justice. Things that matter."

"You said you think 'Firebug' is cute..."

"Not 'cute' in any way that's demeaning. But freaking adorable in a way that, like, I...*adore* you." He blushed. "I mean, I adore the way you think. I just want to follow you around and listen to you say things that are important. If you made a newsletter, I'd be your first subscriber and memorize every word."

"You're making fun of me." Wasn't he? Or had he found out about my former science fair project and "newsletter" was his code word for "podcast"?

"I'm not."

I frowned. Mr. Campbell had said the same thing—that I glowed when I talked about my interests, that he was glad I was pursuing that project because clearly my whole heart was in it.

I'd corrected him that it was *my brain, thank you very much.* The memory made me wistful—I missed every part of podcasting.

"When you get angry—" Curtis sucked in a breath.

"It's cute?" I lifted my chin and propped my hands on my hips.

"Noooo! It's very scary. But it's also awesome. The things you get mad about—they matter."

"Oh." I looked down at a pile of paper-towel confetti. I hadn't realized I'd been shredding it.

"Also, Lampyridae are about the most gorgeous creatures on this earth. Bioluminescence—I know science has an explanation—but every time I see it, I forget what it is. Every time I see a firebug, it's like a demonstration that magic exists." His smile was equal parts sheepish and vulnerable. "Every time I see you, I feel the same way."

I'd told Merri a million times that magic wasn't real—but those weren't the words I was thinking. I wasn't thinking *in* words. I was just...floored. And frustrated I couldn't communicate how keenly I felt this or how much I liked what he said. I awkwardly patted the hand he had resting on the counter. "Um, thank you?"

He flipped his palm over and twined our fingers, using his other hand to take the plastic cupcake tray out of the bakery bag. "Is now when you explain why you call me 'Cupcake'? It's because I'm sweet and decadent, right?"

I shouldered him out of the way, dropping his hand so I could have both free to select—white chocolate with raspberry frosting. "I've never called you that. You call yourself it."

"You should." He selected his own, and half of it disappeared in a bite. "Try this chocolate-cookie one. It's amazing."

"Why gluten-free?" I asked, relieved we were back on safer, endearment-free topics.

"I wanted to compare them. These are pretty great. I bet you couldn't tell the difference."

"I bet I could," I snapped back—foolishly. I'd had exactly one and a quarter cupcakes in recent memory. I barely knew what gluten-*filled* tasted like. But he'd posed it as a challenge, and I wasn't backing down.

"All right, blind taste-test time. Shut your eyes and I'll feed you bites."

"No way."

"You don't trust me?" He pressed a hand to his chest and made puppy dog eyes. "It's not like I was going to smear frosting on your face or feed you Cheetos instead."

I snorted. "Good luck finding Cheetos in this house." I let my eyes slowly drift over his body. Beneath his sweatshirt he'd worn a red dry-fit shirt that teased of the muscles beneath. His joggers weren't as fitted as my running tights, but I could see the outline of his phone in his pocket. He definitely wasn't hiding any bags of chips anywhere.

Curtis grinned at my scrutiny—fine, my admiration—and did a slow spin. When he finished, he lifted an eyebrow. "Like what you see?"

I laughed, then reached for the hem of my oversized, extralong pullover. Since that stupid first day on campus, he hadn't ogled me—hadn't made me feel like "arm candy" or decoration. But that didn't mean he wasn't allowed to—that I didn't *want* him to—find me attractive. I took a deep breath and removed my pullover, taking down my ponytail too. I smoothed my hair and tucked it behind my ears, fought the urge to cross my arms over the front of my fitted shirt. This was me. This body was *mine*. I tossed the pullover to him and he caught it.

His eyes were still glued to mine, waiting for my permission. I nodded. I wasn't going to strut or spin like he had, but I couldn't stop the corners of my mouth from lifting as I watched his gaze grow dark and hungry. We each took a step closer, crossing floorboards and personal barriers.

Curtis's voice was husky when he asked, "So what you're saying is you don't trust me?"

I blinked, confused—because that was the opposite of what I'd meant to communicate. I began to cross my arms, then saw where he was pointing—at the gluten-free cupcakes. I'd forgotten they existed. Instead of answering in words, I slid the tray over a foot and boosted myself up beside them.

"Counters are the perfect height," I reminded him, beckoning with one finger.

"I heard that somewhere." He stepped closer, until his pants were grazing my knees, the fabrics catching in a thousand tiny sparks. "Remind me again: For what?"

I shut my eyes and tilted my head back. "Taste tests."

His laughter danced across my lips. "Firebug, for all your talk about not knowing how to flirt, you're killing me." His arm brushed my leg as he reached across me. I heard the plastic tray crinkle, and the scent of chocolate grew stronger. His thumb grazed my bottom lip, painting it with frosting. "Open your mouth—and don't bite me."

"I make no prom—" I laughed around the bite of cupcake he'd pressed between my lips, cutting off my words. I chewed slowly, and swallowed.

"Gluten, or no gluten?" His nose brushed against my jaw as he touched his lips to my neck.

I frowned. I hated the words I was going to have to say—but they were in the way of what I wanted, so I spit them out. "I don't know." I twined my arms around the back of his neck. "Now kiss me."

There was frosting on his hands—I only realized this when they cupped my face... and I couldn't have cared less.

He kissed his way across my cheek, and his teeth nipped my earlobe. I shivered as he whispered, "It was gluten-free."

My laugh was a goose's honk, loud and wild. I smacked his shoulder. "Seriously? You're still thinking about baked goods?"

"Are you critiquing my sweet nothings?" He grinned and I mirrored it, but it wasn't facial mimicry; it was a moment of shared emotion—of kindred spirits.

"Keep practicing, Cupcake."

I hadn't known it was possible for a smile to be that radiant. That I could make someone so happy with three words and, in turn, their facial expression could light up my insides like one of those simple circuit boards I'd done in preschool. I'd lived sixteen years in this body—but it felt newly mine. And by claiming ownership, I earned the right to these sensations. How had I never known what it felt like to have someone twirl a strand of my hair around their finger? Or rest a hand on my shoulder while their thumb stroked the bare skin above my collarbone? And now that I'd experienced his mouth against mine, how could I ever let that go? Answer: I couldn't. I pulled him closer, kissed him again.

It was a scientific fact that when the brain is deprived of one outlet of sensory input, it will compensate by developing stronger sensory pathways for others. In those who can't see, the visual cortex is used to process objects by touch and sound. I knew this was true—I'd read the studies on neural pathways and sensory deprivation experiments.

But despite that—despite the fact that my eyes were closed—my auditory processing didn't compensate and pick up the sound of a key in the lock or the kitchen door opening.

It wasn't until I heard a scandalized "Eliza!" that I pushed Curtis away and opened my eyes.

"Mom! Dad!" I raised horrified hands to cover my mouth—smearing the frosting on my cheek. "What are you doing here?"

34

Dad dropped his suitcase with a thud.

"What is going on here?" Mom demanded.

Everyone looked at me, but I was still trying to process their presences and believe they were real. Dad looked thinner, Mom's hair was longer. I wasn't sure it suited her. Their subzero parkas were as red as my face. Their fur-lined boots were laced as tight as the invisible bindings on my mouth. They were cradling military-grade, latched containers—these held lab equipment or computers—which dictated they be set gingerly on the table before they crossed their arms. Dad slowly panned the scene before gasping. "Are those *cupcakes*?"

"I know dinner first would be more appropriate, but we just completed a grueling run, so a cupcake appetizer or three is warranted." Curtis was probably seeking a retort, but I was a statue, my knuckles white around the edge of the counter so I didn't give in to the urge to shove the cupcake tray off the other side—like that would somehow make the evidence disappear. He rested his hand on my knee. I stiffened. He flinched from my recoil.

Dad focused on me—he pointed to my iLive band. "Seven miles. It seems your endurance and speed have improved dramatically—but have your hands suffered some grievous injury that prevents you from typing up your log?"

I shook my head. I'd quit logging days ago. In my mind it was a game of chicken, seeing if I could provoke them enough to talk to me. But I'd been aiming for an *email*, maybe a phone call. This was...

"I, uh, tried to talk her into coming to my house for a video-game showdown, but now I'm glad we didn't miss your arrival. Welcome home." Curtis wiped his fingers on the remains of my shredded paper towel before extending his hand, completely unaware of the combustibles he'd thrown on the situation. "I'm Curtis Cavendish, by the way. I'm sure you've heard lots about me this year. Only believe the things that are good."

"Actually"—Dad drew out the word while continuing to stare at the tableau of all my lies—"I've never heard of you."

Curtis dropped his hand, hurt blatant on his face before he covered it up. "Well, I'm the guy who's—" He turned to me, and I could see how fake his smile was, but I couldn't add his expectations to those piled on me. "What word do you prefer: 'smitten,' 'enamored,' 'besotted,' 'mesmerized,' 'enchanted'?"

I looked away.

Later I'd think about what it meant to have those words used about me, but at the time I could focus only on my parents' reactions to hearing them. I wanted to shove him too. But like the cupcakes, instead I pretended he wasn't there, studying my thighs and fingers and the floor.

"But don't worry," Curtis added. "It's entirely one-sided. So the best description for me would be 'fool' or 'shameful secret.'"

"Yes, well..." Dad trailed off. There was sympathy in his voice, but I didn't look up to see if it was in his expression too.

"The cupcakes are mine. Though not entirely illicit. Spoiler: It's part of my research for the Avery Competition. I suppose you'll see my project there."

"As judges, I suppose there's no avoiding it." Mom's voice was brusque.

Had I always had a freckle on the back of my hand? Or was it chocolate? Mud? No, the mud on the hems of my leggings was an ashier color. I liked it better. Chocolate was the color of Curtis's eyes, and I didn't know how I'd ever meet them again. What was wrong with me? At least when Rory had been little and played "You can't see me" she'd pulled a blanket over her head. I was seated on the counter like some blasted centerpiece, and wishful thinking was not going to make me disappear.

"You know what, you guys have a lot to catch up on . . ."

"Yes, we do." Dad unzipped his parka, like Curtis's words had reminded him that this was *his* house, no matter how little time he spent here.

"And I'm in the way, so I'm just gonna leave—" Curtis paused. This conversation was full of invitations for me to join and make things better. Merri would've slid in like an expert, defusing tensions, making introductions, smoothing things over. I could barely look up from my socks. Curtis slowly retrieved his sweatshirt from the chair, his whole body angled at me—waiting. "I guess . . . I'll call my parents to come get me. Or I can walk."

I felt like a tiny woodland creature—one that was caught wide-eyed in the headlights of an oncoming car. Not the kind that dithered—dart a few steps left, then a few steps right—trying to decide which route was best. No, I was the type of small-brained mammal that thought if it stood still, it would be safe.

"Good idea." Mom opened the door and practically shooed him out, along with the bakery bag she'd hastily repacked. "You should take these with you."

I dared to meet his eyes as the door was closing. Just a microsecond of contact before it shut, but the hurt in his was palpable.

"Eliza—" My parents said it together, then stopped and looked at each other, both indicating with pointing and head-shakes that the other should speak first. Mom lost the battle of gestures and willpower. "Didn't you read the studies we sent you on adolescent dating? Were our rules not clear?"

"I did and they were." I could've taken the moment to tell them I *knew*—I knew how flawed that research was and how biased and cherry-picked the material they'd shared had been. I could've countered with studies of my own. But none of that was important right now.

What had I been thinking, letting him leave?

I hopped down from the counter.

"Well, at least she's being honest, Warner."

"Yes, but—"

I pushed between where Mom and Dad were trying to communicate their confusion to each other—without making it overly clear to me—to my muddy shoes resting by the door. I shoved my toes inside, not bothering to lace them, not bothering with a coat.

"Where are you going?" asked Dad.

"I'll be—" I shook my head and pointed outside. Then I was shutting the door behind myself and activating lights from motion sensors as I ran, scanning the sidewalks and across yards for a gray sweatshirt and black pants. I spotted him two houses down, passing the Karbieners' monstrosity of a brick mailbox. "Curtis! Curtis, wait up."

He stopped moving but didn't turn around. I jogged over and shivered as the cold air filtered through my thin shirt. "Hey."

He was studying the mailbox like it was actually interesting—not just a mammoth construction of bricks and solar lights they'd put up after Mr. Karbiener had backed over their wooden post for the fifth time. As hard as he was studying those bricks, I was studying *him*. Trying to figure out the emotions on his face and if it was the streetlight that made the shadows and angles look so harsh. "You're—you're angry."

"And you're cold. Can we move past the part of this conversation where we state the obvious?" He wanted the words to be a joke, but he didn't get the cadence right and I was jabbed by their sharp edges.

Anger on him looked different than on Win or Wink. Wink's anger was injured—it cloaked her feelings of betrayal. Win's was feral and restless, always anticipating an attack. But Curtis's—it was restrained, just barely. He didn't sigh, he *seethed*.

"I'm not sure what happened in there." I pointed over my shoulder. "Or what's happening right now."

"Well, I haven't known what's been happening for a month, so I guess that makes us even."

"Oh. Okay, um." It felt like trying to use a microscope in a room with no light source, trying to make a neutral solution when all you had was acids. "Do you want to tell me what you're confused about?"

"You told me to kiss you—then answered a phone call about math homework."

My forehead wrinkled. "Are you talking about the first time we ate cupcakes? That was weeks ago. You told me to answer the call!"

"No, I said, 'Maybe you should answer that in case it's important'—I wanted you to say it wasn't. I wanted you to say *I was.* I wanted you to tell Huck you were out running with me, to take you on a real date. I wanted your parents to already know my name. Or at least for you to act like they'd be hearing it again."

My throat ached with the impossibility of explaining. "You don't understand what they're like."

"But I do!" He threw his hands up. "You've told me. I listened. Your parents have you convinced that people are only ever going to value your looks and dismiss you because you're beautiful. But how is that any different than what they're doing to you with your intelligence? You are not *only* either of those things. You're more than your brains *or* your beauty."

"You think I don't know that?" I stared at him, feeling heat creep up my neck to sit like flames on my lips. Maybe that knowledge was recent, but it was hard-won and important. And despite looks and brains and everything else I was—it wasn't *enough.* "What part of me do *you* want, Curtis? My brains so you have a challenge in quiz bowl? My body so people can see us on this 'real date' you want?" I made air quote around the words; I resented him saying that because there weren't spectators to our interactions, what we had wasn't genuine. "What is it *you* want?"

Curtis dropped his arms. "Your heart, mostly."

I shook my head. "I need some part of me that's my own."

"What if I gave you mine?" He stepped closer, maintaining eye contact that seared me. "What if I've already given it to you?"

"Don't." I ground my teeth and stepped back. It was like being trapped in the chapter of *Anne of Green Gables* where Gilbert saves Anne from drowning after her reenactment of a romantic poem goes very wrong. He holds out a friendship olive branch and she almost accepts—but can't. I *couldn't*. "Love is irrational, emotional, illogical. It makes people distracted and kills their focus and ambition. It destroys."

He gave a bitter laugh. "It's also one of the best dang things on the planet."

"It's a mistake, a weakness." All the evidence I needed was standing in my kitchen, jet-lagged and furious. My head swam when I thought about what I'd face when I walked back in. Would they stick around long enough to forgive me? "I just...I can't."

"Yeah, you proved that today." He turned his back on me and grasped his neck with both hands. "I'd convinced myself you were scared of dating. I didn't get that you were ashamed of me."

"I'm not!" I pulled on his arm, hating the defeat in his posture and that I couldn't see his face. "I told you I'd be bad at this. You said that was okay. You said it was okay to fail sometimes and that was how we learned."

"You're not bad at it, Eliza." It was worded like a compliment, but it didn't sound like one. I held my breath and waited. "Being bad at it would require you to put in some effort. You're not even trying."

I gave up ineffectively tugging his arm and ducked underneath to see his expression. "I am."

"I refuse to be a joke—not to you." He scrubbed both hands over his face, but his eyes glistened when he dropped them. "You've never made me feel like one. Until now."

"Are you—are we..." I swallowed and licked my lips, searching for any of the sweetness left behind from frosting or kisses. "Are you breaking up with me?"

"No."

I pressed a hand to my chest, almost staggering from relief.

"We're 'not-dating,' remember?" Curtis said. "There's nothing to break up. Maybe this is our...our *apoptosis*. Is that brainy enough for you?"

"Apoptosis": Programmed cell death. Cellular self-destruction to maintain stasis. A natural unnatural end.

I shut my eyes.

Heartbreak wasn't a real thing—anatomically, nothing abnormal or organ-rending was going on inside my rib cage, but apparently no one informed my pain receptors, because my chest *hurt*. Even with my fist clutching the front of my shirt applying counterpressure, it was all I could do not to double over while Curtis was standing there. After he left I didn't bother staying upright, but sank to the curb.

I could've filled a field notebook with the things I didn't say:

I'm sorry

I was wrong

I adore you too

Come back

The cold concrete seeped through the fabric of my leggings. I wanted to go numb. No matter how close I hugged my knees or how far I dropped my chin, I couldn't assuage the pain radiating from my chest—spreading out to my clenched hands and tight shoulders, until it leaked from my eyes and lungs in great, gulping sobs.

35

From my spot on the curb I could hear my front door opening, my parents shuffling in and out as they unloaded
their rental car. They couldn't see me—thank you, Mr.
Karbiener's inability to reverse—but I could hear snatches
of their conversation, their bafflement and the escalation of
their concerns. When they reached "Do you think we need her to
take drug or pregnancy tests?" I forced myself to stand, reenter
the house, and face their judgment.

They were organizing their bags into piles: "bedroom," "lab,"
and "just stack those in the basement."

I quietly shut the door behind me. "I'm back."

"You can't leave without telling anyone," said Dad, and I
ground my teeth to keep from correcting him. I not only *could*, I
had to—because normally there wasn't anyone *to tell*.

"Eliza, good grief." Mom was struggling to get her enormous
anorak to fit beside Dad's in our coat closet. "*This* is what we
come home to? You on the counter with some boy?"

A warped, sickly sound leaked between my lips—half groan,
half laugh. I'd been in the lab thirty-three of the past fifty hours.
Of course *this* was when they came home. I spent ninety-nine
percent of my time in compliance with their impossible rules,

in a state of suspended life and delayed gratification. Waiting to be worthy and for them to come and collect me, like an umbrella they'd left behind at a hotel.

Except their time was so valuable—an umbrella was never going to be worth retrieving. I'd just proved I wasn't either.

"Well?" They were a caricature of parental frustration—Mom's hands on her hips, Dad's arms crossed over a South Pole Station–branded fleece. "Present the facts, Eliza."

I didn't have an answer. Why would they listen to me when they hadn't to Curtis, and why should I offer them words I hadn't been able to say for him? My legs felt shakier now than they had after reaching the top of the hill or when Curtis had suggested we do interval pickups for the last mile. I sank down.

They stepped around the table and peered at me in side-by-side confusion. "Why are you sitting on the floor?"

"Counters, floors—is there something wrong with our chairs?"

"No." But I didn't move. I'd once criticized Curtis for the same thing—*I don't sit on counters*—but now it seemed absurd. Who cared? "What are you doing here? The Avery isn't for another week."

My parents blinked and raised their eyebrows. The way they loomed made me feel like a toddler again. Like I'd asked some foolish question and should already know the answer.

Dad spoke slowly. "You told us you wanted us to come home."

I slid my hands under my thighs. They were so cold from being outside. I wanted a hot shower—a place to cry. And answers that made sense, because this conversation did not. "That was two *weeks* ago. I haven't even heard from you since then."

"I'm sure Nancy's kept you informed," said Dad.

"Um, I'm sure she has *not*," I countered.

258 | TIFFANY SCHMIDT

He stiffened. "Oh. Maybe we should've anticipated that and given her direct instructions to do so? Communication has been one of her larger failings."

"Or maybe you could've *told me directly?*" I ground my teeth and willed back tears.

Mom huffed over to the sink and opened the cabinet beneath, pulling out cleaner. "We've been a bit busy. It's not like we can just pick up a cell phone and call you. Do you know what's involved in coordinating travel from Antarctica? Moving things up a week was a major hassle. We needed to get people to cover our lab, and pack, and arrange transportation. Transports are already starting to ramp down for the season—we had to find one to McMurdo that had room. From there, it was two days waiting for a flight to Christchurch. California. Pennsylvania. It takes *days* to get home. I'm sorry, Eliza, but we can't snap our fingers and grant your wishes."

She'd moved to the other side of the island, so I couldn't see her from the floor. I turned to Dad. "You came home *for me?*"

"Of course we did. Good thing too. We had evidence that something was amiss: iLive band data, your missing log, credit card receipts. Your dentist emailed us that you haven't made an appointment for the night guard he recommended two months ago. You didn't mention you'd been grinding your teeth."

"I forgot," I lied.

"But despite that, I can't say we were expecting you to be..." He pointed to where Mom was attacking the frosting on the counter with a dishrag. I wanted her to leave it. I wanted proof the good parts of the day had happened.

Mom put down her cloth. "We're going to have to punish her, Warner."

"You're right, Violet." He nodded solemnly. "Adolescents do best with clear limits. She needs a consequence."

The looks they exchanged over my head lacked the assured purpose I'd seen them demonstrate in the lab. For a second I wanted to laugh—Frankenstein's monster was misbehaving, and they had no clue how to handle that.

"We can discuss it on the way home from returning the rental car," Mom said. I'd forgotten how they did this, analyzed me in front of me, like I was a problem written out on their laboratory whiteboard and they were brainstorming a solution. "And tell her when we get back."

Which meant I had at least a half hour to call Merri—get her to create a fix-it plan—then call Curtis and enact it.

"But we should take her phone, right?" Dad asked.

"Yes!" Mom plucked mine off the counter with a look of transparent relief. "That's a good one. Phone *and* computer. She can use it for homework, but we'll monitor that."

"And the car—that's a logical consequence. We'll need it, she loses it."

"What about grounding?" Mom asked. "Or does it harm a child's sense of autonomy?"

"We'll look it up on the drive—but if that's still a thing, then she'll be grounded too." They exchanged self-satisfied nods, proud of how they'd handled the situation.

Dad gave my head a stiff pat as he walked past to get his coat. "It's good to see you, Eliza."

Mom picked up the car keys—the set with the Hero High fob Merri had slipped into my locker after I got my license with a note signed, *Love, your favorite navigationally challenged copilot.* Those keys had meant freedom, no more relying on guardians for rides. They disappeared into Mom's pocket. "Now that we're home, things are going to change."

My nod was slow and cautious, because my eyes were wet and I was determined to wait until they'd left to cry. Change. For the better or worse?

36

It wasn't until late Sunday that I remembered the burner phone I'd left in the center console of the car. Then it was an excruciating hour before Dad was back from the grocery store. I was waiting by the door with shoes on when he pulled in. "I'll help you unload."

"Sounds great." He hummed as he set the first round of cloth bags on the counter. "I never appreciate the luxury of fresh produce quite like I do after coming home from Antarctica. Spinach, grapes, *strawberries*."

He followed me out to the driveway as I tried to come up with an excuse to open the driver's door when the bags were in the trunk. He loaded up his arms while I dithered, then winked. "Another thing we don't have at South Pole Station—cell phones. You seem to have an abundance of those." He patted his pocket. "You've got the rest of the groceries, right?"

I sighed. Not that he'd waited to hear it.

I had this memory of them, one I wasn't sure was real—but it centered on a rubber duck. Not a regular one; this one changed color to indicate if the bath water was a safe temperature. It had gone missing. I remembered standing wrapped in a towel on a blue bath mat as my parents had measured the water with a thermometer from their lab and had debated what to do.

"Careful," Dad had said. "That's glass."

Mom had suggested looking up optimal temperatures online. Dad had wanted to search for the duck. "I think it's too hot. She'll be scalded."

I, who couldn't have been more than four, had got fed up and cold. I'd dropped the towel and stuck my arm in the tub. I'd said something like, "Feels good to me," and climbed in.

My parents had stared, aghast. I'd splashed them. The night had ended in laughter.

That's how it felt in our house. They were cautiously taking my temperature, unwilling to plunge themselves into my life—or even to dip a toe—for fear of being burned.

I was twelve years older but still felt as impatient. They were *here*, right here. Why did they feel so far away? How did I convince them it was safe? When could we laugh?

Merri hummed in the back seat of Toby's car on Monday's ride to school. His and Rory's shoulders leaned toward each other in the front as they planned a "paint-and-play" date—where they serenaded and sketched each other or something obnoxiously sweet.

The humming was Merri's attempt at white noise to cancel them out. Or maybe it was a manifestation of her impatience, because she was practically vibrating with curiosity. In the school parking lot, she brushed past the guy who'd been waiting to open her door. "Thank you, Fielding, but I can't talk now. Eliza and I *need* some time."

"Oh, right." He nodded somberly at me. "Merri told me."

I sucked in a breath. "Told you what?"

"That your parents are back?" He looked between his girl-friend and me.

"Oh. Yes, they are." I attempted a smile. "Sorry, I've got Monday brain."

His forehead creased, because when had I ever been the type of person to use the words "Monday brain"?

"I'll catch you later? Maybe in the hall before history?" Merri blew him a kiss and began to drag me across the parking lot. "I promise I only told him about your parents. I wouldn't have told him"—she looked around—"about the *other thing*—because I don't know what's going on. I know *something* is, because when you didn't respond to my texts, I sent Curtis a heads-up about your parents and he responded 'Too late.' He didn't include an emoji, which makes me think it's bad."

I swallowed. Dad had made me a smoothie this morning. Some recipe with oatmeal and flaxseed and yogurt and vanilla the breakfast chef at South Pole Station had taught him. It had been surprisingly good—but now my mouth tasted sour and I regretted every sip. "It's bad."

Merri studied my face. "Do we have time before first period? If not, the library at lunch?"

"Lunch sounds good." Because it meant escaping our cafeteria table, and it gave me hours to figure out what to say and how to say it without crying.

"If you need me to kick him or cause a big spectacle before then, let me know." She squeezed my hand. "Just say, 'There are other factors to consider,' and I'm on it."

She truly would, and that was amazing—but it also meant I was already mentally scanning for any conceivable situation where that combination of words might occur. It kept me distracted, prevented me from focusing on unfixable things... which was probably her goal all along.

Lunch in the library wasn't half as painful as sitting in class with Curtis and having him not look my direction, no matter how fiercely I stared in his.

I led Merri over to the study corrals, then gave her the gist, reducing Saturday to an emotionless list of events: run, bakery, kissing, interruption, breakup, punishment.

"Wow." She sat back. "And you really had no idea you had frosting on your cheek until you went to shower?"

I hadn't known how badly I needed to laugh until that moment. "Nope. You would've thought the crying would've washed it off. Guess not."

"How long are they staying?" she asked.

"I don't know."

"You don't—*you don't know?*" Merri had been spinning her chair in nervous arcs as she chewed on pretzel sticks, but this time it did a full rotation. "They've been back for two days. You haven't asked?"

I gnawed on my lip. "I think maybe they're staying for good? Or, at least for a while. They *fired* Nancy. She was apartment shopping for herself. And they were talking about how 'sharing one car isn't feasible long-term.' *Long-term.*"

Merri *hmm*'d and spun her chair again. "Your family has been doing this 'reverse boarding school' thing for so long—where you go to school and stay home while they go away. I can't imagine anything different. We need more evidence."

I had it. "They brought more luggage than when they came home at Christmas. And they spent *that* trip meeting with colleagues. This time I heard them talking about meetings with my teachers."

"How do you feel about all"—she waved both arms in some chaotic charade—"that?"

I shrugged, suddenly exhausted. "Dad keeps saying things like, 'We need to recalibrate and figure out how to function as a trio.'"

"Gah, that *does* sound long-term." Merri's freckles stood out against her pale face. She lowered the banana she'd been eating. "Do they still not like me? What happens when you're ungrounded?"

I looked for answers on the desktop. Someone had carved *PH + LD* into the wood. Someone had tried to scratch it out. I wondered if it was the same person, or if one half of the equation had been more reticent. But maybe the reticence was temporary—maybe they would've caught up. Not everyone goes full speed ahead. Some of us look before we leap—but sometimes we *do* leap, and run down mountains and kiss the boy standing at the bottom. I sniffed.

"Give Curtis time." Merri checked the clock on her phone, then began to repack the uneaten food I'd pulled from my lunch bag. "And while you're giving him time, think about what *you* want. You can't go back to how things were."

"But if my parents are home—"

"Yeah, think about what you want *there* too."

I did. Constantly. But I didn't know.

That was the *why* behind not asking about their plans. I couldn't decide how I wanted them to answer—and I knew part of me would feel disappointed and guilty either way.

37

After a torturous quiz bowl practice on Tuesday, I'd come home to find my parents in their office on a conference call. The door was shut, so I waved through the glass and went into the kitchen to make a snack before I headed to the lab.

I was rinsing grapes when they emerged, smiling and bright-eyed. It was the invigorated look they wore when they began a new project, so my hackles were up as I asked, "Good day?"

"It was," Dad said. "Very productive. Also nostalgic. While organizing things in the basement, we found a box of your baby photos."

Mom laughed. "When you were an infant, your dad was always looking for signs of genius."

"As were you," he retorted.

"Yes, but I didn't overextrapolate from every one of her accomplishments." Mom sat at the kitchen table and Dad did too, shaking his head and saying, "I'm sure I don't know what you're talking about."

Mom pressed her lips together. In their sparring, smiling was a loss. How dare they let each other know they'd been amused. My stomach twisted; I'd played that same game with Curtis.

"Hmm. Selective memory. For example, Eliza, when you were three months old your father decided that because you didn't fuss when clothing was pulled over your head you'd already mastered the concept of object permanence."

"And your mom was delighted the first time you pushed her away and said, 'No. I do.'—even though it took you five minutes to put on pants. Backward, I might add."

"It was a sign of her independence." Their looks of nostalgia soured. "And now—well, you're certainly independent." Mom sighed. "We understand that's a result of our previous arrangement, and it's a laudable quality for a young woman to possess, but..."

"What your mother's trying to say is, you need to tell us what your plans are."

"What plans?" This felt like the lead-up to something, and because I didn't know what, every possible answer felt hazardous. "I have no plans. I'm grounded."

"Maybe not 'plans' then," Mom mused. "But, sit. Tell us about your day."

It was a task that shouldn't have felt insurmountable. I sank onto the chair between them and tried to pretend their impatience wasn't palpable. I could give them the data I would've put in my log, but Dad had made my breakfast and Mom had watched in concern as I'd unpacked a mostly full lunch bag yesterday, then been relieved when I scarfed my dinner. They'd been up when my alarm went off this morning and said good night to me before bed. "I'm going to run on the treadmill later?"

"Okay. But how was your day?" Dad asked.

I didn't know how to quantify that. "Fine."

"Let's try something else." Mom tapped her lip. "Oh! Why all the running?"

"I was thinking of doing a half-marathon, but..." It wasn't like I needed Curtis's permission, but the idea of training solo—of trading trails for the treadmill—made my body feel heavy. "I changed my mind."

"That's quite the goal." Dad went over to the fridge and got a pitcher of water. He returned with it and three glasses. "Did I ever tell you I ran a marathon?"

"No." I tried to picture it. "When?"

"Chicago. The year before you were born. But one of our research assistants ran the Antarctic Ice Marathon this year."

"Ice marathon? How did she train?"

"There's a gym," said Mom. "But Nahlia ran outside whenever she had time. The pictures are—I bet I have some on my computer if you want to see them. You can't even tell it's her under the balaclava, goggles, and gloves."

"Your mom liked to tease her that the photos were of a stunt double while Nahlia was off in the sauna."

"You have a sauna?" I reached on the countertop behind me and grabbed the bowl of grapes. Dad had been eating fresh fruit almost nonstop. "I want to see pictures. Tell me more about life there."

"*Only* if you'll tell us more about life here." Mom and Dad did that smug-glances thing again as he popped three grapes into his mouth. "We're realizing now, no matter how much data we collected, we weren't seeing the big picture of your life."

"But we couldn't figure out any other way to parent from a distance," Dad added. "We needed something quantifiable—some measure of your well-being."

"I don't think that can be measured." Very few of the best things in life could be—not in any objective way. This moment, for example, couldn't be charted or captured in a diagram; but them admitting a flaw, letting me see them vulnerable—it told me more than years of logs. "But well-being can be communicated. I know anecdotes are imprecise, but they offer more insight than BMI or REM cycles."

"We agree," Mom said. "But that's irrelevant now. Try again, tell us about your day."

It was grapes and water, not Mrs. Campbell's perfect-temperature chamomile; but the other aspects—the attention and interest, the feeling valued and feeling *part* of something—those were the same. *This* was family. Mine.

Dad plucked another grape from the bunch. "Start at the morning, I want to know how you and Tobias May got on carpool-friendly terms—I thought you couldn't stand him. And I asked George Campbell this back in September, but I want to hear it from you too. Is he a safe driver? Are you? I'll have to take you out for a test later. Should I ask him to do the same?"

I grinned around my glass. Finally, answers to my questions: They were staying, and I was glad.

I forgot Thursday was Valentine's Day until I got in Toby's car. He and Rory were sitting starry-eyed in the front seat while Merri clutched a glittery heart-shaped gift bag in the back.

I bit my tongue and spent the drive mentally listing prime numbers. I refused to think of the response journal I'd written yesterday—about Gilbert's pond rescue and Anne's stubbornness. How she said the ordeal cured her "of being too romantic." I wanted to be at that point—cured instead of still stinging.

As soon as I stepped out of the car at Hero High, I was tempted to step back in. I wondered if my parents' tentative attempts at bonding extended to allowing me to skip school. Doubtful. But if they saw how the student body was practically frothing with hearts, they might have understood my motives. When I reached the sophomore hall, it was worse. Every locker had some combination of carnations taped to the front. Red, pink, white—I'm sure the prom committee had assigned meanings to the colors, but all I cared about was if any of the flowers taped to *my* locker were from the guy I hadn't talked to since he left me crying on the sidewalk on Saturday night.

I flipped through the heart-shaped tags impatiently. *Merri. Merri. Merri. Rory. Hannah. Merri. Sera. Toby. Merri. Merri. Merri & Fielding. Lance.*

The last one—the only red one—was signed with a doodle: a cupcake.

I smiled as I pressed the card and carnation against my chest.

"Hey, Eliza?" Merri was chewing her bottom lip, still holding the gift bag for Fielding, so apparently she'd followed me instead of finding him. "I think I should remind you the deadline to order flowers was last week. I know if it were *me*, I'd want to believe it meant things were okay, and..."

"Right." I let go of the flower. It fell to the floor. He'd sent it Thursday or Friday, or any of the days before Saturday. "Good point. Thanks."

"I'm sorry."

I shook my head. "I'm glad you said something."

It wasn't like Curtis had been rude; he wasn't ignoring me—at least not blatantly. He just didn't engage. I wasn't a person he noticed or teased. His feet stayed on his side of the lunch table. He didn't wink at me over quiz bowl buzzers.

Yesterday at lunch, I'd done my best to bait him with talk about the Avery. "Have you started *Frankenstein* yet? You know, for when I beat you?"

I'd wanted it to be playful, but it was twisted by self-doubt and hesitation, and from how the rest of the lunch table blinked, I knew it sounded harsh.

"I guess we'll see." His answer was paired with a shrug, like it *and I* were of no consequence. I used to wish Curtis would stop joking and "be serious"—but now that he was, I hated it.

After lunch Lance had pulled me aside. "You need to give Curtis some space. I've been there—the guy who's pining and had enough. It's time to leave him alone."

My cheeks had burned. "What did he tell you?"

"Nothing. But it was clear he had a crush, and now it's clear he's moved on. Because he has, you're suddenly interested? C'mon, you're better than that."

If it was Merri who'd been hurt and Fielding who'd done it, I wouldn't be half as courteous as Lance. That didn't make his words sting less. I still couldn't decide if his perception of the situation was worse than the truth.

Lance likely also wished he could unsend his friendship carnation. I shoved it and the others onto the top shelf of my locker, then schooled my expression before facing Merri. "I'm fine. Go find Fielding. He's probably panicking."

"You're right! If not panicking, at least freezing. I told him to meet me in the parking lot and not wear socks." She shook her gift bag. "I found a few pairs he's going to love—basset hounds and fencing dudes and Mr. Darcy." She paused and picked up the flower from the floor. "I'll hang on to this in case you ever want it back. See you in bio?"

I nodded. But it was English I was dreading, where we'd get those response journals back.

I got an A, but I barely cared about that. I couldn't tear my eyes away from the line Ms. Gregoire had scrawled across the bottom. It was a quote from Matthew Cuthbert: *"Don't give up all your romance, Anne... a little of it is a good thing."*

38

braced myself when Ms. Gregoire stopped by my desk in English class on Friday. I'd been expecting a question about *Anne* or *Frankenstein*. Instead she asked, "Are you all ready for the Avery?"

"Yup." I looked down at my hands. There were still traces of dirt beneath my nails, but my abstract and display board were finished. By this time tomorrow, it would almost be over. I was more excited about it being past tense than about any awards or accolades in my future.

"Great. I'll see you there." She smoothed down the skirt of her dress, making the cherry blossoms printed on it shimmy, then paused. "You never did tell me what your project was called. What title should I look for on a poster tomorrow?"

"*Isolation and introduction of* Vibrio harveyi's *bioluminescent*"—Curtis's head pivoted toward me as I said the word "bioluminescent," and I wondered if he was thinking of what he'd told me about firebugs and magic and me—"*gene into* Pisum sativum *via clustered regularly interspaced short palindromic repeats.*"

"Oh." She blinked. "I recognized maybe three of those words, but it sounds important."

"It's really not." I didn't know if Curtis was still watching me, because I was studying my desk. This project was the opposite of important. It was the epitome of jargon and showing off just to show off. It served no actual function. "I made some pea plants glow in the dark."

Ms. Gregoire laughed. "Why?"

"To prove I could. Because it will win. Because it's the sort of project a Gordon-Fergus should do." I hadn't meant to sound bitter. I'd need to practice modulating my tone before I presented to the judges.

Ms. Gregoire crouched down so her face was level with mine. "You know one of the things I love most about Anne Shirley? How she's always true to herself. Even that time she's forced to make that awful apology to Rachel Lynde or when she confesses to losing the brooch she really didn't lose—she does it in the most over-the-top Anne-ish way possible."

I gaped at her; those were the same scenes I'd thought of the night I'd decided to change my project. I hadn't told her—hadn't told that to anyone.

"Eliza, you've never seemed all that excited about the Avery— it's just a shame you couldn't find a way to make it your own."

Only I'd used those same scenes to justify the opposite outcome—focusing on the *has to do*, not making it mine.

Ms. Gregoire gave me a sad smile before standing up. "Anyway, I'm sure your parents will be very proud of your glowing plants, and I'll see you there tomorrow."

"You like Hero High, right?" Dad asked me Friday night. He was chopping peppers, and I was sitting on a stool stealing carrots from his piles. This was starting to become a *thing*. Talking, sharing pieces of our days, and opinions on things that weren't science. It was still weird, but getting less so.

"Yeah, I do."

Mom was stirring rice. She glanced over her shoulder and added. "None of the social issues you were having at Woodcreek Charter have carried over?"

I almost choked on a carrot. It scraped all the way down. "You knew about that?" My face grew hot, but I couldn't tell if it was in embarrassment or anger.

"About the bullying and the nicknames?" Dad nodded. "Your teachers emailed us weekly progress reports. Your socialization difficulties came up frequently."

"You *knew*"—I tucked my shaking hands beneath my legs— "and you didn't say or *do* anything?"

"What are you talking about?" Mom switched off the burner and turned to face me. "We had Judith give you a book."

"No, that was during Carlotta's stint, wasn't it?" Dad asked. "Regardless. We had your then-guardian buy a book about social dynamics. It came highly recommended."

"A book?" I wanted to throw Dad's neatly diced veggies at the walls, to dump Mom's pot down the drain. "I wanted my *parents*."

They made eye contact with each other but would no longer meet mine. "You didn't say anything. We assumed if it really bothered you—"

"You assumed. And your assumptions were based on the premise that you *knew* me, which you don't. Not at all." I slid off my stool and grabbed my coat.

"Where are you going?" Mom asked.

"To work on my science fair project," I snapped. "Is that allowed?"

"It's *tomorrow*," said Dad. "You're not done yet?"

"Warner," Mom chided. "When's the last time *you* finished something a full day before deadline? Also, I think she needs some space." Mom nodded at me. "Be home by eight."

Ms. Gregoire's words echoed in my head: *It's just a shame you couldn't find a way to make it your own.* The CRISPR'd pea plants were a project that would win the bet. They were a project that would please my parents. But they weren't *my* project. The podcast was.

And did it matter if I won or lost if the boy on the other half of the bet wasn't talking to me? Was the subject of a book report worth more than my integrity?

My chest felt tight the whole walk to the Campbells', until I opened their front door and Mr. Campbell greeted me with a smile. "Eliza! I've been missing my cohost lately." I followed him into the kitchen, trying to invent a valid excuse for showing up, but he didn't act like I needed one. "I've got a whole bunch of questions written down on the back of an old grocery list. Jennifer accidentally threw it out, and I had to rescue it from the trash, so don't mind the stains." He handed it to me. "Do any of these look good?"

I couldn't read his spikey scrawl through blurry eyes, but I nodded anyway. "They're perfect."

"Is Toby bringing over the mics?" Mr. Campbell asked. He slid a bowl of green beans across the table toward me. "I thought he and Rory were at the movies."

I gratefully accepted the task of snapping off the beans' ends. Anything to stop my hands from fidgeting. Was I wasting his time? The glowing-pea plant project was done, and it was too late to switch back. Wasn't it? Why was I here?

Because my parents' revelation felt like being abandoned all over again. They'd known. A *self-help book* had done nothing to stop those tiny, plastic Barbie shoes from being flicked at me in class. I'd come home with small red welts. A book.

But I hadn't *told* them—they'd heard from teachers, but not from *me*. I was too scared to admit weakness or flaws, or give them any ammunition to be disappointed in me and stay away. I'd wanted them to guess—felt like if they were truly as smart as everyone said, that they should *know* ... Much like how I'd tested Merri's friendship ESP instead of telling her about Curtis.

I groaned.

I was here because here felt safe, and Mr. Campbell made me feel like *enough*. But I owed him an answer. "I love our podcast. But I'm worried it's not flashy. I'm not discovering anything *new*."

"No, but you're creating something that could give new information to *many*."

"Yeah." And I loved it. Had I mentioned I loved it? "It's not going to win though. I think I've always known that."

"Do you care?"

"I—" I hesitated, because the truth surprised me. "My parents will, but I don't." Even if it meant also losing *Anne* or letting them down.

"They called me the other day, you know. They do that every month or so." Mr. Campbell chuckled. "This time they had questions about your friend group. They also wanted to know if grounding had 'ever proved detrimental to the girls developing a growth mind-set.' So, if you're mad about being grounded, I guess blame me."

I hadn't known this. And was shocked they'd allowed anecdotal evidence to determine my punishment. They were trying. Yes, it was taking some "recalibration"—but maybe we could make it work if I met them halfway. If we all stopped running. If I dropped facades and told the truth. If they listened. "It's fine."

"Now, I'm no expert—but when Merri was little, one of her teachers gave me this piece of advice about gifted children—and we both know how much you qualify." He waited for me to shrug-nod. "Gifted children have a tendency to center their identity and value on what they achieve academically. They're used to things coming easily—they don't have to, say, struggle like Rory does with math. Because of that, they don't have as many opportunities to build up fortitude in the face of frustration—or learn what it means to persist. Or that failure can be temporary. We were told to find ways to put Merri in a 'frustration zone,' so she would have a chance to work her way through it. And that we needed to praise her efforts more than her outcomes." Mr. Campbell gestured to the list of questions before resting his hand on my shoulder. "I'm proud of your efforts here, Eliza. Whether or not you win, you've made something great."

"Thanks." I patted his hand and sat up. "But is Merri home? I need her and her laptop. And do you have any cardboard or poster board?" This was probably impossible, but I was going to try—and with their help, I might just pull it off.

"She's upstairs. You go get her, I'll fetch the display board and glue sticks." He paused. "Welcome back, cohost."

Lilly Campbell-Rhodes's headlights lit up my kitchen as she backed out of the driveway after dropping me off. They showed

Mom sitting at the table, her hands curled around an almost-empty mug of tea. "You're an hour late," she said.

"Sorry, I was working and lost track of time." She nodded like she understood. It probably helped that the things I carried supported my answer. I placed Merri's laptop and borrowed pairs of headphones on the table. "Mr. Campbell says you called to ask him about my friends."

"We contact George and Jennifer frequently. More frequently lately, since Nancy proved useless beyond reporting the most basic observations."

I took a step toward the table and a deep breath. "Ask me. Don't monitor my web searches or call my guardian or teachers or friends' parents. Ask *me*."

"Would you have told us?" Mom tilted her head. "About the boy?"

"Curtis," I corrected, dropping my bag to the floor with a thud, setting my new display board carefully beside it, because the glue was still wet. Apparently four hours at the Campbells' hadn't dulled my anger. "And possibly—if you hadn't also been sending me those 'studies' about the dangers of dating. Either you thought I wouldn't read them, or you thought I wouldn't understand their science is garbage. I'm not sure which is worse. If you don't trust me, why should I trust *you*?"

Mom lowered her head. "George suspected *something* was up. But he either didn't know the details or was keeping your confidence. He's so connected to his daughters. His knowledge of their lives—your life—is astonishing."

"Because he's *there*!" I curled my toes against the floor, craving the pounding of trails. "He carpools and volunteers in our classrooms. He listens. He shows up."

After four hours of brainstorming, cutting, pasting, and running to the store for more printer paper, Mr. Campbell was probably still wiping glitter off his kitchen floor. I'd just barely saved my poster from Merri's attempt at "bedazzling"—but since she'd spent the whole night helping me write and revise an abstract for the podcast project, I had zero complaints.

Post-movie, Rory had come in clutch with some drawings for the display board, and Lilly had left Haute Dog early to bring over snacks. Everyone had paused their plans to help me.

I waited for Mom to add an excuse about the "value of her time." Instead, she sniffed. "After Brazil, how could we possibly chaperone other people's children when we'd almost lost our own?"

There were no throw pillows in our house. No cozy couch blankets or plush carpets or kitschy cross-stitched samplers hanging on the walls. Nothing to absorb the magnitude of her revelation. It echoed in the empty spaces, in the cavernous distance between us.

"It's late." Mom and I turned to where Dad was standing in the kitchen doorway. "We have a big day tomorrow. I suggest we get to bed."

To bed. Not *some sleep*. Because maybe Dad knew none of us would.

39

The gymnasium where the Avery Science Competition was being held was chaos. The wooden floor was covered in rows of tables in various states of setup. And everywhere, students, display boards, crates of equipment and parents who were being shuffled to the side: *"Stop being so embarrassing, Mom." "Don't touch that, Dad. You'll ruin everything."*

My parents were sequestered somewhere, getting badges and instructions. It had been an awkward morning and a silent car ride. I'd spent it trying to process the significance and insecurity in Mom's words from last night. Trying *not* to think about Brazil.

They'd looked relieved when they'd dropped me off to set up while they'd checked in with the other judges. "Two hundred and eighty entrants," Mom had said. She'd looked a bit smug when she added, "It's a record for the Avery."

Dad's parting words had been a reminder: "We won't be judging you."

I'd snorted. "Well, that'll be a nice change."

Compared to the projects nearby, my setup was simple. I'd placed mine and Merri's laptops on my table, along with a couple pairs of headphones. That plus my display board and copies of my abstract were all I needed. My presentation was nonexistent. Everything I had to say was in the podcasts.

What I hadn't factored in was how nerve-racking it would be to *not* have anything to do. The other participants were interacting with people who'd stopped by their tables, rehearsing for the judges, answering questions. I was watching people in headphones listen to my recorded voice. It gave me plenty of time—too much time—to wonder where Curtis was and track the progress of the first group of judges.

Then it was my turn. Mom and Dad stood to the back, official scoring tablets lowered. "Well, we certainly know *this* candidate," Dad joked, and their three colleagues gave strained laughs. There were two more judges roaming individually, but they would focus on the finalists only after the initial five narrowed them down.

"If you're ready, Eliza, why don't you begin," encouraged Dr. Greene. I recognized her dark complexion and natural hair from photographs that accompanied the coverage of her cutting-edge research in gene splicing. She would've loved my pea plants.

I cleared my throat. "There are two hundred and eighty student scientists here today"—thank you, Mom, for that helpful fact—"and if any of us walked up to a stranger in a grocery store and attempted to explain our projects with all the technical language that is lauded here, we'd likely be met with blank stares and confusion. That's not good."

The judges glanced at one another, but I continued. "Science should be accessible. If we want people to get as excited about climate change as they once did about the space race, then we need to present it in ways that can be understood.

"When I think of my own relationship with science, my favorite memories are of times when I've shared it. Whether that's examining samples of glaciers with my parents, or explaining epigenetics to my best friend's dad, or analyzing riparian buffers while running trails with...a friend." I swallowed. "For my project I've created a science podcast that welcomes listeners of all backgrounds. It eliminates the technical lingo and explains concepts through anecdotes and allegories. You'll have to judge my success for yourselves by listening to any of the podcast episodes I've created. Headphones are there—and you can select from the topics listed on the screens."

I stepped back as three of the judges previewed the options on my laptop. Mom and Dad approached Merri's borrowed computer with wrinkled foreheads. "I thought she was..." Mom shook her head. "This seems like rather elementary science." Dad shh'd her. They were slower to choose an episode but faster to remove their headphones. They didn't meet my eyes.

Dr. Greene clicked Pause. "This project is difficult to evaluate with the Avery's criterion. We're limited to a few minutes per table."

That was her polite way of telling me not to expect a medal. I shrugged. "I understand, but this was the format that worked best for what I wanted to accomplish."

She smiled. "If you launch it publicly, please send me the link. I'd be happy to come on a future episode as a guest."

I nodded and told myself my parents weren't disappointed or unimpressed—they'd warned me they had to appear impartial. But when they moved with the other judges to the next table after offering me only a small nod, I retreated behind my display board to blink back tears.

"A podcast, really?" The voice from the other side of my board was deep and haughty. "Who'd have thought Gordon-Fergus would go twee and trendy...instead of, you know, *actual science*."

His remarks were met with a shrill laugh, and a female voice added, "Apparently the intelligence genes were not inherited."

"Seriously, if she were smart she would've done an iLive channel. Put on a tight shirt, worn some makeup. At least then I could've watched it on mute."

I hugged myself. I wished I'd worn my hair up or a baggier shirt, but I ground that thought between my teeth. I would not let these strangers make me feel small.

"Her last name is the only reason people pretend to think she's smart," the girl added. "But watch her still win because of nepotism and everyone's practically drooling on her parents."

"Like you're not? *'It's such an honor, Dr. Fergus…'*"

"Shut up!" she squeaked.

I peeked around the display board to see they were both wearing lanyards that designated them as Avery entrants. The girl was twirling a set of my headphones. "Think she's adopted? Because how did *they* produce Miss Teen Science Fair?"

I'd had enough. I stepped forward and cleared my throat. The girl dropped the headphones and the guy almost knocked over a laptop in his efforts to catch them. I stuck out my hand. "Hi, I'm Eliza Gordon-Fergus. I wanted to introduce myself since you were having so much fun talking about me." I flipped a strand of hair over my shoulder and upped my affect. "You must be, like, so smart to make superficial judgments about people you haven't met. Wow."

They looked at each other, trying to decide if I was for real.

I yanked my hand back and glared. "Seriously, though— 'judgmental jerk' isn't a good look. If you want to get anywhere in the *very small* science community, stop treating people like conquests or competitors and respect them as colleagues. Regardless of their gender or appearance or last name…because I'll remember yours."

The girl tried to sneer, but it looked like she was about to sneeze. The guy covered his name badge and stammered, "You're—you're not going to tell your parents, are you?"

I rolled my eyes and shook my head, walking away before they could. Enough standing around and waiting. It was time to find the boy who'd always seen *me*.

40

Excuse me." I stopped a passing Latinx girl. She was the second person I'd seen carrying a cupcake. "Where did you get that?"

"One row over. Look for a poster that says *Gluten Quest*. They're really good. The guy was cute and super nice. That's some science I'd happily get all over."

"Thanks." I was irrationally annoyed that she'd seen Curtis's appeal in a few minutes when it had taken me months. I hurried in the direction she'd indicated, arriving as the judges stepped up to his booth. Which was perfect. There was something delicious about watching him in his element—knowing he was too busy charming the fivesome to notice I was standing behind them with open admiration in my eyes.

He already had Dr. Greene laughing. "I can't wait to hear more. We're ready to begin."

"Someone seems to have confused 'science fair' with 'bake sale.'" These words stung worse than the ones I'd overheard about myself, because it was my father who'd faux-whispered them, my mother who'd laughed. The other judges did not.

Curtis's smile faltered, but he swallowed and began his presentation. "When I was two, my aunt Joan took me to the movies. She bought me Reese's Pieces, and while everyone else in the theater was focused on the screen, I was struggling to find a way to get oxygen in my lungs. This is how we learned I'm allergic to peanuts.

"I'm careful with food labels and carry an epinephrine injector, but because of this experience I'm interested in food sensitivities and safety. I'm grateful that many places, including this university, require everything that contains the top eight allergens—milk, eggs, fish, shellfish, tree nuts, peanuts, wheat, and soy—to be clearly marked.

"But sometimes products aren't labeled, and after reading about gluten in unexpected places like beauty products, Play-Doh, and even medications, I wanted to create something that would bring peace of mind to the estimated one percent of Americans—three million people—with gluten-sensitive enteropathy, aka celiac disease. Using an enzyme-linked immunosorbent assay—also known as an ELISA test"—his eyes sought mine for the briefest of moments, so clearly he *did* know I was here—"similar to what you'd find in a pregnancy test, I've devised a way to detect the presence of one of the main proteins that make up the gluten family. For today I've focused on gliadin—the prolamin found in wheat gluten—but this test could be replicated to screen for secalin and hordein, the prolamins in rye and barley too.

"For my test, you simply take a piece of your questionable item—in today's example, these cupcakes." Curtis's eyes flicked to my parents, and I wondered if he was thinking about the last time we'd shared a room with them and baked goods. His hand shook around the bulb syringe he was using in his demonstration. "Titrate a droplet of your resulting suspension onto the test strip. If it turns red, it indicates the presence of gliadin—which is the component of wheat gluten that helps baked goods rise."

The other judges leaned closer to see the test strip, but not my parents. They were frowning statues.

"If the test strip stays white, the item is free of wheat gluten." Curtis held up his—it was red. He flipped over the cupcake he'd used for the demo. The bottom of the wrapper read *Contains Gluten*. The other three judges applauded. One leaned in to ask a follow-up. I waited until Curtis was handing out cupcakes and test strips, then grabbed my parents by the wrist.

"Why aren't you by your table?" asked Mom.

"And why are you *here*?" added Dad, shooting another look over his shoulder at Curtis.

But Dad's glare had nothing on mine. I whisper-hissed, "You are being unspeakably rude and unprofessional."

"That boy broke your heart," Mom answered. "Did you think we hadn't noticed? Our bathroom shares a wall with yours, Eliza. You're still crying in the shower. I have no intention of being kind to him."

"That boy"—I gave up whispering, because sometimes shouting was necessary—"is brilliant. And kind. I deserved to have my heart broken for the way I treated him. But none of that matters right now...well, except for the brilliant part. Do you not understand the significance of what he created?"

"*If* it works," Dad muttered, but his ears were red and he'd dropped his chin.

"Then maybe you should be over there testing it with the other judges." I hesitated, then went a step further. "Or maybe recognize that you're not impartial and recuse yourselves."

"I think Eliza might be right." I hadn't noticed Dr. Greene joining us, but her words were gentle and she punctuated them with a bite of mini-cupcake. "She's wise beyond her years."

"Of course she is." Mom's face was as pale as Dad's was red. "I apologize. I didn't realize how difficult it would be to remain unbiased."

"It happens to the best of us," said a judge whose name I hadn't caught. "Just ask my son how badly I flubbed coaching his youth soccer team. He was *not* ready to be goalie."

"Yes, well, I'm not sure that's quite the same," Mom said, but Dad was nodding.

"I hope you'll still stay," said the last judge. "Many of these young scientists were excited to meet you. Maybe instead of judging, you could offer encouragement and positive feedback."

"We'd be happy to." Dad squeezed Mom's hand before she could respond. "Thank you for understanding. I hope this doesn't put you in a bind."

Soccer judge shook his head and tapped through some functions on his tablet. "It's no problem to recalibrate scores with a smaller judging pool. I'm just sorry you made such a long trip for no reason."

"Not for no reason." It was Mom who spoke, but they both looked at me as they handed in their tablets and shook hands.

"We need to get back on schedule." Dr. Greene eyed the curious onlookers starting to gather. "But let's catch up at the reception."

The remaining three judges moved to the left as my parents headed down the aisle to the right. Which left me facing Curtis. The only things between us were the table with his project and the stream of people pausing to interact with his cupcake display.

"I'm sorry," I said.

He shrugged. "I won't hold you responsible for their anger, if you won't blame me for Win and Wink's—they're around somewhere and Wink's on a vengeance mission. Win's here under duress."

"Noted." I wrung my hands together and wished I had Anne Shirley's gift for words and flowery apologies. "But I meant sorry for *me*, not them."

"I like cupcakes! Can I have one?"

Curtis shrugged in my direction. "Thanks, I guess, but I need to focus on this." He turned from me to the parent-child duo standing in front of his booth. I left while he was flipping over the cupcake to show the white *Gluten-Free* label on its bottom.

Embarrassment wasn't hereditary—not passed down like detached earlobes or the ability to curl your tongue—but that didn't stop me from keenly experiencing my parents'. They'd resigned as judges, but I had to stand at my table for another four hours and hope people didn't ask me about it—though I knew they would. I walked reluctantly back to my row but perked up when I saw a familiar person standing at my table with headphones atop her red hair.

Ms. Gregoire removed them as I approached. "I wondered where you'd gone. Not crossing roof ridgepoles or buying hair dye from peddlers, I hope."

I laughed and decided to take the book references as encouragement, even though the bet was clearly lost. "I make plenty of mistakes—hence my momentary detour into a project that was pea plants, not podcasts—but I'm not interesting enough to make them like Anne Shirley."

"I don't know about that." Ms. Gregoire grinned. "This podcast is incredible, and there are bound to be some rather amazing adventures in your future, Eliza. I just hope I get to be your teacher while they unfold."

"Are you going somewhere?" My throat tightened at the thought.

"No. *I* have no plans to leave Hero High."

For a brief moment I had the urge to make an Anne-level gushy declaration of appreciation. Luckily I was spared by Ms. Gregoire pointing to my display. "Now tell me about this. I hear you had a most demanding adviser."

I laughed. "She was everything I needed her to be."

"I also heard your adviser is wonderfully impressed by what you've created. The bridge between science and story hasn't been this well constructed in a very long time. It's marvelous."

"Oh, that's all due to my English teacher. She's forever insisting we apply our experiences to the books we're reading. So it felt natural to use personal reactions and anecdotes when trying to explain science concepts."

Ms. Gregoire's smile was brighter than any of the medals I wouldn't be getting. "I'm sure that teacher would be flattered to have helped."

"I hope so." I wanted to find a way to compare her to Anne's beloved Miss Stacy, but the sentiments were lodged beneath the gratitude in my throat.

But maybe she understood my unsaid feelings, because she added, "I spy your parents over there—I have to go tell them how 'bright and diligent' you are." I gaped, recalling that those were the exact words Miss Stacy used to describe Anne.

Ms. Gregoire laughed and left me with a wink and one more quote from the end of Anne's first novel. "Remember, Eliza, '*I don't know what lies around the bend, but I'm going to believe that the best does.*'"

It was Ms. Gregoire's fault I couldn't stop thinking about Anne as my parents hurried me through packing up my laptops, head-phones, and display board.

They'd wanted to leave as soon as the winners were announced, but I wanted my Gilbert moment. Well, I wanted a lot of different Gilbert moments, and mostly I wanted to play the Anne role in scenes where she and Gilbert were in love. But the Gilbert moment I wanted at the Avery was the one where Anne acknowledges her competition with him is no longer about beating him but about having a "worthy foeman"—and that "Next to trying and winning, the best thing is trying and failing."

Because I felt nothing but happiness for Curtis. He deserved his second place and the chance to go to the International Science and Engineering Fair. He'd need the prize money—especially if Win and Wink transferred to Hero High next year—and he'd accomplished something amazing.

I was proud of him. I needed him to know that.

Toting my bin of supplies, I went to find my parents. They were where I'd sent them when their efforts to "help" had tan-gled my cords—standing in front of the presentation they'd shortchanged earlier, reading his research.

"Eliza, it's time to go," said Dad.

"Just a minute." Curtis's table was covered in cupcake wrap-pers and test strips, but he was being mobbed with congratula-tions and hadn't made it back yet.

"Now," Mom snapped. "We're no longer judges, you didn't win. We're leaving before the awards banquet starts and it's con-spicuous. I've hit my embarrassment quota for the day."

"Just—" I snatched an abstract from my bin and flipped it over. I could hear Dad's shoe tapping and Mom muttering. I ignored them and scrawled a few sentences, then tucked it under his display.

Congratulations, Cupcake. You deserve this. I can't wait to see what you do with *Green Gables* and at ISEF.

41

After a silent car ride home I escaped to my room and pulled two things out of my desk drawer: *Frankenstein* and a highlighter. I had a week to finish this book and figure out what to write—might as well get started.

A half hour later there was a knock on my door. Mom leaned in. "I made you a sandwich."

"Thanks. Can you put it on my desk? I'm not hungry."

She did but then sat down in the chair. "Have you thought about what to do with your podcast? It would be a shame to let that effort go unrecognized."

I closed the book. "You hated the podcast."

"We didn't. It was a surprise." She looked down at her hands. "It's possible we'd peeked at your materials in the lab and had been expecting genomic editing."

I lifted my chin. "I liked explaining CRISPR more than using it."

Mom took a bite of sandwich, apparently forgetting it was mine. "Well, we look forward to listening to your episodes."

"You don't have to—as you pointed out, it's very 'elementary science.'"

"We'll be listening to hear *you*, not to learn."

I scowled down at my bed. "You said you'd hit your 'embarrassment quota' because I didn't win."

"No." Mom laughed bitterly. "The embarrassment piece was all on us. You were right to call us unprofessional. Last night we swore we'd be unbiased—but...I'd cast Curtis as a cupcake-wielding villain. I saw his project and it was impossible to be objective." She rubbed her forehead. "I'm sorry. You should know I've written an apology note and have a bakery delivering cupcakes tomorrow—though he's probably sick of them."

I fought a grin. "Don't worry, Curtis will *never* be sick of cupcakes."

"I'm glad." Mom pointed at me. "But that's not why I came in here. I wanted to talk professional names. Have you given any thought to what you'll use if you publish the podcast, or moving forward in general?"

"What do you mean?" I was trying to wrap my head around my parents wanting to spend time listening to me explain things they already knew. Also, *cupcakes?* I wished I could see Curtis's face when they were delivered. Or read their note. Not that I expected notes to change anything—not mine on his table, or their apology. I sighed.

"How about E. Gordon-Fergus? Initials aren't gendered and that might serve you better. Peer review of articles by women get harsher criticism. You know this. You've seen how often my accomplishments have been subverted into your father's. We have to push back to have me listed first on dual publications."

I heard what she was saying. I'd seen blatant examples of it at the Avery. But still, I shook my head. "My first name is *mine*."

Mom looked at me like I was a toddler who'd just discovered that four-letter word, but I didn't know how to express it more clearly. My appearance was a threat. My intelligence was a threat. My last name—it was theirs. It came preloaded with people's expectations. My first name—that belonged to me. Sometimes it felt like the only thing that did, the only part of my identity that wasn't a minefield.

But now I was expected to sacrifice that? "When do we stop changing our behavior and start changing society?"

Mom sat back in her chair. "You are so much wiser than I was at your age."

"You skipped grades and had all those awards already."

"But you know who you are. You've got a sense of self and purpose, of what you want from this world. That came from *you*. We weren't here to help mold it."

I looked down at the book, the monster on its cover. I had no idea who I was. Didn't they see I was lost and lonely?

"Warner, come in here, please," Mom called. "It's time."

Her ominous words made my head shoot up as Dad entered with a gift bag in his hands. "We're doing this now?" He waited for her nod before turning to me. "We're proud of what you've taken on alone, Eliza. Not just the podcast, but everything. Your teachers speak highly of you and believe you're capable of independent study."

"Independent study?" I was staring at the bag. We didn't do gifts. Certainly not ones with wrapping paper. They'd brought me South Pole Station–branded pencils and a hat at Christmas, but handed them to me directly from their suitcases. It wasn't like they'd had chances to shop—and it wasn't like I knew what they wanted.

Mom cleared her throat. "When I was gestating there were so many helpful books that detailed the stages of your fetal growth by week. But then after you were born…Parenting books lack consensus. None of them are empirical. They couldn't tell us what it meant that your first word was 'go' or why you threw a tantrum in the grocery store. The advice on how to get babies to sleep was contradictory. Everything was full of caveats that this recommendation or schedule or advice might not work."

Dad chuckled. "We knew the mechanics—recommended amount of sleep and milk and 'back is best' and what temperature to keep your room, black and white contrast toys for brain stimulation, and duration of 'tummy time'—but you weren't compliant. You rolled early and slept on your stomach. You were hungry after I fed you a six-ounce bottle. You refused to adhere to your nap schedule, but fell asleep every time you were in a car. Tummy time made you spit up all over the black and white toys you ignored."

I'd never heard any of these stories, and I clutched each like a treasure. "What did you do?"

"We threw out the books and decided we were highly educated people who would parent our own way. We eschewed the raised eyebrows and comments about 'stability' and 'consistency'—and brought you with us to Iceland, then New Guinea, Peru, etc. We thought it was for the best."

"Until it wasn't," I said.

"You're older now—Brazil...it was an anomaly," said Dad.

"No," Mom interrupted. "It was a mistake." I cringed and she clarified, "*Our* mistake. You were young and curious, sick of being trapped in a lab. Of course you were going to wander off at some point. We should have known—and we should've noticed faster."

I ground my teeth against the memory of being lost and scared and possibly almost abducted. I hadn't understood Portuguese. I'd never learned what the old woman who'd rescued me had yelled at the man who'd been following me in his car, but whatever she'd said, it had scared him away. Then she'd called the police and begun the process that had ended with me being reunited with my parents and us on a flight to Pennsylvania. It was the second-worst day of my life. The worst was a month later, when they'd gotten on a plane back to São Paulo without me.

"You're not that little girl anymore," Dad said.

"And we're better listeners now," Mom added. "At least we're trying to be. Sometimes you have to be blunt with us—like in that letter you wrote on the airplane: *'If you love me, you won't make me go on any more trips. I just want a home.'*" She shut her eyes, like the scared words I didn't remember writing still hurt, eight years later. "What you've typed in your emails lately about missing being a family. We've heard you."

"I appreciate that." I sounded stiff, because I wasn't sure what they were building to, but clearly whatever was in that gift bag wasn't going to be a tourist trinket.

"We want you to come with us again," Dad said.

"Where?" I was making myself dizzy looking from one to the other—they were smiling, but clearly I'd missed a step between baby books and Brazil and whatever was currently being offered.

"South Pole Station," Mom said. "I know it's anomalous, but we've thrown our weight behind it and thankfully we've got some friends in high places at the NSF."

I kinda loved the idea of Mom and Dad having the National Science Foundation on speed dial. I kinda hoped someday I would too.

"You'll technically be classified as part of our 'research team,' but you'll do your high school classwork first. We'll have to move quickly though—it's getting close to sunset and there are only a few weeks and flights before we hunker down to 'winter-over.' You'll need to take a cold-weather survival course when we get there—and there are rules. I've got a field manual and participation guide for you along with the gear we've started to collect." Mom poked Dad's leg. "Give her the bag."

It contained a binder full of papers and a pair of high-tech gloves. I set these on my bed.

"There's more in the basement. I'll bring it up," Dad said.

"'Try everything on." Mom leaned forward in her chair. "We'll make a list of whatever doesn't fit. We've set up an appointment for a comprehensive physical tomorrow, and your dentist is going to rush that mouth guard. You'll need to do an interview with the NSF—it's a formality, but they're bending rules for us, so be agreeable. I've got at least a dozen more items on the list to check off before Tuesday."

"*This* Tuesday?" I tugged on the left glove. It felt oversized and clumsy when I tried to open the binder.

"Did you miss the part about winter and flights? The last plane in or out is in two and a half weeks." Mom pointed to the binder. "There's a lot of information to absorb, but we've got layovers in Los Angeles, Sydney, Christchuch, and McMurdo—you'll have plenty of time to read on planes."

"You want me to come?" I couldn't make my brain process this. "But I didn't win today."

"What does one have to do with the other?" Mom asked. "I'm not seeing causality here. Do you, Warner?"

He shook his head.

"Never mind. It's just—" I paused and looked at their eager faces, at the table of contents in front of me—*United States Antarctic Program* emblazoned above the NSF logo. "I'm overwhelmed. Most scientists wait their whole life for this sort of opportunity. I never thought at sixteen…"

"Luckily your parents have some clout." Dad laughed.

I winced. This time, when people accused me of nepotism, they'd be correct. But was that a reason to reject the opportunity to be with them? No way.

"So, are you excited?" he asked.

Was I? Absolutely. But also flabbergasted and reeling. "Still taking it all in."

"I'm noticing you haven't said yes yet." Mom looked like *she* might be grinding her teeth as she waited for my answer. "We really want you with us, Eliza."

"You do?" Before Brazil, we'd had fun. It hadn't all been labs. I'd learned to ski on Icelandic glaciers, them patient and teasing. I remember splashing in the thermal pools after they'd taken water samples. Chasing one another down the beach as we measured sand dunes on Prince Edward Island. Their explaining the chemical processes of dye as we watched the weavers in Peru.

Brazil had been a fluke—and a collective mistake. I'd known I wasn't allowed to leave the lab without permission. And afterward...*I* had been the one who'd asked not to travel. They'd respected that request. Just like now, when they'd gone to so much trouble to include me after reading my emails about wanting us to be a family.

Their anxious faces split into grins as I affirmed my decision out loud. "Yes, I want to come with you."

They hugged me—a rarity that made us all slightly uncomfortable—then Dad lugged up a crate of brand-new gear. *My* gear. He also returned my computer and phones. "Might as well enjoy these while you can—you're not grounded anymore."

They left me to try stuff on, but my thoughts snagged on Dad's words. In a way, wasn't my time at South Pole Station going to be its own type of grounding? I'd have restrictions on where I could go, I wouldn't have a cell phone, internet access would be limited. I shook off that interpretation—the experiences I'd gain would more than make up for it.

I pulled out a parka and waterproof pants. There were multiple pairs of long underwear—silk and Merino wool—plus socks, gloves, gaiters, hats, mirrored sunglasses, ski goggles. But after trading my wrinkled dress pants for a pair of blue wool long johns, I didn't move to try on the rest. *I was going to Antarctica.* And if the few pages of the binder I'd flipped through were any indication, life there would be simple, ordered, scheduled, logical. Meal times, laundry times, two-minute showers twice a week. No Curtis. No worries about dating or subtext in conversations. No stressing about friendships and if I was taking too much of Merri's time. No more classes, or the adrenaline rush of quiz bowl. No pressure to do something with the podcast. No more creepy guys at the grocery store. No temptations or cupcakes or romance...

My stomach twisted. Probably from hunger, since I'd barely touched lunch at the Avery, but looking at Mom's sandwich made me queasy. I put down the binder and picked up my phone, because before I did anything else, there was someone I needed to tell.

42

The phone rang once. Merri answered with "How is he?" before I had a chance to say hello.

"How is who?" I should've written out a script. Figured out the words I'd use to convince her my going with my parents was positive.

"You're calling from the hospital, right? It's been killing me not to bug you. Fielding took my phone away and has been holding it until you called. I asked him to, but still. How's Curtis?"

I wanted to ask *What?*, but she wouldn't lie about this, so I skipped to the vital question: "*Why* is Curtis at the hospital?"

"He—" Merri faltered. "He had an allergic reaction at the science fair reception. Weren't you there? They had to EpiPen and rush him out. I thought you'd gone with him..."

The reception was hours ago. *Hours.* "Is he under Montgomery or Curtis? Never mind, I can ask for both. Which hospital?"

I heard her ask Fielding, but he took the phone to answer directly. "Mercy General. Want me to pick you up?"

"No, I'm fine." It was such a bad lie and I couldn't care. I ended the call and charged out of my room.

"So, what doesn't fit?" Mom already had a pen poised above a notepad.

I stared blankly. "Curtis is in the hospital."

Dad set down his mug. "Is he okay?"

"He's allergic to peanuts." It wasn't an answer, but it was all I knew. "I'm going."

"But—" Mom tapped the pad. "We don't have time—"

Dad tossed me the car keys. "Drive safe. Call us if..." He shrugged. "Call us if there's a situation where George Campbell would want his daughters to call him."

I nodded numbly.

"Wait. Coat." He grabbed mine from the closet and handed it over with a squeeze of my arm. "I hope he's okay."

I called "Me too!" over my shoulder as I tossed the coat onto the passenger seat. I was backing out of the driveway when my phone rang. "Hello?"

"Hey, it's, uh, Lance. Merri called and told me some stuff. I owe you an apology."

"That doesn't matter right now, and you weren't wrong." I hit my blinker.

"Right, well, I'm calling because Merri said you were going to visit Curtis. He got discharged an hour ago. Go to his house, not the hospital."

"Oh." While I was glad he'd been sent home and for the health things that connoted, going to his house felt a lot more intimidating than an ER. "He's probably sleeping then."

"You should go over. He'll want to see you."

"Okay." But my hand trembled as I did a three-point turn in the Karbieners' driveway. "Thanks."

"Tell him I'll stop by tomorrow, and I say congrats on the science-medal thing. Oh, I heard yours was great too."

"His was better," I admitted.

"I'm telling him you said that. Not that he'll believe me."

Two minutes after I hung up with Lance, I pulled into Curtis's driveway. That's when I realized I was still wearing my left glove. Plus the button-down shirt I'd worn to the Avery and a pair of baby-blue long johns. For shoes, dressy loafers. Well, Curtis had said he liked me for more than my looks; here was his chance to prove it. Though I was leaving the glove in the car.

Wink answered the door. Her hair was twisted into a messy knot on the top of her head and her tired expression sharpened. "Nice of you to stop by."

"*Wink!*" She'd only opened the door a few inches, so I couldn't see Win, but his voice carried all sorts of warnings.

"Sorry. That wasn't as sarcastic as it sounded." She swung the door wide and pulled me in. "You try spending four hours in the ER with Win and not have him rub off on you."

"I think I'll pass."

"Curtis will be glad you're here." She paired this with a tentative smile. "My parents are in with him. I'll go tell them."

I turned to Win. He was slumped at the table, a bowl of cereal that he was stirring into soggy glop in front of him. "I'm the one who got him that plate of dessert." His shoulders were up, like he was bracing for attack. "He was so busy being congratulated or whatever. I thought maybe if I fed him, we could move it along and leave."

"It wasn't marked." I looked over to where Mr. and Mrs. Cavendish had emerged from the hallway. Win's dad crossed the room to sit beside his son and put a hand on his back. "Allergens were supposed to be marked. You couldn't have known."

"Yeah, but—" Win's chin quivered, and I turned away from the table to give him privacy.

His mom was behind me, wringing her hands and shifting her weight like she wasn't sure which of her sons needed her more.

"May I see Curtis?" I asked. "Please."

"Yes!" The raspy answer came from the first room off the hallway and made his mom smile.

"I was going to ask you to come back tomorrow, but he bargained hard for a short visit." She rubbed her forehead. "Please don't tire him out."

"I won't." I held up my hand like I was making some sort of vow, then ducked past her before she could change her mind.

I'd never been in the boys' bedroom, but I didn't pause to take in the décor. The only thing I cared about was locating Curtis. He was propped on pillows in the twin bed by the window. Shirtless—but instead of muscles, I focused on the blotchy hives on his chest, the bandage from an IV on his arm. His lips were swollen, his eyes shadowed with fatigue.

I stopped inside the door and squeaked the word "Hi" in a small, uncertain voice.

"If you came to admire my medal, it's on my dresser. Bring it over here and I'll model it while you congratulate me."

"Yeah, that's not going to happen." I snorted nervously. "I came to see if you were okay."

"Ah, is this like when Gilbert gets sick with typhoid fever? Did you suddenly realize you cared 'cause I might die?"

"You know I care—but you're not dying." I narrowed my eyes, like I could glare away any secondary reactions or spot their symptoms before he suffered. I wondered if his parents were taking time-lapse photographs of his hives. "The hospital wouldn't have released you if—"

He held up a hand, and it stopped my outward gruffness and inner panic. "Firebug, I'm fine."

My eyes itched, but I nodded. He wouldn't lie to me. He hadn't ever lied to me.

"Anyway, since it's my big victory and you won't let me wear my medal, should we keep going with these post-typhoid scenes from *Anne of the Island*? How about when Gilbert brings up that he proposed to Anne two years ago, and asks if her answer has changed." Curtis pushed up on his elbows, the pillow slipping from behind his head to land at his lower back. "If I re-asked you my question from last week, would *you* give the same response?"

I turned to his dresser and picked up the medal. I couldn't see it through blurry eyes but traced trembling fingers over the engravings. I couldn't have both—Curtis *and* Antarctica. There wasn't time for a "real" date before we left on Tuesday.

"That's not my favorite book in the series. Too much talk of weddings and far too many proposals." I set the medal down and smoothed the ribbon. "It doesn't matter though; I'll be writing about *Frankenstein*." *If* I decided to do a paper; I'd be gone before Friday's due date. But Mary Shelley's novel didn't bother me anymore. My parents were taking me with them, which proved I was more Anne than creature.

"Eliza, *Green Gables* is *your* story." His voice was hoarse, and he paused to sip some water. "I just like teasing you."

I shook my head. "We had a deal. You won."

He shrugged. "I picked a different book. Already turned in my project. *Anne's* yours if you want it."

I took a step toward him. "Why?"

He ducked his head. "I couldn't think about Anne without thinking of you—and that *hurt*. I needed to do a different book as much as I think you *need* to do this one. But since the bet was off, I didn't do *Frankenstein* either."

He'd been hurting. I hated that, and hated myself for being relieved I hadn't been the only one feeling that way. I looked around the mildly messy half of his room for the answer. "What book did you do?"

"Not telling. You'll have to wait and find out with the rest of the class." His smirk lacked its usual swagger—instead of making me want to pinch him, I wanted to check his pulse, tuck him in, pass him more water.

It wasn't the right time to announce my departure, and if that meant not knowing, then maybe guessing titles was the type of puzzle that would keep me busy on sleepless hours in subfreezing temperatures.

"You should start thinking of new wagers, because I'm going to beat you again next year, and I want bigger stakes." He shifted, this time to lie back—but that pillow wasn't in the right spot. He winced, and I darted past Win's bed, which clearly doubled as a laundry hamper, to kneel beside Curtis.

I hadn't realized I'd needed an excuse to touch him until I had one and couldn't stop. I fixed the pillow, then brushed his hair off his forehead and traced a finger around his jaw. My caresses were soft, but my words were hard. "Do you think next year you can manage to celebrate in ways that are less potentially fatal?"

"There's my firebug." He grinned and covered my hand with his. "Though it's really not my fault. Who puts peanut butter in Rice Krispie Treats? That's unnatural."

"I don't know, but when I find out..." I let the threat hang because I couldn't think of a consequence big enough, and I didn't want to picture what had happened—EpiPens, IVs, blood

308 | TIFFANY SCHMIDT

oxygen levels, steroids. He'd been suffering while I'd been trying on socks and reading about crevasse safety.

If this allergy scare happened two weeks from now, I'd find out after the fact via email. If at all. I'd be the one begging for anecdotes and data to try and reconstruct everything I'd missed. I wouldn't know where Curtis went for runs and how the woods changed with the seasons. Or what the Lunch Bunch was up to. Merri was waiting for me to get home and call her; in a week, I couldn't.

Curtis dropped my hand. "But seriously, where do we stand— you, me, your parents? They aren't big fans of me or cupcakes— but I heard *you* stand up for me."

"Yes, I did." I'd also grilled my parents on what they thought after reevaluating his project. They'd begrudgingly admitted it was "impressive" and his medal was "merited." That was still several levels below a glowing endorsement, but add in the forthcoming apology note and baked goods and it was a start.

"Don't you see how arbitrary their rules are?" Curtis asked. "I did some research. I can send you science that says the exact opposite of what they told you—that healthy teen relationships teach valuable social skills and coping mechanisms."

"I know." I looked at him through lowered lashes. "And it's seriously attractive that you looked up the science of dating."

"Don't play with me, Eliza."

"I'm not." I stroked the hair off his forehead again and fought the urge to call out an excuse: *"You had a fuzz."* I could invent a whole blanket's worth of lint to keep doing it—or simply tell him the truth. "You make me want to be irrational, illogical, emotional."

He slid a hand up to cup my elbow, pull me closer. "Even if it's a weakness?"

"It's not. I was wrong; you make me stronger, better. Happier."
Merri did too. She made me more compassionate, more creative.
And being in classes with my peers had taught me patience and
forced me to broaden my focus and consider others' perspectives.

No doubt there'd be so much to learn at South Pole Station—
people with diverse backgrounds and expertise, but...they
weren't *my* people. My Lunch Bunch. I clutched the corner of his
bed, all too aware that when I got home I wouldn't be able to climb
under my covers and hide—because my parents would be waiting
and my comforter was buried beneath gear and paperwork.

Curtis was beaming up at me. I narrowed my eyes. "Don't let
it go to your head."

He laughed. "Can I at least have a mutant pea plant?
Please." He made prayer hands and puppy dog eyes. "I want a
glow-in-the-dark plant—you know how I feel about bioluminescence, Firebug."

I rolled my eyes when he waggled his eyebrows. "That can
be arranged."

He fist-pumped. "Yes! But why did you change projects?
When do I get to be a guest on your podcast? And...what are you
wearing? That's quite the outfit."

He gestured for me to spin around, and I smacked his arm.
"Long story."

But a more important one bubbled up beneath my skin. It
was about a girl with no parents—hers had been scared they'd
mess up, so they'd run away. And now she was facing the boy
she liked most in the world, and he was asking her for the thing
she feared most: to be vulnerable. She was thinking of running
scared too.

But what if I didn't? What if I stayed? What if I tested
that boy's theory that sometimes it's okay to make mistakes,

sometimes it's okay to be uncomfortable? It means you're trying and learning.

I leaned down and kissed him. Really just a grazing of my lips against his—an exchange of breath and tingle. I didn't know if it was a goodbye or a new beginning. But it was a promise either way.

The knock against the doorframe was brusque, and Win's voice chased it. "Remember other people have to sleep in here, so don't get gross. Also, Mom said to tell you, 'Time's up.'"

The words felt too real, too true. So before I stood and obeyed, I leaned down to kiss him again. "Rest up, Cupcake."

Win walked in as I slipped out, his eyes red and penitent. "Hey."

"Hey," Curtis echoed, then grinned mischievously. "My medal's on my dresser. If you bring it over, I'll model it for you."

I grinned as I glanced over my shoulder. Unsurprisingly Win had skipped the medal.

He'd gone straight for a fierce hug instead.

43

Mom and Dad were waiting in the kitchen. She looked up from her laptop, and he set down a half-finished apple. "How is he?"

"He'll be okay." I hung up my coat and joined them at the table.

"I'm glad," Mom said. "I realize Curtis is important to you, and—"

"Before I left, you told me I didn't 'have time' for this." The comment still burned.

"I shouldn't have said that." Mom looked at the blank screen of her laptop. "I tend to hyper-focus and don't always have facileness when switching mental gears."

I didn't either. Especially when it was to acknowledge something or someone who got in the way of my goals. Adults—my parents, teachers—had always praised me for my ability to ignore distractions, but they were wrong. *I'd* been wrong. The evidence of that was how everyone—from Lance to each member of Curtis's family—had praised me for *showing up*. Because they hadn't expected me to. Because by being there, I'd made them feel better.

That changed tonight. I wanted people to have different expectations for me. The type that made me a good person, not just a smart one. I lifted my chin. "I will always have time for the people I care about." Like the Campbells had for me last night. Their names hadn't been listed beside mine on my Avery abstract, but they might as well have been. It was a team effort—I couldn't have done it alone.

"That's a kind goal but maybe not a practical one," Dad said gently. "Antarctica's going to make that tricky."

Mom pressed her lips together. "It's a nice sentiment, and tonight I was wrong, but there will be times I tell you no and mean it."

"I know. But I'm not always going to listen." Before they could look at each other or call Mr. Campbell and ask if this was a "typical teenage rebellion," I clarified. "I can't be what you want me to be a hundred percent of the time. Anne wasn't who Matthew and Marilla wanted her to be either. At least not at first. But she refused to change her identity for them—and they learned to love her for who she was. And no offense to Gregor Mendel, but I'm podcast, not pea plants."

"Who's Anne?" asked Dad, while Mom said, "I don't know any of these people—well, besides Mendel, obviously—and I'm not sure how they're relevant."

"*Anne of Green Gables.* It's a book. Read it later if you want, but I need you to *hear me* now. I don't want to be your project. I want to be your daughter. I want autonomy to make my own choices and learn from my mistakes. Stay up too late and yawn through class, eat too much junk food and get a stomachache. Watch ridiculous TV shows and scoff at the things they get wrong."

"Why would you want to do any of that?" Mom asked. "It sounds horrible."

"But if I never get to experience them, how will I discover what I do and don't like, or learn my limits? How will I get to know myself if I'm never allowed any self-exploration?"

"And that boy, Curtis—he fits in this schema?" Dad was spinning his apple on the tabletop. "Romantically?"

"Maybe—No, that's a lie. Yes, he does."

"But he hurt you," Mom said. "Despite this, you want to experience more heartbreak?"

"I want the chance to try and avoid it."

"High school relationships rarely last," Dad said. "Statistically—"

"I'm not a statistic. I'm a person. I'm *your* daughter. Maybe Curtis and I can overcome statistics, or maybe we won't want to. We could date for a week, or a year, or a lifetime. We could grow apart or want different things or decide to be friends or have a devastating breakup. But any of those options sounds better than not knowing."

"Long-distance relationships don't have great odds either." Dad sighed. "But you're not coming with us, are you?"

I shook my head.

"You're choosing a future with romantic breakups over scientific breakthroughs." Mom shut her laptop so she could lean forward and study me, disapproval all over her face. "You're choosing a boy over family."

Merri would've admired the poetry in those statements, but I shook my head. "It's not about him. It's about *me*. I'm choosing myself. I want to see where things go—with Curtis, with school, with friendships, with interests. If I have a breakup—it won't break me. For every flawed study you've sent me about the risks of teenage relationships, I can counter with an experiential anecdote—" Sera reaching for Hannah's hand before an oral presentation. Toby signing up to perform a piece inspired by Rory at the spring concert. Fielding smiling and laughing while the melting dregs of Merri's snowball dripped from his mussed hair. They were happier people—better people—because of their partners. Not that anyone needed a romantic partner to be complete, but it wasn't a barrier to self-actualization either. "I've been *your* experiment for so long. Now it's my turn."

Mom pressed her hand to her mouth; Dad slumped back in his chair. I tensed for their response.

"Do you comprehend the effort we've put into getting you clearances or the exceptions that have been made for you?" Mom asked. "If you come with us, you could be part of something extraordinary—it will be a stepping-stone to your future success. You're trading that for *high school*?"

"I don't need to be extraordinary." I flattened my hands on the table to keep them from shaking. "Our definitions of a successful life don't match. I need to figure out who I *am* before I figure out what I want."

"Your mom and I can't stay." Dad's voice was quiet as he tossed his apple into the bucket for compost. "We've made commitments—"

"I know. I'm not asking you to. I want to know about your life at South Pole Station, but mine is *here*."

"I see." Mom's eyes were glassy. "Well, if that's your choice..."

"Are you angry?" I wasn't sure I wanted to hear their answer, but if I didn't ask, the question would haunt me.

"No!" I was grateful Dad replied first, because Mom looked less certain. "You've got a life here—we were asking a lot, for you to give that up to be with us..."

"Even though we weren't willing to make that same sacrifice for you," Mom finished with a sigh and dabbed at her eyes. "But I'm not okay with things reverting to how they were before—reports and clinical conversations. I want to know what's going on in your life."

"Good, because I'm done with logs." I stripped off my iLive band and made a show of dropping it on the counter. "I want you to know me."

"There's one problem," Dad added. "We fired Nancy."

"That's okay." I looked around our showroom kitchen with a schemer's grin. I wouldn't miss it.

"You're a minor," Mom stated. "Nancy may have been dull as paste, but you need a guardian."

I held up a hand to stop her. "Just listen. I have an idea..."

44

You didn't pack your passport or tickets, did you?"

This was the third time Mom asked, so I held up my phone. "My tickets are on here, and my passport is in my carry-on, next to my gear crate, which are waiting in the car."

"Oh, good." Mom checked her pocket for her own passport. I'd forgotten she was a nervous traveler. She got motion sickness too—I used to refuse to sit next to her on small planes or boats.

Dad's method for dealing with her panic was to ignore it. He calmly took a sip from a mug shaped like a poodle and said, "We haven't decided if we're going to rent the house or hire a caretaker. It's temporary, you know."

Mr. Campbell nodded, and Mrs. Campbell offered my mother a refill on her water.

She demurred. "We'll likely be back in mid-November, but I can't give you a precise date because it's dependent on our research and the weather."

"Don't worry," Mr. Campbell said. "We'll be fine. I'll pick Eliza up from the airport in a few weeks and keep her safe as houses until you're back. Jennifer and I are happy to have her."

"She feels like one of ours already." Mrs. Campbell hugged me, but I didn't miss how her comment had tightened my parents' expressions. They'd been taken aback by how readily and eagerly the Campbell family had accepted my proposal that I move in with them after an early-spring-break trip to see South Pole Station and eke out a little more time with my parents.

Even three days later, five hours before we began our multi-day journey, my parents had paused on the Campbells' front step to ask, "You're not going to call them 'Mom' and 'Dad' or anything like that, are you?"

And sitting in this kitchen, not twenty minutes after I'd reassured them I wouldn't, they visibly relaxed as I stepped out of Mrs. Campbell's hug and crossed to stand behind their chairs.

"A little help out here?" Merri demanded from the doorway. She was balancing her school bag with a box she must have snagged from the car parked in her driveway. She dropped both on the foyer floor and grinned at me. "First, you skip school. Then, you don't even help move your stuff? I hope you're not going to be a diva houseguest."

"Why don't you girls bring Eliza's things in?" Mr. Campbell suggested. "We'll order pizza for dinner before the Gordon-Ferguses leave for the airport."

I started to follow Merri outside but paused in the foyer. "She won't be any trouble," Mrs. Campbell was reassuring my parents. "She never is."

"I know I'm biased," Mom answered slowly, "but I truly think Eliza is remarkable. Do you ever look at your daughters and swell with pride and think, 'How did I make that amazing human?'"

Biting back a grin, I stepped out the front door and almost stumbled off the step when a barrage of voices yelled, "Surprise!"

I laughed around the hand I'd clasped to my mouth. Fielding, Sera, Hannah, Toby, Rory, Lance, Win, Wink, and Curtis stood around my car with bags and boxes in their hands.

"What are you all doing here?" I asked.

"Helping you move," said Lance. "Though I thought you'd have more stuff. This is only going to take five minutes."

"My dad's ordering pizzas," Merri offered. Lance shifted the box he was holding to give her a thumbs-up.

"Personally, I thought I'd come stare at you a bit." Curtis peeled himself off the passenger side of my car. His hands, I noticed, were empty. His lack of helping had nothing to do with any lingering maladies—he'd been fine when we'd gone running yesterday. "In case you get frostbite and your nose rots off, or you fall in love with some research project and decide not to come back."

"We should be so lucky," said Toby. He raised his hands and added "Kidding!" even before Rory elbowed him.

Merri and I exchanged glances—she was the only one who knew that'd almost come true.

"So, Eliza Marie Gordon-Fergus, I have something middle-name serious to ask you."

Personally, I wanted to ask Curtis where he'd learned my middle name. Instead I waited for the wink or flicker at the side of his mouth that meant he was trying not to grin. But his expression was earnest and focused; he was ignoring or oblivious to the way our friends were disconcerted, Sera and Hannah cutting off their conversation midsentence and Toby and Wink putting down boxes to watch.

The attention prickled at my spine, sharpening the edges of my tongue so it sounded like a curse when I said, "Proceed." I swallowed and added a belated, "Please."

"Will you..." He cleared his throat and shuffled his feet, but when he raised his chin, he met my eyes, and this time there was zero hesitation. "Will you—"

"Yes." If this was a battle of confidence, I'd grant us a tie. This time at least. I wanted months—years—of competitions. Of matching wits and intelligence and challenging each other to be better. But at the end of each day, I wanted to be on the same side. I wanted us to be a team, not competitors. I crossed the snow-crusted grass to meet him by my car and didn't pause for a second before I twined my arms around his neck and pulled his mouth to mine. I kissed him long enough to tune out the whoops and cheers of our audience. Then I pulled back and said, "I'm assuming you were about to ask me out."

He chuckled against my forehead and pulled me tighter. "Either that, or pick me up a souvenir from the South Pole. Maybe a keychain or a snow globe. *My Girlfriend Went to Antarctica and All I Got Was This Lousy T-shirt*?"

I laughed. "I'll see what I can do. Anyone else have souvenir requests?" But when I turned to the driveway, it was empty. Our friends were graciously giving us a moment. Which would likely be the last nonteasing moment either of us experienced for a *very long time*. Poor Curtis—at least I got a two-week reprieve.

Speaking of: "Hey, since I won't be here to see it, can you tell me what book you did your project on now?" I tugged on his hand, then interlaced our fingers.

"A poem, actually." He looked down at the driveway. "Tennyson's 'Lancelot and Elaine'—I wrote a modern, gender-swapped version."

I tilted my head. "Isn't that the poem from when Gilbert saves—"

"Yeah, it's *Anne*-adjacent and also super emo and unrequited. Which is how I felt at the time." He squeezed my hand and gave me a sheepish smile. "Be very glad you're not here to see me present it. I certainly am."

I leaned in. "Never unrequited, just…'unprepared,' 'unex-pressed,' 'uncourageous'—what word do you like?"

He leaned in too. "'Unforgettable.' 'Unreplaceable.'" He laughed at my pursed mouth. "Yes, I know that's not a word. Still true."

I breathed my correction against his lips, making the kiss *irreplaceable*, just like he was.

The front door cracked open, and a white mitten waved from the gap. "Is it safe to come out yet? Have you stopped mauling my brother?"

"Yes, Wink," we said in unison. Curtis swung our clasped hands as everyone trooped out for another load.

"About time," muttered Lance. "Though now I'm the *only* single person in the Lunch Bunch."

Rory and Merri exchanged looks, but somehow I couldn't roll my eyes when Merri said, "Maybe you should talk to Ms. Gregoire."

"Ew, gross. She's, like, old." Lance recoiled, spilling socks out of the box he'd squeezed. "You are weird, little Campbell. Fielding, she is *weird*."

"That's not what I meant!" Merri protested, scooping up sock rolls and pelting him with them.

"Hey!" I jumped to intercept a pair Lance was firing back. "Those were clean."

"I'll wash them while you're gone," Merri answered from behind Fielding, who was acting as a human shield.

I laughed and went to check if the trunk was empty.

"Hey, E!" Win called from the other side of the driveway. "Did this fall out of one of your boxes?"

He was too far away for me to read the title of the thick black book, but I didn't recognize it. "Nope. Not mine."

"Oh, that's…" Huck emerged from the house. His eyes locked on Win, and he froze. Huck cleared his throat and raised a hand, then sheepishly lowered it. His dimples flickered in and out like he couldn't settle on an expression. "That's mine."

"You brought homework?" Rory grimaced. "I thought we were watching a movie and avoiding manual labor. What *is* that book even? Did I forget an assignment?"

Huck hadn't moved to take the tome Win was holding out. They were at the top of the driveway—standing a garage door's width apart and apparently either having a staring contest or playing an impromptu game of freeze tag. Win was the one who crossed the ten feet of asphalt. He didn't stop until the toes of his Vans almost grazed those of Huck's suede wing tips.

Finally Huck blinked and unfroze. "Thanks. Um, yeah, thanks."

I waited for Win to flay him with sarcasm or grind his vulnerability with sandpapery abrasion. Instead he ran a hand through his hair, and his voice was missing all his trademark snark when he answered, "No problem. How is it?"

Merri sidled up next to me at the trunk, and from the smile on her face, I knew to brace my side for the elbow she was about to gleefully dig in. "Do you see sparks flying? I see sparks. Frissons, frissons, everywhere. Curtis, back me up."

This was my cue to tell her she was being absurd, that there was no such thing. I *shh*'d her instead, stepping around the car to spy closer.

"Did my brother just ask about a book?" Curtis's awed words were so quiet I barely caught them, though he'd whispered directly in my ear, causing shivers on my skin.

I *shh*'d him too.

"I haven't started it yet." Huck scratched the back of his

neck, suddenly remembering he'd left Rory's question hanging and turning to answer her. "It's not homework. It's this extra-assignment thing from Ms. Gregoire. I'll tell you later."

"Oh!" Rory's eyes widened and searched the driveway to meet Merri's, then mine. She knew her sister would nod and smile, but I didn't think she'd expected me to as well. "If Ms. Gregoire wants you to read it, you should. Like, *right now*."

Huck shook his head. "I'll do it later. But maybe the movie can wait. It looks like there's a lot of boxes out here." The person he turned to for confirmation wasn't me—the owner of the completely reasonable number of boxes that were already unloaded—but the guy still standing way too close. "Do you guys need some help? I'm Huck, by the way. Huck Baker."

Win's answering smile was enormous before he adjusted it down to a grin. I couldn't hear what he said though, because they'd dropped their voices.

"Did that happen? Is this really happening?" I wasn't sure if it was Merri or Curtis asking, but both were gawking.

"Leave them alone." I pulled them back a step. "Merri, you are twelve kinds of obvious. Curtis, your brother will never forgive you if you interfere."

"Fine. But I'm singing the 'Sitting in a Tree' song to Win on the way home, and good luck, Huckleberry." Curtis spun the box he was holding. The last one. Should we put it back in the trunk as some sort of decoy for Huck? No, that was absurd. They'd had their meet-cute, and I'd done my part by distracting my nosy duo. The rest was up to Huck and Win…and maybe whatever book Ms. Gregoire had assigned.

"Can I take this in through your balcony, Short Stack?" Curtis asked. "I've heard about how you climb it, and I want to try."

Merri laughed. "Sure. Knock yourself out—not literally though. Check to make sure it's not icy before you step on the wall."

Once he was gone—whistling loudly as he walked past the pair of flirting boys—I pulled a small gift bag from the back seat. "This is for you. I'm not saying I was wrong about magic or Ms. Gregoire, and I'm not saying you're right either. Just that some things are open to interpretation."

Merri shoved aside tissue paper and pulled out a notebook. Embossed on the cover was a quote from Einstein: *Imagination is more important than knowledge. Knowledge is limited. Imagination encircles the world.*

"I got myself one too—I figure since I'm going to be unplugged for the next two weeks, I might want a place to write stuff down." I fished mine out of my carry-on and held it up. It was green with a quote from *Anne of Green Gables* emblazoned across the front in a carroty-orange font: *It's delightful when your imaginations come true.*

It was a different *Anne* quote about imagination that I'd used as the centerpiece of my English paper: *"I've just been imagining that it was really me you wanted after all...It was a great comfort while it lasted. But the worst of imagining things is that the time comes when you have to stop and that hurts."* I disagreed—if I'd learned anything from Anne's impetuousness, from my own forays into rule-breaking, it was that rejection was worth the risk of asking to be valued. Imagination was worth the pain of reality.

Merri hugged her notebook to her chest. "It's perfect. They both are." She grinned and hip-checked me as I bent to put mine away. "And so we're clear, what I'm taking away from this conversation is that you, me, Fielding, and Curtis are going on *soooo* many double dates when you get home."

"Maybe." I nudged her shoulder with mine. "But I owe Curtis a solo date first. Want to help me plan it?"

She nodded frantically. "I have so many ideas already."

"Eliza!" Mom called from the Campbells' front door. "Do you want to show me your new room? I want to make sure you're settled."

I started up the path with Merri beside me. *Settled.* The word rested lightly on my shoulders and felt right against my tongue. I'd spent so long as a restless outsider…but now I was *settled*, and right where I belonged.

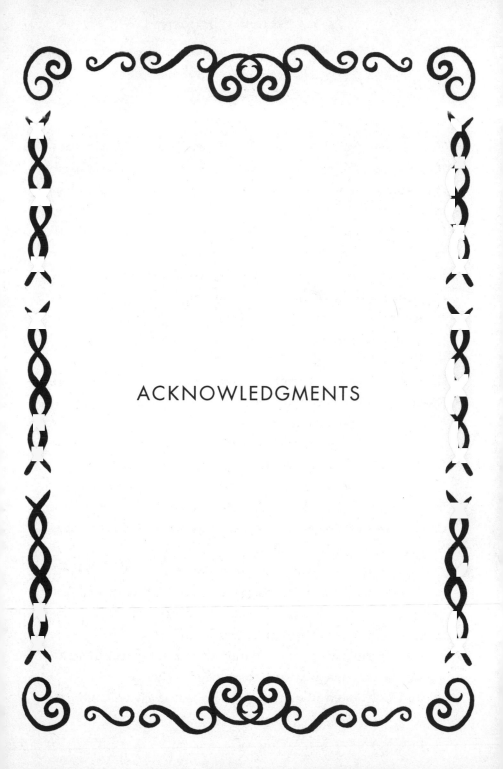

ACKNOWLEDGMENTS

There's a song from the *Anne of Green Gables* musical that repeats, *"Gee I'm glad I'm no one else but me."* As an awkward, bookish child and an awkward, bookish teen, I spent so much time wishing to be others—characters in books, kids in my classes. I never felt like I fit—not in my skin, not in my family, not even with my friends. I daydreamed of futures that felt impossible. You're holding a piece of an "impossible" daydream in your hands, and I am filled with gratitude for everyone who has helped to make it a reality.

"Kindred spirit" is a term that neither Anne Shirley nor I use lightly, but I've been blessed to have so many in my life: Jen Zelesko, Nancy Keim Comley, Shannon Kimmel, Stacey Yiengst, Kristin Wilson, Jenn Stuhltrager, Carly Mendelssohn, Heather Hebert, Tiff Emerick, and Lauren Strohecker.

If I could have my own version of Anne's "Story Club," I would fill it with all my writer friends who've helped me with this book. First and always, Emily Hainsworth and Courtney Summers. Jessica Spotswood, Annie Gaughen, Amanda Hollander, Jess Capelle, Lauren Spieller, Bess Cozby, Reese Kimmel, Emerson Morley, and Grace Reed.

To my real-life STEM heroines: Rae Ann Cook, Elisabeth Beadell, Jenny Warner, Amy Carroll, Deborah Gross, and Gail Yates—your intelligence and courage inspire me. And to my favorite STEM heroes—Matt Schmidt and Matt Fowler—who were endlessly patient as I asked questions and checked wording. Any errors in application are mine, not theirs.

To the wonderful team at Abrams: Anne Heltzel, Andrew

Smith, Jessica Gotz, Marie Oishi, Melanie Chang, Brooke Shearouse, Jenny Choi, Kim Lauber, Trish McNamara O'Neill, Nicole Schaefer, and Michael Clark—you all are the makers of dreams, and I'm so lucky to work with you and the fabulous crew at KT Literary and BG Literary; hugs to Barry, Tricia, Jen, and Kate.

And, always, always endless chapters of gratitude to the librarians, readers, teachers, and booksellers who have spread the word about this series. Especially Josh Berk—author, librarian, and quiz-bowl-host extraordinaire.

I'm forever grateful to Lucy Maud Montgomery for her stories and Prince Edward Island for summers spent on beaches and red clay roads where imagination and magic flourish. It has been one of my greatest joys sharing both these stories and places with my Schmidtlets.

Finally, St. Matt— I may have fallen in love with Gilbert Blythe *first*, but I love you *more*.

TIFFANY SCHMIDT

Tiffany Schmidt is a former sixth-grade teacher. She lives in Pennsylvania with her family and spends her time baking cookies, chasing her sons and puggles around their backyard, and writing the kissing scenes first. Tiffany is the author of the Bookish Boyfriends series, including *A Date with Darcy* and *The Boy Next Story*, as well as *Talk Nerdy to Me* and the forthcoming *Get a Clue*. In addition to Bookish Boyfriends, Tiffany has written four other books for young adults.